THE GUILLOTINE
AND THE TERROR

DANIEL ARASSE

=

THE GUILLOTINE
AND THE TERROR

TRANSLATED BY CHRISTOPHER MILLER

ALLEN LANE
THE PENGUIN PRESS

*Christopher Miller would like to thank Charles
Drazin and Robin Buss for their valuable suggestions
and corrections. His errors are all
his own.*

ALLEN LANE
THE PENGUIN PRESS
Published by the Penguin Group
27 Wrights Lane, London W8 5TZ, England
Viking Penguin Inc., 40 West 23rd Street, New York 10010, USA
Penguin Books Australia Ltd, Ringwood, Victoria, Australia
Penguin Books Canada Ltd, 2801 John Street, Markham, Ontario, Canada L3R 1B4
Penguin Books (NZ) Ltd, 182–190 Wairau Road, Auckland 10, New Zealand

Penguin Books Ltd, Registered Offices: Harmondsworth, Middlesex, England

First published in France as *La Guillotine et L'imaginaire de la Terreur* by Flammarion 1987
First published in Great Britain by Allen Lane The Penguin Press 1989
1 3 5 7 9 10 8 6 4 2

Copyright © Flammarion, Paris, 1987
This translation copyright © Christopher Miller, 1989

Filmset in 11 on 13pt Imprint
Printed in Great Britain by
Butler & Tanner Ltd, Frome and London

A CIP catalogue record for this book is available from the British Library
ISBN 0–713–99008–2

for René Démoris,
who first encouraged me to write this.

Contents

My heart rends; my blood freezes; my hand shrinks from the task of recording still more of these hideous murders. Ah! how I pity the historian who takes it upon himself to reveal them to our descendants!

Galart de Montjoie,
Histoire de la conspiration de Robespierre

An army of apostles of the revolution comes flocking in from all around, stalwart *sans-culottes* one and all. Saint Guillotine is quite wonderfully active, and the beneficent terror accomplishes in our midst, as though by a miracle, what a whole century of philosophy and reason could not hope to produce.

Citizen Gateau, administrator of military provisions,
27 *Brumaire* Year II

Introduction

The guillotine is the ultimate expression of Law . . . it is not neutral, nor does it allow us to remain neutral. He who sees it shudders with an inexplicable dismay. All social questions achieve their finality around that blade.
Victor Hugo,
Les Misérables, I, 1, 4

This is not, in any traditional sense, a work of history. It is, more precisely, a collection of stories – stories told at the foot of the scaffold by those about to ascend, or by people returning from the spectacle. It is, in short, a study of the comments elicited by what its artisan-manufacturer once (in a letter) termed the 'great machine'. These expressions of enthusiasm or revulsion form the documents on which our interpretation is based. They have, for the most part, already been published, but little use has been made of them by historians of the Revolution, who have concentrated on issues apparently more significant. In using them, I am concerned less to establish facts than to give a reading of the projections that have tended, from its very inception, to condense (in the Freudian sense) around the guillotine.

One seemingly simple question lies at the heart of this book: Why does the guillotine inspire fear? What makes it so abhorrent? What is it that so horrifies us? I felt that an answer to our question might be found in that dramatic exploitation of its power to appal, in which, no sooner invented, it was enthroned centre stage: the Terror.

Taking my cue from the conference 'The Machine in the Imagination' (Lille University, 1981), I have considered the guillotine as an *object of the imagination*. By this I mean that there have accrued to it 'values' which, though they derive from the function of the machine, go well beyond what that function implies. As my work progressed, I found that my initial inquiry – why does the guillotine frighten us? – was diversifying into a whole series of questions relating to areas which are themselves of the first importance: theatre, medicine, politics, metaphysics – the guillotine, a veritable *object of civilization*[1] touched on all of these.

I

My aim, in drawing attention to the years 1789–94, is threefold: to bring to light the common origins of the revulsion the machine inspires and the reputation it has earned; to attempt to explain its abject prestige; and, in so doing, to point out its doubly anachronistic nature. It is anachronistic that France should have continued to use a machine nearly two centuries old, which, alone among engines of destruction, had scarcely been modified since its invention – indeed, outside France it has become a symbol of the nation. But even in the late eighteenth century, when a society priding itself on its 'philosophical' outlook originated this 'simple mechanism' for chopping heads off, the guillotine was already an anachronism.

The Guillotine: The Mutilated Body

The guillotine was perceived from the first as barbaric, for it brought together two virtually incompatible characteristics: a cold technical precision, and the savagery of physical mutilation. The use of sword or axe rendered the headsman's attentions personal, and unforeseen consequences could and did arise. The guillotine, by contrast, made simple use of the basic laws of mechanics. Applied mechanics, by eliminating all human contact in the course of the execution, spared the executioner his guilt of blood; but the human body was none the less mutilated in a highly symbolic fashion, and the condemned man deprived of his last moral and physical confrontation with his fellow man. The guillotine effected the most abstract of executions through brutal butchery and hence is the subject of an extreme tension between its rational technology and blood-letting purpose.

The machine is consequently perverse, but not *unreasonable*, since reasons were found for it, reasons that constituted a spectacular perversion of medical science: from Guillotin to Louis and even Cabanis, it was the medical profession that proposed, invented and, in the last analysis, exonerated a machine for decapitating people. The medical science of the Enlightenment created in the guillotine one of its most accomplished products, and in so doing revealed its true nature as an art of death. Yet it should not be forgotten that the medical profession resolved upon the guillotine out of humanitarian considerations. Here, in embryo, lies the logic of today's 'art of death': the electric chair, the fatal injection ... The guillotine is not in itself monstrous, but became so relative to the society it served.

The Guillotine: The Medical Body

In his entry under 'Anatomy' in the *Encyclopédie*, the good and great Diderot justifies the practice of dissection, and, in this context, remarks on how different a corpse is from a healthy live body. With the logic becoming a philosopher he recommends the dissection of the living, citing in support various examples from classical antiquity. This argument leads him to suggest that the progress of medicine might be advanced if criminals were to be punished by vivisection. He defends himself explicitly against possible accusations of inhumanity, and his reasons offer considerable insight into the notion of humanity such as it appeared in the last thirty years of the Enlightenment.

What indeed is humanity, if not a habitual disposition of the heart to use one's faculties to the advantage of the human race? Once this premiss is admitted, how can the dissection of an evil man be inhuman? Since you call the malefactor to be dissected inhuman on the grounds of his having turned against his fellow men the faculties he was to have used to their advantage, what name will you give to that Erasistratus who, for the sake of the human race, overcomes his revulsion, and seeks enlightenment in the entrails of the malefactor? ... I should like to see established amongst us the custom of turning criminals over to the members of this profession [surgeons and anatomists] for dissection, and I would desire these latter to have the courage to perform this task. Whatever one's opinion of the death of a malefactor, it would be as useful to society in the lecture hall as on the scaffold – and this form of punishment will be no less fearful than any other. Anatomy, medicine and surgery could only gain by this procedure. As for the criminals, there will be few who will not prefer a painful operation to the certainty of death.[2] Who, rather than undergo execution, would not submit themselves to the injection of liquids into their blood, or to the transfusion of that fluid? Who would not allow their thigh to be amputated at the joint; or their spleen to be removed; or some portion of their brain to be extracted; or their mammary and epigastric arteries to be joined; or a section of some two or three ribs to be sawn out; or an intestine to be sectioned and the upper part inserted into the lower; or the oesophagus to be opened up; or the spermatic vessels to be tied, the muscle not included; or some other operation to be attempted on some other internal organ? For the rational, the advantage of these experiments will be reason enough.

The detail of these surgical proposals, their almost triumphant accumulation, reminds us that the period was – in the wheel and the stake – familiar with horrors scarcely less appalling than this scientifically conducted dissection. The fact remains that Diderot the *philosophe* not only has no thought of abolishing executions or mitigating penalties, but is primarily concerned with the profitability of executions. It is easy to perceive how, in this context, the painless and mechanical instantaneousness of the decapitating machine might pass for a notable advance in philanthropic thinking.

⟨ The point is the more easily grasped if we remember that, in a memorandum written in 1775–6 on the treatment of rabies, Guillotin himself takes up Diderot's idea, proposing that convicts should undergo 'all such experiments as have been . . . attempted with animals', and expressing the hope that they might in this way be reintegrated into society.[3] Experiment of this kind would no doubt seem 'unjust, cruel, terrifying or unnatural, but it is merely alarming'. Guillotin's justification of his thesis seems commonsensical, and serves as a reminder of the appalling suffering engendered, prior to the abolition of torture, by executions: 'A biting sensation, the painful symptoms of illness – are these to be compared with the appalling torments undergone by a man whose bones are being broken, who is forced to expire in the anguish of despair?' The machine was undoubtedly a step in the right direction and it foreshadowed a radical change: between 1776 and 1789, Guillotin rejected any attempt to extract profit from torture, confining himself to a single goal, that of replacing death by torture with a humanitarian device, the guillotine.

The Guillotine: The Body Politic

Like it or not – and the critics of the Revolution do – the guillotine is one of the key images by which the French Revolution has been represented – apart from the slogan of 'liberty, equality, fraternity', no other stereotype of the Revolution is so widely recognized. As early as 1820, Victor Hugo remarked on this: 'For our fathers, the Revolution is the greatest achievement ever to arise from the inspiration of an Assembly . . . For our mothers, the Revolution is the guillotine.'[4]

The Terror, the climax of the Revolution and its most revolutionary phase, is indelibly associated with the names of Robespierre and Saint-Just, and it is represented in the collective memory by an instrument which Cabanis had already in 1795 described as its 'ensign'. Now that the French Republic has abolished the death penalty and no longer makes use of its decapitating machine, the time has perhaps come to inquire how and why the guillotine contributed to the pristine beginnings of the Republic.

Sources and events clearly show that, between August 1792 and the apogee of the Terror in the summer of 1794, the guillotine was used in accordance with a perfectly coherent policy. It would be a mistake to attempt to 'excuse' this policy as the consequence of the ambitions of one particular faction, as a mechanism of government that had gathered its own uncontrollable momentum, or, in Mathiez' somewhat sentimental expression, as a symptom of 'despair'. The terrorist use of the guillotine neither deserves nor requires excuse: contemporary texts on the systematic use of the guillotine as a *governing machine* suggest that the immense and macabre theatre formed around it was intended, by a process of revolutionary regeneration, to forge a new *public conscience* (Saint-Just) after the centuries of abasement that the people had suffered under tyrannical rule. The day of King Louis XVI's execution, 21 January 1793, constituted not only an inauguration but also, and more importantly, a kind of *First Supper*, at which a body was sacrificed, a body monstrous less with regard to the crimes that the king had committed *in propria persona* than in the exorbitant privilege accorded it by the theory of monarchic power, that of incarnating in one body the body of the nation as a whole. By sacrificing a body deemed sacred by the theory of the divine right of kings, the Revolution performed a sort of inverted sacrament, at the same time both founding and consecrating the Republic, a new concept of national representation. The swathes cut by the Terror had established the Revolution as part of the civic identity of every citizen (Saint-Just).

There was indeed a 'logic of the guillotine': what speeches in the Assembly announced, the guillotine, with unparalleled force of conviction, publicly exhibited and confirmed.

This is not an attempt to rehabilitate the Jacobin guillotine. My aims are several. I wish to show how the guillotine became an image of the most radical phase of the French Revolution, a phase which distinguishes it from the less savage, more reformist American revolution; how, over and above such simplifying assimilations as Montagnard/fanatic or Terror/error, the guillotine's technical and visual character allowed it to acquire what we might term an *iconic resemblance* to the Jacobin Revolution; how the revolutionary guillotine was thus able to represent an ideal of Revolution; and, lastly, how this very resemblance explains the religious enthusiasm which, for a few months, greeted the profitable exploits of a machine which certain of its admirers dubbed Saint Guillotine...

PART I

The Birth of
the Machine

How true it is that it is difficult to benefit mankind without some unpleasant-ness resulting for oneself.

Dr Bourru in the funeral oration for Dr Guillotin,
28 March 1814

The Roman
Guillotin
Sets about his task,
Consults the masters of his craft,
Barnave and Chapelier,
Even the executioner:
See his hand create
The machine
That, simply, will exterminate
Ourselves: it shall be called
The Guillotine.

By this flourish, the Chevalier de Champcenetz, a member of the Académie française, who went to the scaffold on 23 July 1794, brought his satirical song to a neat and unexpected conclusion, and created a neologism destined for immortality. Even before its appearance the decapitating machine bore the name of its author, Joseph Ignace Guillotin, born 28 May 1738 at Saintes, to Joseph Alexandre Guillotin and his wife, born Catherine Agathe Martin. Family tradition has it that the conditions of his birth determined his later renown. Madame Guillotin, out walking in Saintes, was startled by the screams of a man being broken on the wheel. The shock is said to have hastened Joseph Ignace's birth, and the 'executioner was thus his midwife'. Guillotin the premature baby born to expedite the issue of death: it is an apt fable.

History is simpler. In retrospect Guillotin's medical and political career seems to lead directly to the proposal by which on 1 December 1789, his name entered history. A Jesuit since 1756, he left the order in 1763, and, turning from the ministry of the soul to that of the body, took up the study of medicine; he was awarded his Doctorate in Paris in 1770. His election as deputy of the Third Estate in 1789 came as no surprise. He was already a Parisian notable, the man who, in late 1788, in his fiftieth year, had put before the king the '*Pétition des citoyens domiciliés à Paris*, in which he claimed for the Third Estate a number of representatives at least equal to that of the other Estates. This event led to his being summoned to appear before the Parlement de Paris; he was triumphantly acquitted. It was only to be expected that he should take part, with Marmontel and Lacretelle, in drawing up the *cahiers de doléances* (lists of grievances). He subsequently distinguished himself in the Estates General on more than one occasion, and no doubt expected his proposal of December to make himself known in his own right...

His were humanitarian motives: he was at one with his contemporaries in desiring, if not the abolition of the death penalty, at least an easing of the ordeal and an end to torture. His idea was simply that an instrument widely known through its use in slightly different forms in Italy, Germany, England and even France, should be brought up to date. Its design was familiar from its representation in art.[1] Guillotin had, in fact, no part in the development of the machine: its true designer was Dr Louis, the permanent secretary of the Academy of Surgery. But the rhyming of 'machine' with the feminine form of his name married Guillotin to the guillotine for ever.

The machine was not built till the spring of 1792. And at each of the three stages in this long gestation – proposal, manufacture, and inauguration – disappointments occurred. A gap grew between the idea as it featured in Guillotin's plan and its mechanical embodiment. From the very beginning the simple device had unexpectedly taken on a meaning so determined by the powers of the imagination that, in the funeral oration on Guillotin delivered on 28 March 1814, his colleague, Dr Bourru, drew the following moral:

> Unfortunately for our colleague his philanthropic gesture, which was approved and bore fruit in an instrument to which the populace has appended his name, made him many enemies. How true it is that it is difficult to benefit mankind without some unpleasantness resulting for oneself.

He had clearly not taken into account what might be called a serious defect of rational philanthropy...

1

1789: Guillotin's Proposal

Some men are unlucky. Christopher Columbus was unable to have his discovery named after him; Guillotin was unable to prevent his invention from bearing his name.

Victor Hugo, *Littérature et philosophie mêlées*

Guillotin's speech to the Constituent Assembly proposing the reform of the penal system of the *ancien régime* is not extant. Our knowledge of it is confined to the six articles of the proposed bill:

Article 1. Crimes of the same kind shall be punished by the same kinds of punishment, whatever the rank or estate of the criminal.

Article 2. Offences and crimes are personal, and no stain shall attach to the family from the criminal's execution or loss of civil rights. The members of the family are in no way dishonoured and remain, without exception, eligible for all kinds of profession, employment and civic dignity.

Article 3. Under no circumstances whatever may order be made for the confiscation of the goods of a condemned man.

Article 4. The body of the executed man shall be returned to the family, should the family so request. Normal burial shall in all cases be permitted and the register shall not specify the circumstances of the death.

Article 5. No one may reproach a citizen with the execution or loss of civil rights incurred by a relative. Should anyone dare to do so, he shall be reprimanded by a judge.

Article 6. The method of punishment shall be the same for all persons on whom the law shall pronounce a sentence of death, whatever the crime of which they are guilty. The criminal shall be decapitated. Decapitation is to be effected by a simple mechanism.

The king had shown the utmost caution in penal reform. These six articles revolutionized the system, and Guillotin spoke in their favour as an enlightened doctor forwarding the 'philosophical' humanization of justice. Though his arguments are not extant they may be reconstructed without difficulty, for he no doubt recapitulated certain themes which had been much debated over the course of the previous years, while the simple mechanism whose readoption – and modernization – he proposed was well known in eighteenth-century Europe.

The Humanitarian Machine

Guillotin did not go so far as to propose the abolition of the death penalty, a fact which should not surprise us. The treatise on *Crimes and Punishments* by Beccaria, an Italian, was, it is true, already famous, and for the previous twenty years or so debate between philosophers and jurists had raged around it. But France was not yet ready for the abolition of the death penalty. Robespierre's attitude testifies to this. In 1791 he was to speak eloquently in favour of abolition, but in 1783, in the competition organized by the Academy of Metz for the suppression of ignominious penalties, he proposed only that sanctions should not vary with rank:

> The wheel, the gallows ... disgrace the family of those who perish by these means, but the blade that severs the head of the criminal debases his family not at all: it may even yet be seen by his descendants as a badge of nobility. Would it not be possible to turn this attitude to account, and extend this means of punishing crime to all classes of citizen? We thus eliminate an unjust discrimination ... Let us substitute for a penalty which adds its own particular brand of infamy to the shame inevitably attached to public execution another kind of penalty, one to which our imagination is accustomed to lend a certain lustre, and with which it does not associate the idea of family dishonour.[1]

Robespierre won the second prize, Lacretelle the first. In 1777 Marat had taken up a position still closer to Guillotin's. In response to the competition organized by the Society of Citizens of Neuchâtel, he put forward his *Plan de législation criminelle*, one of whose principal themes was the establishing of 'penalties at once lenient and certain'. On the issue of the death penalty, Marat is unambiguous:

> Capital punishment should be infrequent ... Life is unique among the benefits of this world in having no equivalent; justice therefore requires that murder be punished by death. Execution should never be cruel; it should study rather to be ignominious. Even for the most serious crimes (liberticide, parricide, fratricide, murder of a friend

or a benefactor), the machinery of execution shall be fearful, but the death shall be an easy one.[2]

Fearful machinery/easy death. Guillotin was well able to suppose that his proposal accorded with the intellectual and philosophical thought of the time: a retention of the deterrent value of capital punishment while mitigating the suffering caused.

Today the execution of Damiens, which took place in 1757, is often considered a turning-point. The law on regicide provided that Damiens, from whom Louis XV had received a superficial knife-wound, should be hung, drawn and quartered. The disastrous sequel is well known: Damiens would not die. The horses were unable to dismember him, and finally he was cut up with a knife. This horrific outcome was partly due to the perhaps excusable inexperience of the head executioner Charles Jean-Baptiste Sanson, his son Charles Henri and the numerous assistants whom they had called in to deal with this exceptional case. No one had been hung, drawn and quartered in Paris since Ravaillac, and the technique had not, therefore, been handed down. The incident created an uproar, and in 1758 the *rapporteur* of the Hôtel du roi, Mauriceau de La Motte, was hanged and his goods forfeited to the State for having 'spoken against the government itself, against the King and his ministers', and for having prepared posters about the execution of Damiens.

The exceptional nature of the Damiens affair deprived it in the long term of any real significance. Sanson's incompetence was punished by a term of solitary confinement. What was more shocking, in the run-up to the Revolution, was that people were still broken on the wheel and burnt at the stake: in Paris itself, in 1783 a homosexual; in 1785 a thief and arsonist, and a man who had murdered his wife; in 1787 a parricide ... The time was ripe for a machine which might bear the legend: Humanity, Equality, Rationality.

For originally the chief merit of Guillotin's proposal lay in its humanity. It was humane to the victim, whose pain it was intended to reduce to what Michel Foucault has termed 'zero-degree torture'.[3] It was humane towards the spectators, whom the guillotine delivered from their part in the horror of execution by torture – the inhuman spectacle of public execution was restricted to the sudden spurt of blood. And it was humane above all, if that is the term, to the executioner, who was freed from his monstrous 'duel' with the victim; his relation to the body of the condemned man was neutralized by the impersonal nature of the machine, and he had only to trigger off a mechanical process, 'with clockwork precision' (Foucault). This was not least among the benefits conferred, if we are to judge by the *Journal des Etats généraux*, which commented thus on Guillotin's speech:

> Monsieur Guillotin dwelt at length on the tortures in which man shows himself more ferocious than wild beasts. The torment of red-hot pincers and such like, these things I pass over in silence. May their very names be soon forgotten. He spoke of the horror inspired by those beings we term hangmen. Imbued as I am with similar sentiments ... I found it inconceivable that there should have existed beings capable of dishonouring mankind to such an extent as cold-bloodedly to soak their hands in the blood of their fellow men merely in response to orders.

The point is clearly made: over and above the alleviation produced for both victim and spectator, the machine rendered conceivable a figure until then inconceivable – the hangman and torturer (*bourreau*) transformed into executioner (*exécuteur*). It is to the guillotine, in short, that the hangman owed the right conferred in 1790, by decree of the Assembly, to stand for election to the Assembly, a right he gained along with other categories such as actors and Jews, among which he alone was in the singular.

Precursors of the Guillotine

In proposing his 'simple mechanism', Guillotin was on safe ground. Contrary to popular belief the decapitating machine considerably pre-dated 1789 and was widely known. It was simply a question of importing the most modern and effective model. The most detailed description of the mechanism is to be found in *Voyage en Espagne et en Italie* published in 1730 by Labat, a Dominican:

> The *mannaia* is used for decapitation. The device is entirely reliable, and, where an unskilful executioner sometimes requires two or three strokes to detach the head from the trunk, with the *mannaia* the condemned man is not kept waiting. This form of execution is for gentlemen and ecclesiastics. It is rare for such a person to be put to death in public, whatever his crime. The sentence is carried out in the prison courtyard, with the gates closed and in the presence of very few.
>
> The instrument named *mannaia* is a frame 4–5 feet high and some 15 inches across in its operational state. It consists of two uprights some 3 inches square, slotted on the inside to allow movement of a sliding cross-piece. The two uprights are connected by three mortice-and-tenon-jointed cross-pieces, one at each end and one some

15 inches above the lower cross-piece. On this the kneeling victim rests his neck. Above this cross-piece is the sliding cross-piece which runs in the slots of the uprights: Fixed to its underside is a wide blade some 9–10 inches long by 6 inches wide which cuts well and is finely honed. On top of it, firmly attached, is a lead weight of 60–80 pounds. This deadly cross-piece is raised to within 1 or 2 inches of the top beam, to which it is attached by a short length of cord. At a sign from the chief of police, the executioner simply cuts the cord and the cross-piece, dropping vertically onto the condemned man's neck, cuts it clean through without any danger of the stroke miscarrying.

Father Labat is as precise as a carpenter. It is not inconceivable that this graceless technical description was intended to instruct some future craftsman: Labat praises the machine as humanitarian and aristocratic, and his description was perhaps intended to influence the authorities in France towards a mitigation of the death penalty for the aristocracy. What is certain is that Dr Louis knew this passage, and may well have made use of it.

The decapitating machine held a strange fascination for clerics. In his *Voyageur français* Abbé de La Porte gives a less detailed description of a similar machine used in Scotland:

> Noblemen are decapitated in a manner unique to this country. The instrument used is a square piece of iron, whose blade is honed to a fine edge. On the other side is placed a piece of lead so heavy that great strength is required to shift it. At the execution this is raised to the top of a wooden frame ten feet high, and, when the signal is given and the criminal's neck is on the block, the executioner allows the mass of iron to fall: this never fails to remove the victim's head at the first stroke.[4]

Historians of the guillotine have shown that cruder versions of it existed during the fifteenth and sixteenth centuries in Italy (the *mannaia*), England (the Halifax gibbet) and Scotland (the Maiden), and even as early as the twelfth to thirteenth centuries in Naples, Holland and Germany.[5] Memoirs and chronicles testify to the fact that the device was well known throughout Europe well before the Age of the Enlightenment. With the exception of the Maiden, its use represented an exceptional aristocratic privilege, which allowed the victim to avoid the contaminating hands of the hangman and ensured that the execution was of unmatched, indeed mechanical, efficiency.[6]

Clearly, Guillotine's 'simple mechanism' derives from this kind of device, and in particular from the English version, to which Dr Louis refers in his *Avis motivé sur le mode de décollation* of March 1792: 'This is the course adopted in England. The criminal's body is laid prone between two uprights surmounted by a cross-piece from which the convex axe is made to fall onto the neck by means of a trigger.'

The Assembly Has Doubts, and Guillotin is Mocked

At the time the English legal system enjoyed considerable renown, and we might have expected its example to have ensured the swift acceptance of Guillotin's bill. Far from it. The first article was passed, but the rest were debated at length. Articles 2, 3 and 4 were adopted shortly afterwards on 21 January 1790; but the sixth and most enlightened of the proposals, referring to the 'simple mechanism', was not debated until March 1792. This delay is significant, for the Assembly's refusal even to debate the article clearly indicates the radical transformation of contemporary ideas concerning capital punishment implicit in Guillotin's proposal for the use of the machine.

The condemned man who died beneath the blade of the machine had hitherto been privileged indeed, since the aristocratic entitlement to decapitation was supplemented by the use of a device whose very rarity emphasized the status of its victim. Guillotin's egalitarian proposal would have abolished this privilege. But it infringed, too, upon another principle of long standing, the principle that, even for the death penalty, the punishment was to reflect the circumstances of the crime and the social class of the criminal.[7]

Guillotin had argued that the machine made for an easier death. There was, however, another form of death which was, at the time, considered an 'easy' one: hanging. Hanging too might have served as the uniform penalty, and Verninac de Saint-Maur, amongst others, proposed this: 'This punishment [beheading], which has in our country been the preserve of the high nobility, has acquired a certain social standing, a cloak of respectability which makes it all but an honour. Rather than elevate the masses to the dignity of the block, we should reduce the nobility to the modesty of the gibbet' (*Le Moniteur*, December 1789).

Guillotin was rudely awakened to the fact that a doctor and a philosopher did not necessarily add up to a legislator. And worse was to follow. The guillotine's first appearance met with unexpected derision. Its proponent immediately became a figure of fun, and the butt of numerous epigrams and songs.[8] The Goncourt brothers cite a piece they call a 'satirical novel', which parodies Guillotin's speech to the Assembly:

My dear fellow countrymen, so many of my patients have died of my attentions that I may reasonably claim to be among the best informed of men as to the ways of departing this world ... I have at last invented, with the help of my machinist, the delightful machine you see before you ... Under the platform there is a bird-organ, set up to play the jolliest tunes, as for example: 'My goodwife when I dance'; or again 'Farewell, my Lady of France'; or perhaps 'Good-night to my friends then one and all'. The chief protagonist being once mounted on the rostrum, shall stand between the two columns, and shall be requested to place his ear against this stylobate, the better to hear the ravishing sounds that the bird-organ pours forth; and his head shall be so discreetly chopped off, that it will itself, long after its truncation, be in doubt as to this event. Only the applause that shall doubtless resound through the square will suffice to convince it of its state.[9]

The attention of Guillotin's satirists was not inappropriately drawn to the moment in his speech when he vaunted the extreme expedition of the device. The following morning, the *Journal des Etats généraux* reported: 'Monsieur Guillotin described the mechanism. I will pass over the details; in depicting its effect, the orator in him momentarily got the better of the legislator, and he declared: "The mechanism falls like a thunderbolt, the head flies off, the blood spurts forth, the victim is no more." No such flourishes are permitted in the penal code.' This crowning moment of Guillotinesque eloquence was seized upon by the humorists. Two weeks later the *Moniteur* of 18 December notes that Guillotin's peroration was greeted in the Assembly with gales of laughter. It is given there as follows: 'Gentlemen, with my machine, I can have your heads off in the twinkling of an eye and you will feel not the slightest pain.' Elsewhere the same passage becomes: 'The form of death I have invented is so gentle that, were one not expecting to die, one would scarcely know what to say of it, for one feels no more than a slight sensation of coolness at the back of the neck.'

It is no accident that the humorists fixed upon the mechanical instantaneousness of death; and no doubt, if we follow Bergson in supposing that comedy resides above all in the idea of the 'mechanical clamped onto the living',[10] there is something comical about it. But in 1789 the derision signalled above all a rejection of the way the guillotine suddenly transformed the image of death, in both its social and private aspects. The underlying reasons for this rejection did not immediately emerge, as the debate was postponed, but from 1793 onwards the uses to which the Revolution put the machine brought these motives to light. They thereafter defined those concerns of the imagination that the guillotine so effectively focused.

2

1792: The Making of Louisette

'Have you, as a surgeon, a precise notion of the guillotine?'
'No sir.'
'This very day I have been over it minutely,' continued Doctor Velpeau
impassively. 'It is, I can assure you, a flawless device.'

Villiers de L'Isle-Adam,
Le Secret de l'échafaud

The machine was not built and used till 1792, and the bureaucratic
delays, administrative calls to order, and budgetary contention that
accompanied this long gestation seemed to bury any philosophical
significance it might have had under the banality of standard administrative procedure – unless it was precisely this banality that defined
the machine's true significance.

Articles 2, 3 and 4 of Guillotin's bill were passed on 21 January
1790. They constituted a substantial reform: in addition to excluding
considerations of rank in the apportioning of punishment, Guillotin's
law established the personalization of punishment, abolished confiscation of goods and secured the rights of the family over the dead
man's body. The rights of the condemned man and his family were
thus, for the first time, acknowledged.

There remained the issue of the death penalty, for which article 6
merely reaffirmed the rule of equality established by article 1. Beccaria's
treatise had elicited greater and more detailed reaction in French
intellectual circles than elsewhere in Europe, but no action had
followed, and France in the Age of the Enlightenment trailed in the
wake of Russia, where the death penalty had been abolished in 1754,
Austria (1787) and Tuscany (1786).[1]

The debate finally took place a year later on 30 May 1791; the length
of the delay was indicative of the Assembly's reluctance to consider
the issue. The highlight of the debate was Robespierre's speech in
favour of abolition, which was admired for its 'philosophical sensitivity'.[2] Showing that capital punishment was neither just nor an effective deterrent, he refuted the objections of Prugnon, and was supported

by speeches from Pétion and Duport-Dutertre. But the time was not ripe for abolition.[3] The Assembly, unmoved by Robespierre's sensitivity, maintained the death penalty, and, on 3 June, following the report of Lepelletier de Saint-Fargeau, determined that 'all persons sentenced to death shall be decapitated'. The adoption of Guillotin's 1789 recommendation was probably motivated by the ignominy traditionally attached to the alternative 'easy' death, hanging. The decision had the further merit of not infringing the established right of the nobility, merely extending it to the populace at large, who thus acceded, in best egalitarian fashion, to the 'dignity of the block'.

Four months went by before the decree of application was formulated on 25 September. The civil servant responsible for enforcing the law was then consulted – the executioner whose eligibility for the Assembly had so recently been recognized. His professional opinion was essential and, with it, the proposal moved from the theoretical to the practical stage: the humanitarian idea was to come face to face with the conditions in which it had to be carried out. Five more months passed before Charles Henri Sanson pointed out, in March 1792, two difficulties implicit in the new law. The first was technical: to be instantly effective the blade had to be of high quality and this would be expensive. The second was personal: if the execution was to observe the letter and spirit of the law, both headsman and victim had to be equal to their roles. But there could be no guarantee that the commoner would show the same stoicism as the nobleman; even the executioner might be moved, and, in this operation, such emotions were dangerous, and could be disastrous for all concerned: executioner, victim, and, above all, the public. Charles Henri knew what he was talking about. Not only was he remarkably incompetent at hanging people, but he was also rather shaky on decapitation: in 1766 he had proved unable to dispatch the unfortunate Lally-Tollendal, and his father Charles Jean-Baptiste had had to take over. This case had been turned to polemical advantage by Voltaire, and we will see that Dr Louis too bore it in mind.

Sanson's report[4] is an indication of how attitudes towards capital punishment were transformed by the introduction of a single universally applied method. The inevitable increase in the number of those sentenced to decapitation transformed the conditions, if not indeed the nature, of the event. Previously, every execution had been unique; in every case, victim and ordeal were individual, and the staging of their convergence formed the centrepiece of a rite in which the executioner might show more or less skill according to the demands made on him by the torture to be applied. Execution would henceforth be repetitive, but neither operator nor instrument (the sword) were such as to guarantee that each repetition would be identical. And here was the nub of the problem: the egalitarian penalty was in grave danger of producing the most horrific and singular consequences. The law could not be applied in this form.

The specialist's arguments were irrefutable. On 3 March 1792 the Minister of Justice, Duport-Dutertre, noted his agreement[5] and passed the report on to the Assembly. The man responsible for resolving the Assembly's doubts was the *procureur général syndic* Roederer, who turned to Guillotin, requesting by letter that Guillotin 'soften a punishment of which the law had not intended to make a cruel ordeal'. Guillotin's explanations proved insufficiently detailed – after the fiasco of 1789, he may have preferred to dissociate himself – and Roederer therefore appealed to the person best qualified to design the machine, the Permanent Secretary of the Academy of Surgery, Dr Louis.

Louis responded with speed: his notorious *Avis motivé sur le mode de décollation*[6] was ready on 17 March 1792. At no point did he consider the eventual effect his machine might have on the public imagination. The 'reasons' given for his proposal were historical, geographical and surgical. The only effect to which he referred was that which had necessarily to ensue (instantaneous decapitation); the only function of the machine was to meet 'the express will of the law'. His judgement that the decapitating machine was the instrument best suited to capital punishment was founded on his conception of the human body as a system of interlocking parts – and from this point of view it is true that a convex blade, particularly when set at an angle, is the correct technical solution to the problem posed by overlapping cervical vertebrae. Louis emphasized the element of spectacle traditional in public executions, but he did not consider the emotions that might be elicited by the effect the machine was designed to produce: namely, to slice mechanically and impersonally through living flesh. It was as if the notion of 'deprivation of life' were enough to guarantee the neutrality of the process. In this, as in other matters, we may see in him an adherent of enlightened medicine. The author of the *Encyclopédie* entry for 'Death' had already vouchsafed his opinion that death was not 'so fearful a thing as we imagine', adding that what generally most frightened us was 'the convulsions of the disintegrating machine'. Admittedly, this writer was not able to imagine the spectacle of the guillotine when he wrote: 'When the sickle of Fate is poised to end our days, we neither see it nor feel its stroke. And what sickle is that of which I speak? It is a figment of our imagination! Death does not come armed with a cutting instrument; no violence accompanies death. We die by imperceptible degrees.' As we shall see, the 'cutting instrument' had an impact on the imagination that the demonstrable possibility of dying otherwise than 'by imperceptible degrees' did nothing to diminish. What is clear is that the alliance of medicine and technology was expected to put an end to the fear of death by changing the conditions under which it was encountered.

Louis' *Avis motivé* proved decisive, and on 20 March 1792 the Assembly passed a decree of emergency.[7] The text of the decree included not only the humanitarian considerations we have seen above, but an important political consideration: the need to provide against 'seditious movements' which might arise in the absence of clear legislation concerning capital punishment, or in reaction to the underlying motive for the machine's introduction – the movement towards national uniformity in civil and political procedure.

Thus was inaugurated the last phase of the guillotine's gestation, the financial phase, which, despite the decree of emergency, lasted another month, for a manufacturer had to be found and it was not in a manufacturer's philosophy to undertake the project at a loss. On 25 March Louis handed to Guidon, the carpenter in ordinary of the Domaine, a detailed technical specification that in several points resembled Father Labat's account of the Bolognese *mannaia*.[8] Guidon sought to exploit the sensational nature of the order by inflating his estimate to a ridiculous 5,660 *livres*, although this included, it should be said, top-quality oak for the machine and scaffold (1,500 *livres*), a staircase comprising twelve stairs (200 *livres*), cast copper grooves (300 *livres*), labour (1,200 *livres*) and, for 1,200 *livres*, 'a small-scale demonstration model, so as to avoid, wherever possible, untoward events occurring with the full-scale machine, and to demonstrate its practicability'.[9] Roederer passed this estimate on to the Minister of the Treasury with the following note: 'Mr Guidon founds his request in part upon the difficulty of finding workers for a task whose purpose they find offensive. This sentiment does indeed exist; but workers have come forward who have offered to build the machine at a much lower price than his, requesting only that their names not be made public ... If you were so kind as to authorize the Directory to negotiate directly with some other craftsman, this might be best.'[10] The craftsman chosen was a German, Tobias Schmidt, a piano-maker, who on 10 April proposed an estimate of 960 *livres*. The offer was, predictably, accepted the very same day.

It was none too soon. 'Humanity' required that the machine be built as quickly as possible: one condemned man had been awaiting execution for two months, and, as Justice Moreau wrote to Roederer, 'every moment by which his wretched existence is prolonged must be another death to him'; it was necessary 'in the name of justice and of the law, in the name of humanity to put an end to the effects caused by this delay, which are detrimental to the law, to the safety of the public, to the judges and indeed to those under sentence'.[11] Roederer's reply was reassuring: things were moving. The machine took less than a week to build. On 17 April tests were conducted, using corpses, in a small courtyard in the hospital of Bicêtre, on 'a machine humanity cannot contemplate without shuddering, but which justice, and the good of society, necessitate'.[12]

We may see in this remark of Dr Cullerier the real reason behind the extraordinarily long gestation of the machine. Justice and the good of society on the one hand, and humanity on the other, were in direct opposition, indeed, humanity itself, author and sponsor of the machine, could not contemplate it 'without shuddering'. Bound by its own decisions, the Assembly could do nothing other than commit the government to building the machine. In his letter to Dr Louis, Roederer is explicit: the government 'is unfortunately required to decide on the method of decapitation'.[13] This is far removed from the enthusiasm which had led Prudhomme to declare that 'an instrument of death which might better reconcile the claims of humanity and of the law can scarcely be imagined, at least until such time as the death penalty is abolished'.[14]

Prudhomme's rider is an important one in that humanitarian concerns were, while the death penalty persisted, faced with an insoluble dilemma: they were seeking a humane way of performing an inhuman act. On 20 March 1792 as a consequence of the 'uncertainty as to the method of execution of article 3 of the 1st title of the Penal Code', the Assembly was forced to suspend all death sentences handed down by the courts: the death penalty proposed by law found itself suspended by the very regulations meant to implement it; only a respect for procedure still obliged the government to build the great machine, whose greatness was by now limited to its physical dimensions.

Nothing better illustrates the discredit into which the guillotine had fallen than its thus becoming the 'bastard daughter' of the Enlightenment. No publicly avowed father came forward to recognize his progeny. Those proposed would not allow the machine to bear their names, and those who claimed paternity were rejected.

Guillotin was horrified by the name given to the machine,[15] and carried his 'philanthropy' so far as to provide his friends with tablets of his own making which would give them the option of suicide if ever they were in danger of going to the guillotine.[16] Clearly 'his' machine had somehow escaped his merciful intentions, and equally clearly he had discovered an easier death than that provided upon the scaffold of philosophy. By usurping Guillotin's name and promoting him to a feral immortality, the machine acquired a spurious lineage in which Guillotin's contemporaries were quick to see the punitive hand of fate: 'By what contrivance of fate did a man of no talent or reputation bestow upon his own name the most hideous immortality?'[17]

The machine's true designer, Louis, was more fortunate, for it was also dubbed 'Louison' and 'Louisette', but the names did not stick. Louis was none the less alarmed by the risk he ran:

> I considered the guillotine as an act of humanity and did no more than rectify the shape of the blade and make it diagonal so that it cut cleanly and performed its function. My enemies then attempted, stopping at nothing in their use of the press, to have the fatal machine named Petite-Louison, though they were unable to substitute this name for that of guillotine. I was foolish enough to be greatly upset by this vile act – and it is vile, though they tried to pass it off as a joke in perfectly good taste.[18]

Tobias Schmidt, meanwhile, proved entirely free of the 'absurd prejudices' with which Guidon had justified his inflated estimate, and, not content with winning the first contract, was anxious to obtain exclusive rights to the guillotine, one of which was now to be supplied to each *département*. To do so he was relying on a law voted on 7 January 1791 which established a patent guaranteeing author's rights over useful discoveries and inventions. The contract was a lucrative one, since it involved eighty-three machines, and competition was already severe. While Schmidt refused to go under 824 *livres*, another Parisian carpenter had submitted an estimate of 500. Finally Schmidt won the contract: he had already demonstrated his competence with the prototype, and he could count on the administration's legendary conservatism with regard to suppliers. The patent, however, was refused. On 24 July 1792 the Minister of the Interior replied to his request with a revealing letter: 'Humanity is repelled by the idea of granting a patent for an invention of this kind. We have not sunk to such a barbarous level. Although Monsieur Schmidt has made a useful discovery (of a funereal variety), since it can serve only in the execution of sentence, the government is the proper organ to which he should propose it.'[19]

We have come full circle. The guillotine as it figured in Guillotin's proposals and the machine as built and woven into the Republic's social fabric had been entirely discredited. The machine born of humanitarian intentions had become a discovery whose kind is qualified by a clearly pejorative demonstrative ('this kind'), and which is described as 'barbarous' and 'funereal'. A moral transformation more radical can scarcely be imagined.

And yet the machine was still, undeniably, invested with a value of which the minister's note, though it stressed the negative aspect, contained the seed, a value which was to allow the guillotine to undergo a further striking metamorphosis less than one year later. By suggesting that the patent be offered to the government, the minister pointed to the guillotine's true nature as a *machine of government*, and we shall see how, under the Terror, it acquired a new value, no longer under the auspices of humanity, but in the name of a revolutionary government seeking through its use to found the Republic and establish the reign of liberty.

3

25 April 1792:
Sanson Inaugurates the Guillotine

Today the machine invented for the purpose of decapitating criminals sentenced to death will be put to work for the first time. Relative
to the methods of executions practised heretofore, this machine has
several advantages. It is less repugnant: no man's hands will be
tainted with the blood of his fellow being, and the worst of the ordeal
for the condemned man will be his own fear of death, a fear more
painful to him than the stroke that deprives him of life.

The criminal who is to suffer the first effect of this new machine
is Nicolas Jacques Pelletier, of previous criminal record, declared on
the 24th January of last year, by final verdict of the third provisional
criminal assizes, guilty in fact and in law of attacking, aided and
abetted by a person unknown, on the 14th of October 1791, towards
midnight, in rue Bourbon-Villeneuve, an individual whom they beat
with a cudgel, and of having stolen from him a wallet containing 800
livres in *assignats*.

In reparation for which, he is sentenced by the court to be conducted, dressed in a red shirt, to the place de Grève, and there to have
his head cut off, in conformity with the provisions of the Penal
Code.[1]

It was a sensational event. The curiosity naturally elicited by any
novelty was reinforced by the fact that the Revolution was here putting
a full stop to time-honoured habits and practices. The execution of
Nicolas Jacques Pelletier was undoubtedly a public manifestation of
the Assembly's will to put an end to the *ancien régime*. The inauguration
followed hard on the heels of two highly significant abolitions: on 5
April of the Sorbonne, and on 6 April of all religious congregations. On
22 March the Abbé Chappe, inventor of the telegraph, had bestowed his
invention on the Assembly. In this context the decapitating machine
belonged among those measures that served to show the intellectual
and social progress brought about by the Revolution. The Assembly's
action in reforming capital punishment transcended the sphere of
parliamentary activity, opened itself to public scrutiny, and invoked

the witness of the people to the benefits conferred by an enlightened regime.

The authorities were well aware of the importance of the event. In their uncertainty as to how the innovation would be received, they resolved to take every precaution. These were specified by Roederer to La Fayette, commander of the National Guard:

> Sir, the new method of implementing the penalty of decapitation will certainly draw a considerable crowd to the place de Grève, and measures must be taken to prevent the machine from being damaged. I therefore consider it necessary for you to order the gendarmes who will be present during the execution to remain after it has taken place in sufficient number in the square and its exits to facilitate the removal of machine and scaffold.[2]

The violent and atavistic reactions of the populace might, then, still diverge somewhat from the enlightened notions that had inspired the invention of the guillotine, and the government was aware that the institution thus transformed was not wholly rational in nature. More important was the fact that the machine rather than the executioner was to be protected. Roederer's concern is understandable if we bear in mind how troublesome and costly the machine's manufacture had been, but he was also concerned to ensure that the machine remained operational and thus cost-effective. There is from the start the suggestion that the guillotine belonged to a pre-industrial consciousness mindful of the value of its tools, so it is not surprising that we can detect, at the height of the Terror, a concern with turnover manifesting itself in praise for the productivity of the worker (the executioner) and occasional demands for an improvement in the performance of his equipment. The guillotine, that product of the Enlightenment, was also one of the first machines considered in economic terms, the cost-effectiveness of its output being evaluated according to the time taken.

The inauguration was a great event. Yet the newspaper reports are perplexing, for they emphasize the disappointment of the people, who seemed to the press to be 'calling for Monsieur Sanson to return to the *ancien régime*; to be saying: "Give me back my wooden gibbet, give me back my gallows."'[3] No doubt the papers were less than impartial in suggesting a return to the *ancien régime*. This much is certain, that in the spring of 1792 the guillotine, while departing from the previous ritual of capital punishment, had not yet acquired its own – one which was to be just as meticulously planned and full of meaning. The inauguration nevertheless comprised two fundamental innovations.

First, the machine was extraordinarily new – it was the emblem of the philosophical principles underlying the justice of the Revolution; and yet it was inaugurated on an ordinary criminal who is remembered by history only for being the recipient of this honour. The machine was thus, from the first, reduced to the commonplace; it became what the law wished it to be – an impartial sword of justice. In consequence decapitation itself was reduced to the commonplace. No one noticed the fact, but 25 April 1792 corresponds in some measure to the night of 4 August 1789, when, on a wave of popular enthusiasm, privilege and feudalism were brought down. Pelletier's death was of great significance, as was made clear by the rhetoric surrounding the first political guillotining, that of Louis David Collenot d'Angremont, who was sentenced by the court set up to try the crimes of the tenth of August and decapitated on 21 August 1792. The guillotine was moved from the place de Grève to the place du Carrousel, 'scene of the crime, and therefore the place best suited to its expiation'.[4] 'Scene' and 'expiation': the cause of the Revolution thus restored to capital punishment its ritual dimension. What is more, the scaffold was not dismantled after the ceremony and on 23 August the Commune decreed that it would remain in place till further notice. Politics had made of the guillotine a show which would run and run. Its two qualities – ceremonial glamour and the mundane repetition of the spectacle – were to be fully exploited during the Terror.

Second, accounts of the inauguration refer to neither the personality of the condemned man nor to the person of the executioner; the emphasis was now on the machine itself. A redistribution of roles had taken place in which the executioner's role was transformed. It was his duty, hereafter, to remain in the background, and to return to the limelight only should some unexpected incident occur.[5] The master craftsman of old was reduced to a simple functionary: he had become the 'agent of public works', a simple 'representative of the executive' as Camille Desmoulins is said to have remarked.

The scale of this change is illustrated by the pamphlet *Plaintes de l'exécuteur de la Haute Justice contre ceux qui ont exercé sa profession sans être reçus maîtres*, which was published in Paris in 1789. It takes issue with the way in which the Governor of the Bastille, de Launay, and three representatives of the monarchy were butchered in July 1789: on 14 July Jacques de Flesselles, the Merchant Provost; on 22 July Joseph François Foullon, Comptroller-General of Finances, and his son-in-law, Louis Bénigne Bertier de Sauvigny, *intendant* of Paris.[6] This triple massacre had caused sufficient revulsion for Camille Desmoulins to refer to it in his *Discours de la Lanterne aux Parisiens*, in which he censured this outbreak of popular justice as over-hasty and alien to the intentions of 'enlightened' revolutionaries.

The *Plaintes de l'exécuteur de la Haute Justice*..., which is clearly royalist in tendency, is also an early indictment of a nation 'in danger of passing in Europe for a people of hangmen'. The interest of this pamphlet resides in the melodramatic eloquence of its satire, which, at the outset of the Revolution, firmly establishes the image of the executioner-torturer whose inhuman savagery supposedly corresponds to the demands of the people. Reading it, we are better able to grasp what underlies Chateaubriand's understated conclusion to his own record of those days of July 1789: 'I was horrified by these cannibal banquets.'[7]

The guillotine put an end to such festivities. The transformation of the executioner's task restored not only *his* dignity, but also that of the people, freeing it from the stigma of 'cannibalism'. And, as we shall see, it restored a measure of dignity to the victim himself, offering him, upon the theatre of the scaffold, a new and dignified role.

One thing was certain: the effectiveness of the machine. Its inauguration had gone off without a hitch;[8] it had, if anything, been too successful. It was immediately clear that the extreme rapidity of the process, a feature so commendable in the merciful eye of the law, made it all but invisible. From this, important consequences were later to follow. A 'twinkling of an eye' makes for a very brief spectacle. The rational guillotine cheated the *spectator*; at the height of the Terror this was to become one of the chief reproaches made against it and certain refinements were introduced to prolong the spectacle in exceptional cases.

Moreover, by conforming to Guillotin's prescription ('the head flies off ... the victim is no more'), the rapidity of the machine brought with it a drastic corollary. The ordeal of traditional forms of execution was in some sense a supplication to the Almighty, and the torment endured, which was perceived as an appeal for divine mercy, might redeem the sin committed.[9] No such redemption through the body was afforded by the guillotine, which, in abolishing suffering, so far from allowing of *appeal*, constituted a direct *response*, the secular response of Law to Crime.

The secularization of death in public raises a whole series of questions, which we shall do well to consider now at their origin before returning to them when they take on their full significance in 1793.

For many, what was essential in the death of an individual was the sacred relationship holding between the dying man and his soul, and between his soul and God. While, on the one hand, the sacred was protected by the invisibility that the guillotine's prompt action (incidentally) conferred, on the other, the *hora mortis*, the moment of transition between life and death, during which the dying man might yet attain salvation, was annihilated. By doing away with the notion of a *dying man* (since it involved an immediate transition from life to death), the machine raised issues so profound and complex that they were to be debated in a variety of contexts.

We will consider them later. Let us, for the time being, take note of the divide between the imagined and the real effect of the machine. As early as 1792 an engraving was produced to publicize the innovation proposed by Guillotin. This remarkable document, depicting what did not then exist, reveals clearly what the guillotine was intended to be and how it was intended to be used. An explanatory note accompanies the engraving;

> Executions will take place outside the city in a place set aside for this use; the machine will be surrounded by barriers to prevent the people approaching; the area within the barriers will be guarded by soldiers with arms 'at the order', and at the moment of absolution the signal for death shall be given by the confessor to the executioner. The executioner will look away and, with a stroke of his sword, cut the cord from which is hung a drop-hammer armed with an axe.[10]

These arrangements were clearly intended to ensure the privacy of death. Individuality was retained to the last: each death was unique, and only the confessor could decide when it should occur. By ensuring that physical dissolution and religious absolution were perfectly simultaneous, he dispatched the criminal directly to his salvation.[11]

For those who had in mind a ceremony of the kind described here, the 1792 inauguration must have come as something of a disappointment, if not indeed a shock. A considerable divide had opened from the very outset between what had been imagined and what was seen, shown, and done: the decapitating machine had brought into being a 'secular commonplace' whose consequences could not be predicted. But when the time came for the guillotine to operate upon a body unique in its inviolable and sacred majesty, that of the king, this mechanical commonplace redoubled in symbolic value; or perhaps we should say that it gained a second, and this time specifically *political*, resonance.

PART II

Mechanical Effects

'Titus Manlius, the Roman, died beneath such a machine.' The engraving mentioned above carries this historical reference, which is, needless to say, historically inaccurate. The death of Titus Manlius is narrated by Livy in the eighth book of the *History of Rome*. Manlius, who had engaged in single combat in defiance of his father's injunction, was sentenced to death by his father, and died under the axe.

But the reference is more than merely fanciful. It is derived from contemporary iconography. Two representations of Titus Manlius' death were well known in the eighteenth century; both German, they show the young Roman decapitated by a machine very similar to the one invented in 1789, which may indeed have been modelled on them. The two engravings, by Pencz and Aldegrever, date from the sixteenth century, and the curious presence of the machine can without doubt be ascribed to the great reputation it enjoyed at that time. During the Renaissance efforts were made to trace the machine's invention back to classical antiquity. In his treatise on *Emblemata*, published in 1551, Achilles Bocchius cites the machine as proof of Spartan nobility. The Spartans go smiling to their deaths: '*Dignissimum Sparta virum!*' Whether Titus Manlius or the Spartans, then, exceptional courage was the quality required of those honoured by mechanical decapitation. To the aristocratic privilege connoted by decapitation were added the attributes of martial glory. The use of the machine further augmented the dignity of a form of death virtually restricted to a caste, while the offices of the confessor were there to ensure that the religious aspect of death was not neglected.

It would have been hard in April 1792 to imagine that a machine, whose belated introduction in France had been a victory for humanitarian and rationalist sentiment, would, in the space of a few months, have become 'the vile guillotine, that atrocious sport, that abominable pastime of hangmen and populace' (Dr Soemmering), that 'blade dripping with carnage ... detestable instrument of so many cruel deeds' (Sédillot the Younger); that it would make of the condemned man 'an object of disgust', and that the ceremonial (meaning here procedures)

32

associated with its use would 'debase the man before striking him down, ... prostitute him under the gaze of the people' (Oelsner).

This catastrophic devaluation of the guillotine's prestige, which occurred between 1789 and 1795, may be ascribed very largely to the Terror. For two years, the Revolution made the use of the machine automatic and in every sense mechanical, putting it to political uses which its originators certainly could not have intended. Cabanis, though he had been present at the Bicêtre testing and did not disapprove of the guillotine on medical grounds, called it 'the ensign of tyranny'.[1] The guillotine was even made *responsible* for the Terror, whose judgements could not, in Chateaubriand's view, have been executed had it not been for that 'graveyard mechanism' whose very invention necessarily bespoke the hand of Providence. It was, admittedly, a paradoxical sort of Providence: 'The invention of a machine for murder, at a moment when it was actually necessary to crime, is memorable proof of this communication between reciprocally co-ordinated events, or rather a proof of the latent action of Providence when it seeks to change the face of Empires.'[2]

We cannot, however, simply identify the rejection of the 'monster' with Thermidorian reaction. The sources are there to show that this debate was not conducted on exclusively political, but also on philosophical grounds. The authors were, in many cases, doctors. This should come as no surprise – and not only because the machine had been invented by doctors. The medical profession had come to think that its long experience of death made it a kind of repository of knowledge about death and its signs, and consequently too of the relations between body and consciousness, between body and feelings of identity, even between body and soul. Dr Louis had himself in 1752 written letters 'about the certainty afforded by the signs of death, in which the citizen is relieved of his fear of being buried alive, with observations and experiments on drowned persons'. The subject of 'apparent death' was much debated in the eighteenth century, and it is appropriate that Dr Louis should have been the man to elaborate a machine that inflicted death unequivocally. But here imagination asserted its claim by disputing whether death under the guillotine was, in fact, instantaneous, and chose to detect, in the severed head, signs that it was not dead but *dying*. To whom, if not to members of the medical profession, were these doubts to be submitted?

This is not all. In such a man as Cabanis, a doctor but also a *philosophe* and above all an *Idéologue* and member of the Council of Five Hundred, the significance of the metaphor of the body politic and of its representation in elected and constituted bodies cannot help but strike us.

In the political and social upheaval of the Revolution, the doctor became the authorized spokesman of a science which touched on the most fundamental aspects of the changes under way.

The guillotine stands precisely at the junction of body and body politic. From the field of medicine its blade passes through the political to attain the metaphysical, bringing into focus a number of ideas that were current at the time.

1

The Instant, the Series, the Body

[The Terrible Instant]

> And since gibbet and guillotine have been compared, let us say
> something about that. Hideous as one may make the convulsions of
> the hanged sound, hanging has yet these merits: it avoids the prospect
> of torrents of blood, and the moment of death is not so appallingly
> rapid.[1]

The comparison may not be sensitive, but it is shrewd. Why though had
the rapidity of the guillotine, its principal virtue, become so 'appalling'?
The prolonged ordeal of death under torture gave place to unerring
and instantaneous decapitation. The 'instant of the guillotine' spared
the victim suffering and the spectator a horrific spectacle. What was so
appalling about this?

Perceptions changed drastically for the paradoxical reason that the
blade fell so swiftly as to be *invisible*. The focal point of the act of the
imposing ceremonial of death was over in 'the twinkling of an eye'.
The guillotine 'strikes off heads faster than the eye can see',[2] and the
theatre of the guillotine culminated in a moment of invisibility.[3]

For Cabanis, the very speed of the operation attenuated the exemplary
value of capital punishment. 'The spectators see nothing. For them
there is no tragedy; they have no time to be shocked.'[4] But there is
nothing neutral about this invisibility, it is not a matter of indifference ...

♪ The 'window' (this is the technical term) of the guillotine in operation
might be considered the *blind spot* around which there crystallizes a
terrible *visibility*. At the end of his *Réflexions historiques et physiologiques
sur le supplice de la guillotine* Dr Sédillot draws a 'harrowing outline of
the unprecedented crimes' committed during the Terror. At the heart
of this description, at its culminating point, the moment when the
blade falls, Sédillot exhibits the merest blank, sets before the reader's
eye a full point: '.', the tiniest typographic element, the *nec plus ultra*
of the laconic. The break in the sentence is synonymous with the
punctum temporis of the blade's descent, and a perfect analogue for the

indescribable 'instant of the guillotine' around which 'the tragedy of the guillotine'[5] unfolds. Nothing less than the literary genius of a Chateaubriand was required to render that instant, to offer an account in sound of what it was impossible to see: 'There came a great silence ... "Son of Saint Louis! You go to Paradise," exclaimed the pious churchman who bent to the monarch's ear. Then the blade's precipitate descent was heard.'[6]

It is not that there was nothing to see; but what was seen was something other than the operation of the guillotine, and this difference had the most unexpected and unimaginable effects. Within the frame in which the blade falls, something does indeed happen, something intolerable. What slices through this blinding immediacy, what lies between the last quiver of life and the instantaneous and fatal 'afterwards' of truncation is something it is neither possible nor permissible to see or imagine; it is an unknown quantity, more precisely a taboo.

By its instantaneous action, the guillotine sets before our eyes the invisibility of death at the very instant of its occurrence, exact and indistinguishable. We shall see later how this public display of the sacred moment in which a person dies was perceived as a monstrous obscenity, a prostitution of the most intimate moment in an individual's life, that of his death; here we merely note that this characteristic of the guillotine goes some way towards explaining how 'fearful' it seemed even when at rest.

As Gastellier noted, the 'plummeting acceleration' of the guillotine's axe-head was no less than 'the speed of lightning'. It was such that 'from the first point of contact to the last, there is no distance; there is only an indivisible point: the axe falls and the victim has died'.[7] And there lies the frightening paradox of the guillotine; this 'zero distance' defining an indivisible point *in time* is, *in spatial terms*, a height of fourteen feet. Raised to the top of the uprights, the blade defines a space which expresses the instant, which is a *spatial metaphor of the instant*. The guillotine is perhaps the only machine thus to exhibit in plain view the essentially destructive, rending, agonizing potential of every instant.[8] This formidable configuration takes us back to the etymology of the word: *instans*, that which stands over, that which threatens. The image of the machine is the more frightening in that its very reliability suggests but a single instance of time, that of death and its unerring stroke, a mechanized and more 'productive' version of the immortal reaper's scythe.

The Thinking Head

There is more. The instant of the guillotine gave rise to a monstrous lease of life: 'Several French observers are, as I am, convinced that execution by the guillotine is among the most dreadful, both in its violence and its duration.'[9]

The author of this opinion, a surgeon named Sue, was not motivated by a taste for paradox; he was, despite appearances, taking a serious part in a debate that caused considerable upheaval in the medical establishment in the years after 1794. Its origin was a question raised by Soemmering, a German, who was quickly seconded by the Frenchman, Oelsner. Their question was this: Is death perfectly simultaneous with decapitation? Does the decapitated head immediately lose consciousness?

This question continued to be asked for as long as there was a guillotine to ask it about. Its relevance in the eighteenth century is clear: we have already cited the fear then current of apparent death being mistaken for real. The *Encyclopédie* specifies two kinds of death: incomplete and absolute. The two could be distinguished only by assiduous attention to 'the signs of death'. The distinction leads to an unexpected conclusion: 'That there is no remedy for death is an axiom widely admitted; we, however, are willing to affirm that death can be cured.'[10] True, the author of the article on 'Death' expresses the view that 'it would be most absurd to attempt to revive a man whose head had been cut off', but this opinion was not universal. Auberive, author of a brochure entitled *Anecdotes sur les décapités* which was published in Paris in Year V, cites many cases of decapitated heads speaking. Admittedly, he rejects these 'inspired inventions of poetry', but dwells at some length on an experiment conducted early in the eighteenth century, in which a person had been decapitated and subsequently 'brought back to life', and quotes in corroboration the well-known anecdote according to which the severed head of Mary Stuart is supposed to have spoken.[11]

For an 'enlightened' mind, then, the notion that life and consciousness might survive decapitation was not self-evidently false. The guillotine focused such doubts, and, in at least one case, several people felt that they had evidence of consciousness surviving. The executioner's assistant held up Charlotte Corday's head to show it to the people. When he slapped it, it appeared to blush at the indignity. A scandal erupted. Public anger led to a similar response at the highest level. The inhumanity of the act, and the lack of respect shown to the victim contributed to the indignation, but Corday's reddening cheeks did much to diminish people's confidence in the humane efficiency of the machine.

In the nineteenth century, the subject of the decapitated head and its fleeting vestiges of life held considerable appeal. It was brilliantly exploited by Villiers de L'Isle-Adam in 'Le Secret de l'échafaud', in which the good Dr Velpeau enlists the aid of his colleague La Pommerais, who is about to go to the guillotine. Velpeau wishes to know 'if some gleam of real memory, thought or sensibility survives in the brain of a man after his head has been cut off', and consequently proposes a simple experiment: immediately after his colleague's decapitation, Velpeau will pick up the detached head and, enunciating very clearly, request him to reply by winking three times with his right eye 'while keeping the other wide open'.[12] Needless to say, the response turns out to be uncertain, the sign being hard to make out.

Villiers de L'Isle-Adam writes about two doctors because his story is explicitly based on medical tracts concerning the guillotine written during the Revolution.[13] The proponents of the thesis of survival justified it by reference to a distinction between the objective duration of an event and the subjective impression this duration makes on the agent.[14] If, then, the decapitated man retains consciousness, the instantaneousness of the guillotine may be only relative, and from the two premises 'that (1) the seat of feeling and its apperception is in the brain; that (2) the operation of this consciousness of feeling may persist, even if blood-circulation in the brain is terminated, weak or partial', Soemmering concludes that 'in the head separated from the body by this form of execution, feeling, personality, and sense of self remain alive for some time, and feel the after-pain that affects the neck'.[15]

The surgeon Sue goes one better: the term 'after-pain' becomes 'after-thought'. The transition is pregnant with horror: 'What could be more horrible than the perception of one's own execution, followed by the after-thought of one's having been executed?'[16] The 'temporal syncope' that characterizes the guillotine's action produces an immediate and irreparable break in the unity of the body, but – and here lies the horror – the continuity of consciousness is uninterrupted, and its survival enough to discredit the fatal efficiency, the temporal punctum, ascribed to the fall of the blade. What a philosophical monster the guillotine's instantaneousness now becomes! By suggesting a distinction between the time-continuum of the intact body (at an end) and that of consciousness (which continues), the instant of the guillotine creates a temporal divergence in which the unity of self is fragmented.

This is only the first of the several catastrophic effects the guillotine so mechanically produces:

1. Its mechanism makes the impossible possible and breaks a taboo. The victim, with his after-knowledge, is consciously aware of that which is *par excellence* unknowable, that is, his own death. Physiological reasons, for example, the larynx no longer being supplied with air by the lungs, do, of course, prevent him from communicating this 'astonishing idea' (Sue). It is striking to find in Soemmering's account an image that fiction was subsequently to appropriate: 'I am convinced that if air continued to pass regularly through the vocal organs, and if these organs had not been destroyed, the heads would speak.'[17]

How potent the imagination, and what havoc it wreaks with scientific and medical procedure! Two conditionals, two ifs, add up to a certainty. Clearly, we are no longer in the realms of simple physiology, but in those of the sacred and the taboo. For, if our conditionals are fulfilled, the guillotine forces into articulate discourse an impossible statement, the unspeakable 'I am dead' which can only be expressed as a metaphor. The guillotine produces this monster, a head without a body which possesses in fact and not fiction the unthinkable consciousness of its own death. The duration of the traditional execution constituted the *hora mortis* of the condemned man. Not so with the guillotine; on the contrary, if Soemmering is right to suppose that 'the decapitated man retains the impression of his own existence for as long as the brain retains its vital energy', this impression can only be that of death already past.

This then is the guillotine's monstrous creation, a head that can think without a body, but think, or so we might suppose, one thought only: 'I think, but I am not.' The guillotine slices in half the reassurance of the Cartesian *cogito*. The 'factory of death' (Gastellier) gives its victim to think of death as the death he has died.

2. If the victim's head is thus pensive, the victim is not dead but dying. The duration of the ordeal of execution is restored, albeit for a short time and a truncated self, and, by a hideous paradox, the mechanical instant recreates the span it was invented to abolish.

At least one text testifies to the presence of this image in the mind of a man condemned to verify its truth. On the dawn of his execution, Camille Desmoulins wrote a touching letter to his wife, in which he returns again and again to the idea that he is already in a state of death-in-life; he uses the metaphor of his cell as a coffin in which he is already inaccessibly enclosed. But in the last lines of the letter, which anticipate the end of *Le Rouge et le Noir*, he revives the image of the dying man's presence in death. His wish is the more moving in its fiction, for the beauty of the image serves primarily to deny the separation that must ensue: 'Adieu, Loulou, adieu my life, my soul, my divinity here on earth! ... I feel the shores of life recede from me. Lucile is still in sight, I see her yet – my beloved, my beloved Lucile! My manacled hands embrace you, and from my severed head my dying glances rest upon you.'[18]

3. Medical science calculated the duration of 'survival' thus: 'To judge by experiments performed on the amputated limbs of the living ... it seems likely that feeling may persist for a quarter of an hour, given that the head, because it is thick and round, does not lose heat very quickly ... The dying see and hear long after they have ceased to be able to move their limbs.'[19]

Soemmering's medical style is less moving than Desmoulins's letter, but it points none the less to the same horror, which the condemned man in his anguish desires and the doctor recoils from, that is, the survival of consciousness in a head 'already dead'.

The shadowy regions onto which the guillotine looks out are amply suggested by a question Soemmering poses but does not venture to answer: 'The question whether the brevity can at all redeem the terrible intensity of the suffering must remain unresolved. What then are they for, these abominable tortures we inflict on the poor wretches, as one might say, after their death?'[20] Though he does not reply, the answer is clear. What the Enlightenment philosophers and indeed the atmosphere of the times combined to reject as the invention of obscurantist and medieval religion, the guillotine had reinvented. For the Western mind, these 'abominable tortures' inflicted 'after death' can be only one thing – the tortures of hell.

Scientifically, 'infallibly', the philosophical machine produces a mechanical hell – it is properly termed 'infernal' – at the invisible heart of its instantaneous action. It creates a time-lapse through which the pangs of hell are brought to life, and in which enlightenment gives place to a Stygian darkness.

The Machinery of Consciousness

The debate initiated by Soemmering and Oelsner was more philosophical than scientific, and an answer was shortly forthcoming from the Enlightenment. 'Philosophy' had to be defended – if necessary, at the cost of condemning the guillotine itself. But the medical science of the Enlightenment, in setting out its arguments, came face to face with another, insurmountable contradiction whose impact upon medical theory was considerable.[21]

The doctors of philosophical medicine ascribed no expressive value to the movements observable in the faces of the decapitated. The notion of 'survival' was merely 'bizarre'. Its premises were unscientific. It was a 'purely metaphysical idea', and to be dismissed as 'a figment of the imagination'.[22] Facial expression in the decapitated was not an indication of existing feeling; it was mechanical reaction or reflex. Such 'convulsions' were a 'remnant of mechanism and wholly without perception' (Gastellier). By ascribing these movements to the work of the bodily machine, philosophy rescued the work of the decapitating machine from ignoming and ensured that the concept of 'machine' lost none of the prestige it then enjoyed.

Charlotte Corday's last blush could thus be dismissed,[23] and Gastellier cited as proof of his thesis a remarkable case, that of the man who receives a sword-thrust in the nerve-centre of the diaphragm, and whose face as a result is seized by a form of convulsion called the 'sardonic' or 'sardonian grin': 'He dies laughing, or at least gives this impression, and yet we know he has little enough to laugh about. It is a purely mechanical convulsion and, although the brain is perfectly intact, the patient undoubtedly dies unaware of what is happening to him.'[24]

This last remark is somewhat disturbing. Not only does the term 'patient' suggest the excessive prominence of medical phraseology in this account of death, but the final affirmation is clearly open to doubt. The sardonic laughter of the dying man may express no joy whatever, but we cannot on this account deduce that he is unaware of dying. Gastellier's confident manner seems to be intended above all to reassure the reader, and his logical legerdemain signifies only that enlightened medicine could not conceive of even the 'intact' brain registering thought independently of the body, still less of this occurring in the body's absence.

Much was at stake here. Over and above the issue of an 'afterthought' of death, the question arose whether any part of the body might be identified as the seat of consciousness. The irresistible stroke of the guillotine made the question inevitable: 'Where is the soul located within the body?' (Sédillot). The question was an important one, since Descartes, sharing a widely held opinion, had located the soul in the pineal gland, that is, precisely at the point first encountered by the guillotine's blade. It is no surprise to find the mechanistic notion of the body intersecting so neatly with the machinery of death, but the very efficiency of the machine here again transcends its purpose and touches on the sacral: though the presence of the confessor as close as possible to the head of the condemned man now seems, in consequence, eminently rational, the concepts that the guillotine thus conjures up smack more of the late Middle Ages than of the Enlightenment.

Sue argued that man was the only 'organic being' endowed with three kinds of life: moral, intellectual and animal, each of these having a bodily location which was the 'preferred' theatre of its activities.[25] For Cabanis, on the other hand, the vital principle 'had no specific or exclusive seat', and for Sédillot the soul could not be physically located. Consciousness was to be explained in terms of the co-ordination of the totality of the parts to the body,[26] and far from the brain being the centre of sensation, the self existed only in that 'general life' of which the essential connective organ was the spinal cord.[27]

If separated from the body, then, and in particular from the spinal cord, the brain is no longer complete: 'It is no longer in contact with the extended spinal cord' (Sédillot). The unity that constitutes the sense of self within the body is broken. Cabanis, in his *Rapports du physique et du moral de l'homme*, denounces as 'metaphysical' any attempts to assign the mental function to a localizable organ, and no longer sees the brain as the 'intellectual workshop' that Sue had celebrated. The brain is merely another internal organ; 'the laboratory of life' is distributed throughout the 'torso as a whole'. A reassuring conclusion follows: 'Theory and experience would seem to demonstrate that: (1) the brain loses all vital energy immediately it is separated from the body; (2) it does not feel the after-pain that affects the neck; (3) sensation, personality and self are no longer present in this organ.'[28]

Thus the 'dying head' is dispatched into metaphysics by downgrading the status of the brain. Undoubtedly, one of the guillotine's achievements was to have made this debate necessary. It is a debate in which a traditional concept of medicine, based on an emblematic reading of the body's signs, is challenged by a more modern theory of the body with a radically different notion of the organic. We will see at a later stage how closely this description and model of the nervous system coincided with the new image of the body politic outlined by the Republic; for the time being, let us note that the guillotine contributed to the emergence, or institution, of a new configuration of the body and its sensory apparatus, a new conception of the relations of the mental and the physical. One remarkable product of this debate was Cabanis's *Rapports du physique et du moral de l'homme*, which delineates what contemporary medicine would term a 'somatic' approach to disease and the psyche.

Self as Series

By redistributing the 'vital functions' through the body as a whole, philosophical medicine opened the way for a surprising but entirely logical conclusion that capitalizes on the instant of the guillotine. The victim of the guillotine dies *before* decapitation; he dies 'at that quite possibly incalculable instant when the falling blade strikes the horizontal spinal cord as a contusive instrument before cutting it'.[29] Only after our survey of the medical debate is the logic of this conclusion clear. It is the final paradox reached by medical science in its determination to avert the horror of the opposite hypothesis.

For the self was not easy to dispose of. On the contrary. Thus Auberive:

> We know as little of the moment which unites as of the moment which parts the two substances ... A clever anatomist might perhaps be able ... to prove to me that the movements cannot be voluntary, and in so doing disprove all the facts I have related, even the one concerning Mary Stuart. But he will not on that account have shown that thought does not survive; he will not have shown that sensation is extinguished; he will not have shown that the single blow that divides the two parts immediately breaks the incomprehensible unity in which the two substances are bound.'[30]

Auberive, it is true, could hardly be described as an enlightened philosopher,[31] but there is more to his obstinate refusal to be convinced by the anatomist's arguments than merely a spiritualist reaction against the often explicitly materialist physiology of the late eighteenth century. His insistence is better understood as representing the claims of subjectivity and a sense of individuality as against the levelling pronouncements of science. Enlightened conclusions as to the machine's effects never quite destroyed the lurid fascination of the 'afterthought' and a hundred years later the spectre of a consciousness 'that the blade had not impaired' still haunted the severed head. The 'secret of the scaffold' remained. 'Is it or is it not the self which, after the cessation of the haematoma, acted upon the muscles of the bloodless head?[32] Dr Velpeau replies, as does Cabanis, that 'the self is present only in the whole', but Villiers de L'Isle-Adam's plot turns upon the fact that the hypothesis of enlightened medicine can never be confirmed, and he is not merely availing himself of artistic licence; Cabanis himself had already acknowledged that 'we have no experimental certainty in this, but only the conviction afforded by analogy and argument ... No decapitated man has yet proved able to come forward and give an account of his experiences.'[33] Well, no...

Though empirical certainty could not be found, the debate was a bitter one. Clearly more was at stake in the medical debate of Year IV than the scientific subjects ostensibly discussed. The self centrally at issue is not conceived of exclusively in terms of a nervous system, but in relation to the 'self-image', the individualism that the last twenty-five years of the century had so exalted. The use of the guillotine brought two drastic setbacks to this movement: the uniformity of death, and the suggestion that the notion of machinery might apply to consciousness itself.

The many far-fetched tales that Auberive amassed in his *Anecdotes sur les décapités*, only to set them aside as unreliable, have at least the poetic merit of affirming that every death is unique, and unique with the uniqueness of the individual. The 'sense of self'[34] serves to indict the banality of the guillotine, which divests the individual of his individuality even in his hour of death. The victim once attached to the plank became part of the machine. The uniformity prescribed by the law eliminated any variation supplied by 'human agency'. It mechanized death. The self succumbed to this conformity: 'It would indeed be extraordinary had the victims all fallen as uniformly as ears of grain under the scythe of the mower.'[35] Auberive's protest sheds some light on one of the guillotine's most revolutionary aspects – the very political use to which the Terror put the levelling and production-line capacities of the machine, which were employed in the 'public interest' and against what Robespierre, in words most untypical of Rousseau, terms the 'baseness of the individual self'.[36]

Moreover, by showing that the uniqueness of the individual could be mechanically destroyed, the guillotine also suggested that consciousness derived from the machine of the body. The existence of a 'machine consciousness' was physically demonstrated by its annihilation. This was not an easy point to admit. Cabanis is exemplary in this regard: whereas in the preface to his *Rapports du physique et du moral de l'homme* he had postulated that a knowledge of the bodily machine was required for any study of mental functions, in both the third essay of the *Rapports*, which he read at the Institut National in Year IV,[37] and his *Lettre sur les causes premières* of 1806-7, the question is raised in more alarming terms: 'Does the moral constitution of man ..., of which the self may be considered the link or foundation, share in death the fate of the organic aggregation [of parts], or does it survive the dissolution of the visible elements that compose it?' Still more surprising, in the light of the confidence evinced in his *Note [...] sur le supplice de la guillotine*, Cabanis declares himself 'far from convinced' that 'the self, or more precisely, the sense of self' is destroyed 'at the moment of death'.[38]

So the instant of the guillotine forced an enlightened scientific and methodical approach into an impasse. Its failure does, however, indicate the extent to which Cabanis's confident replies in his *Note* were determined by extra-medical concerns. The medical debate of Year IV was, it would seem, inhabited and moulded by a political analogy, and the relation of self to the body was considered in terms derived from two competing models of the relation of national consciousness to the body politic and social.

Bodies Physical and Politic

In contending that the self survived execution, Sue had, as we have seen, developed a theory of the three 'life forces' in man – the moral, the intellectual and the animal – each endowed with a physical location and attaining unity in the figurative and physical 'head'.[39] The theory dates back to the Renaissance, but what concerns us here are its political implications. The idea that the head incarnates the unity of the functions of the body finds a clear analogy in the notion of the 'body royal'. The king is seen both as head of a nation constituted by three functionally distinct classes, and as the incarnation of a state comprising three powers: legislative; executive; judicial. The role of the head in Sue's threefold division is strikingly similar to the function of the person of the monarch in the theory of absolutist monarchy.[40]

Cabanis, as a convinced republican, was bound to reject this political model, and the medical debate on the effect of the guillotine cannot be considered independently of the political background. Running parallel to the use made of the machine by the revolutionary government, the links between medical and political thought and between the imagery of the body and the body politic form a complex network. Cabanis is here a revelatory, indeed an exemplary, figure. A widely respected spokesman for the new doctrines concerning the working of the nervous system,[41] he felt honoured by his nomination to the jury of the Revolutionary Tribunal on 22 March 1793 and, though he resigned for reasons of health on 23 April, the distinction implied by his nomination remained. His political career was under way; his subsequent role as *Idéologue* in the Council of Five Hundred was far from negligible, and his long speech of 16 December 1789 on the *système représentatif* shows the extent to which the growth of a new concept of political representation was mapped onto the modern notion of the body and its metabolism.[42]

Cabanis conceived of society as an animate machine whose 'every part must be vivified'. The *système représentatif* was, in his view, the most important discovery of the 'social art' of recent times, because it guaranteed a healthy communication between parts and whole. Structured as a 'whole whose every part matches', the system creates a 'true national and general representation' of the people, which is considered a 'common resource'.[43] In this way a constant interchange between people and government is established and the advent of a despot, that 'absolute representative', is excluded.[44]

'Pure democracy' is a mere perversion, comparable to organic derangement or to a regression.[45] To avoid the 'continuous worry and agitation' which would result therefrom, a representative system founds its dynamic coherence in the power that it bestows upon the executive. Tyranny is excluded because of the supervision of the legislature and judiciary, and the system thus has the strength that derives from 'unity of thought and action'.[46] Robespierre had already formulated the republican position with great clarity: 'A single, unified will is necessary. It must be either republican or royalist.'[47] And what separated the monarchic from the republican unity of the executive was precisely the differing concept of the political body in which the nation was represented; the body of the king, which for absolute monarchists was the incarnation of the nation, or for republicans, the body of representatives elected by the people as a body.

And here the ideas of Cabanis, which arise at a junction of the medical and the political, take on their full significance. The language of politics draws on the metaphor of physiology, and the language of medicine makes play with social imagery.[48] Thus, when Cabanis postulates that the cerebral system is 'everywhere present, and everywhere governs', this is no longer analogous to the government of a king and his 'omnipresent body'.[49] The cerebral system no longer has any particular centre in the body; it is not an 'independent and absolute cause', and the healthy 'economy' of the body requires just such an interchange as that organized by the système représentatif: 'In order to act and ensure that its actions affect the other systems, it [the cerebral system] must in its turn undergo their influence. All these functions are linked and form a circle which does not allow of interruption.'[50]

The term 'interruption' returns us to that irresistible physical interruptor, the guillotine, and points clearly to its inevitable political signification. No doubt the reasons that led Cabanis to reject the horrific thesis of the 'thinking head' were genuinely medical, but to acknowledge or suppose that consciousness might momentarily subsist in the brain after decapitation would also be to acknowledge consciousness as an 'independent and absolute cause', making of it an 'absolute representative', which might in its turn entail the obligation to acknowledge that the body politic too should come under this 'fixed form of existence'. It is therefore not surprising that Cabanis, a staunch republican, firmly rejected the idea in a magazine article which was bound to receive a political interpretation. Nor, on the other hand, is it surprising that, in his *Mémoire sur les rapports du physique et du moral*, which was presented to a specialist audience, he adopted a more cautious position; or, finally, that in his speech to the Council of Five Hundred, he recommended the restoration, within the system, of a strong executive, of a head, of a headquarters capable of authoritative local decision-making. Cabanis supported the *coup d'état* of 18 *Brumaire* and its aspiration to expunge the 'hideous traces of the revolutionary government' while also ensuring that 'royalism did not raise its ugly head'.[51] The firm government of Bonaparte might momentarily have seemed a perfect solution . . .

And so one of the most unexpected effects of the machine intended to make death, along with the self that died, uniform, was a new, reconstituted, exacerbated self, the self exalted by Romanticism and the *'enfants du siècle'*. This is perhaps the point of scission between the gentle, contemplative, Rousseauist self and the wild, exalted Romantic ego. At all events, it is remarkable that Chateaubriand should end the first volume of his *Essais historiques sur les révolutions anciennes et modernes* with a passage that anticipates *René*. Written 'under the influence of a death sentence, as it were, between sentence and execution' – the sentence and execution of Louis XVI – the *Essais* conclude with what Chateaubriand himself was pleased to call 'the dark orgy of a wounded soul' for whom 'individual independence is all'.[52]

Perhaps in this feverish reaffirmation of the self there lay a remedy for the 'upheaval' of the Terror, in which so many selves had gone to an identical death, uniform as ears of corn. As early as 1793 a German print had made of the tomb of the king a political metaphor presaging this renewal of self. Prone, truncated, the king's body lies at the base of the monument, on the summit of which the body royal is displayed in all its pristine, unitary glory. On the left, set back somewhat, is the guillotine, a paradoxical machine, a mechanical instrument, which, while destroying the singularity of the body, was destined, under the pressure of history, to emphasize the singularity of the self . . .

2

The Death of the King

You will die as other men do. And nevertheless, you are gods, and though you die, your authority lives on ... Man is mortal, it is true; but the king, we affirm, never dies. The image of God is immortal.

Boussuet, *Sur les devoirs des rois*

For the philosopher, it is a matter of some interest to see how kings comport themselves at death.

Le Thermomètre du jour, 18 February 1793,
quoted by Chateaubriand in *Essais historiques
sur les révolutions anciennes et modernes*

21 January 1793, the death of the king.

The procession momentarily halted, and then continued on its way through the ranks of the silent and motionless people, to the point where rue Royale opens onto the place de la Révolution. There, a wintry ray of sun had penetrated the mist and illuminated the hundred thousand heads that filled the square, the regiments of the Paris garrison drawn up into a square around the scaffold, the executioners awaiting their victim, and the instrument of death whose beams and posts, painted blood-red, stood out above the crowd.

This instrument was the guillotine. Invented in Italy, imported into France through the humanity of a well-known doctor and member of the Constituent Assembly, Guillotin by name, it had replaced the hideous and ignominious method of execution practised before the Revolution. In the view of the legislators of the Assembly, it had this further merit: no man's blood was shed by the – often unsteady – hand of his fellow, and the murder was executed by an instrument without life, insensible as wood, infallible as iron. At a signal from the executioner the axe fell by its own weight. This axe, whose momentum was multiplied a hundredfold by two weights attached to it under the scaffold, slid in two grooves with a movement part horizontal, part vertical,[1] like that of a saw, detaching the head

48

from the torso by the weight of its fall and with the speed of lightning. Time and pain alike were expunged from the sensation of death.[2]

The relative sobriety of Lamartine's fiction in these two paragraphs, written more than fifty years after the events they narrate, offers a remarkable insight into the tensions governing the way in which the execution of Louis XVI was perceived. Above the crowd stands a new machine, the description of which is confined to historical and technical detail, and whose solitary distinction is its philosophical and humanitarian 'merit'. In the square, the 'apparatus' of state ceremony is deployed; the great day has drawn a large crowd. The restraint of Lamartine's account gives the greater weight to the symbolic overtones: from rue *royale* to place de la *Révolution, a sun* (king?) penetrates the shapeless mist, a mist as amorphous as the crowd of one hundred thousand *heads* gathered for the decapitation of a single *head* (of State) – the decapitation to be effected by a *blood-red* device surrounded by the armed guard in *parade* formation. At the centre of this contrast between the grandeur of the occasion and its soulless, mechanical instrument, the guillotine determined the symbolism of an unprecedented act – the execution of a king; but in so doing it also defined its own.

The king's death was, as Albert Sorel noted, invested with a 'solemnity', a 'pomp . . . scarcely less regal for being counterfeit'. Louis was still 'treated as a king, and in his very death remained an isolated figure among the French'.[3] But Sorel was wrong to suppose that the Convention had instigated the pomp and ceremony only 'reluctantly'. On 3 December 1792 Robespierre had clearly announced that the 'punishment of Louis' must have 'the solemn character of a public vengeance'.[4] The death of the king thus invested the guillotine with a solemnity and grandeur commensurate with its function as the instrument of the people's justice. 21 January, still more than the execution of Collenot d'Angremont, fully inaugurated the political use of the guillotine, and its mechanical character, combining as it did the properties of scaffold, gibbet, and blade, came to play a well-defined emblematic role.

Body Royal: Sacrosanctity of the Law

The theory of the divine right of kings and of the supernatural powers attaching to the body of the king[5] had taken something of a battering during the Enlightenment. Yet the prestige and sanctity of the king remained potent forces. Not only was regicide long considered a crime in its own right, but the exceptional status of the royal body was recognized in law: paragraph 2 of the 1791 Constitution maintained the principle of the inviolability of the king's person. And the terms in which, during the king's trial, his advocate de Sèze referred to that principle, indicate how sacred, how untouchable the king remained: 'Our current notions of equality lead us to see in the king an ordinary individual. But a king is not an individual, he is a privileged being, a moral being, a being for whom a nation, seeking its own happiness, establishes an existence entirely different from its own; and for him, its head, the nation stipulates, though he is but one, as it would for an entire nation.'[6] Louis XVI forbade de Sèze to speak these words, for they constituted very precisely the principal accusation brought against the king in the Convention by Robespierre and Saint-Just. It lies at the political heart of the Revolution, and we must examine it closely.

The Montagnards revived the concept of the sanctity of the body royal, and used it to make the king's status seem not so much exceptional as monstrous. In the words of Grégoire, whose speech of 21 September was instrumental in abolishing the monarchy: 'Kings are in the moral sphere what monsters are in the physical.'[7] The Revolution set up its own legitimacy and sanctity on the ruins of the sanctity of the king's person, which it turned to its own advantage, establishing itself by annihilating him.

The debates preceding the execution had allowed revolutionary eloquence to 'draw a sacred circle [*sacer*] around an exceptional being',[8] and on him the guillotine's blade descended as if on an expiatory sacrifice.

As early as 13 November 1792 Saint-Just set aside the constitutional guarantee of inviolability, on the grounds that, by 'conspiring against liberty', Louis XVI had himself torn up the Constitution. More important, inviolability could only subsist between citizens, but not between king and people.[9] In Robespierre's view the inviolability of the king rested upon 'a fiction', the inviolability of the people upon 'a sacred natural right'.[10] The fictive inviolability of Louis removed him from the register of citizens, and he could not therefore be judged as one: only his crimes made a citizen of him, and he should therefore be judged as 'a foreign enemy'.[11] On 3 December Robespierre took his arguments one stage further. The king needed no trial, judgement on him having already been rendered. 'Louis was king, and the Republic has been founded ... Louis denounced the people of France as rebels ... Victory and the people have discovered in him the solitary rebel. Louis cannot be brought to trial – he stands condemned already; if he is not, the Republic is not absolved.'[12] The representatives of the people therefore do not have 'a verdict to return', but 'an act of national providence to perform'.[13]

❡ The logic underlying this revolutionary argument is a doctrine of natural rights that excludes tyrants from the natural order. In Saint-Just's laconic summary: 'There is no innocent reign ... every king is a rebel and a usurper.' Robespierre confirmed the point: the only relationship that can exist between a people and a king is insurrection.[14] The circle in which the king was placed was now drawing exceedingly tight: if he was not to be judged under civil law, but by the law of the people, if the nation was not to judge him 'a civil servant, while maintaining the form of government', but to destroy, in his person, 'the government itself', the only possible sentence was death.[15] If justice thus made a 'cruel' exception to its own rules, it was to take account of the monstrously exceptional status arrogated by the king: his person was in itself sufficient to abort the nascent Republic.[16] Louis had excluded himself from the law of nature, and had to die to regenerate a society that he had corrupted by his tyrannical usurpation of power. Varennes had led to the massacre of the tenth of August: 'The blood of the best citizens, the blood of women and children, had flowed for him on the altar of the homeland.' The king had become a monstrous barbaric deity whose cult demanded human sacrifices, whereas the sacrifice of this monster was, on the contrary, 'in the natural order of things',[17] a sacred duty that quite transcended the requirements made by judicial conventions at least partly inherited from despotism; it was a duty far above 'constitutional niceties'.[18] The orator here speaks simply as the spokesman of the people, a people defined not as a collection of individuals, but as a natural entity rejecting the royal monster: 'I have heard the voice of the public calling upon you to accomplish the sacred duty which the will of the nation confers upon you.'[19]

Finally, on 23 December, after the demand had been made by the Girondin, Salle, for an appeal to the people, Robespierre brought together all the strands of this argument which condemned Louis without the need for a trial: 'There are sacred forms which are not those of the Bar.' The case was made, and Louis the Last went to the scaffold to 'consolidate liberty and the peace and calm of the public with the punishment of a tyrant'.[20]

And so the Assembly became a sanctuary, a temple, where the representatives defended a sacred cause. Corrupted by the monstrous tyranny that had usurped a sovereignty naturally theirs,[21] the people had to be regenerated, and Louis, the author of this usurpation, stood already condemned; he could not so much as be summoned before a court.[22]

All this political theory progressively ensnared the king in a condemnation that was by then a foregone conclusion. The vocabulary of Saint-Just and Robespierre is implacably consistent, and tends to confirm that the execution of Louis XVI had little or nothing in common with that of the English king, Charles I. As Robespierre claimed, the execution of Louis XVI was without precedent: 1793 was a revolution not least in the very principles of civil society presented as a return to the natural and sacred sources of human society. The essential, theoretical underpinning of the Revolution was the re-appropriation of the sovereignty in favour of the people. This required that the sanctity with which the theory of the divine right had invested the person of the king revert to the people. The arguments surrounding the king's death hinged on the ideology of monarchy: on 21 January 1793 the poles of sanctity were reversed, and the people gained what the king had lost.

The Revolution sacrificed in the king's person the supernatural qualities supposed to reside therein. The 'circle of sanctity' which its spokesmen drew around him in their speeches was a menacing variant of the sanctity which monarchic theory had itself bestowed, and which defined his inviolable divinity: 'I am the State.' When, in his *Réflexions sur le métier de roi*, Louis XIV had written that 'in France, the nation as such does not constitute a body; it is entirely subsumed in the body of the king', he identified 'an abstraction with a body'.[23] That the king should prove unable to cure the king's evil (scrofula) was by then irrelevant; the king no longer represented the State (on a symbolic level) – he was the State (on an 'imaginary' level). The king embodied the nation, and this 'real presence' made of the monarchy a mystery resembling that of the Eucharist.[24]

The transition effected by monarchic theory between the king's symbolic representation of the nation and his becoming, in the imagination, the nation itself, was sanctioned in both senses by Louis XVI's execution. It was not simply the abolition of monarchy, nor the result of a debate about the principles of political philosophy. The 'grace of State' (Démoris) which accorded a supernatural legitimacy to the power of the king necessarily legitimated the destruction of a body which had come to seem monstrous to the now regenerate nation. The king was the devil incarnate, and exercised a 'hideous fascination upon souls'.[25] His impure blood, shed not in the imagination, but actually slaking the soil of the square, would redeem the homeland: 'Louis must die because the homeland must live.'[26] And, after the king's death, Robespierre went on to exhort the Assembly to persevere in the defence of this 'truly divine religion' of which the people's representatives were the 'missionaries': they should 'put forth the sacred energy to which the punishment of kings should elevate them'.[27]

The baptismal significance of the immolation of the king is clear in this last statement. The death of the king was something more than the abolition of the monarchy; it was a sort of founding sacrifice whose religious significance is confirmed by the consensus of revolutionaries and royalists as to the significance to be accorded to the event. Even before Albert Sorel declared that Louis had acquired a 'halo' upon the scaffold and that his death was a 'transfiguration', royalist propaganda – or at least royalist sentiment about his death – gave the king the status of a martyr, the status almost of a Christ.[28] On 17 June 1793 Pope Pius VI made this version of the event official, deploying the phraseology proper to cases of martyrdom: 'Oh day of triumph for Louis! For to him the Lord has vouchsafed patience under persecution and victory in martyrdom. We do not doubt that he has exchanged the fragile crown of royalty and the ephemeral lilies of France for an eternal crown woven of the immortal lilies of the angels.'[29]

Madame de Staël, describing the celebrations that marked Federation Day (14 July 1792), revealingly compares them to the day of the king's death, as though the king's attitude on the former occasion had foreshadowed his eventual fate: 'The king then went on foot to the altar which had been erected at the far end of the Champ-de-Mars ... As he mounted the steps of the altar, it was as though we saw the holy victim offering himself up for sacrifice ... from that day forth, the people never saw him again till he appeared on the scaffold.'[30]

The Consecration of the Guillotine

Having considered these many levels of discourse, the great 'abundance of words that each and every one lavished upon this unique circumstance' (Madame de Staël found this shocking), we can now appreciate the character and condition of death which the rhetoric of the Revolution had prepared for the king. We can understand how the use of the guillotine served to identify the revolutionary character of his execution, and, above all, how the decapitating machine came, through the execution, to acquire new connotations which, though unexpected, determined its later image. For at the heart of this execution stood the sanctity of the king, and, by it, the instrument of his death was for ever coloured. The king, desanctified in death, sanctified the Revolution at its foundation, and the instrument through the frame of which this transition and transfer occurred attained thereby to its own symbolic consecration.

That Louis XVI should be decapitated by a machine was, first and foremost, a very powerful example, and a definitive negation of the exceptional status of royalty. Though the event was staged with all due solemnity, the process and instrument were standard. True, the ritual had been observed in holding a political execution on a political site, and the scaffold had therefore been transferred from place du Carrousel to place de la Révolution;[31] but the machine had not changed: uprights, crossbeams and blade were none of them new; they had already been used. It was already commonplace, and wholly lacking in the exceptional status conferred by the sword, the wearing of which was a badge of class, the wielding of which, especially on signal occasions such as this, required a 'sovereign' mastery. The guillotine restored Louis to the ambit of common law. It was not so much death that was the same for Capet as for the rest, but the instrument by which he suffered it. The significance of the machine was the clearer for its having become the central protagonist. The role of the executioner was, by comparison, secondary. This effect had been foreseen and indeed promoted from 1793 onwards, but its impact was greatly enhanced by the royalty of the victim. Between king and executioner there was, in the late eighteenth century, a long-standing relationship that might have given their meeting upon the scaffold an almost traditional sense.

Joseph de Maistre gives perhaps the most illuminating account of that sanctity which invests the king and his headsman, persons indissociably connected in any system of power based on 'divine right': 'All greatness, all power, all subordination reside in the executioner: he is the horror and the cement of human association. If once this unfathomable influence is withdrawn from the world, at that instant, order gives place to chaos, thrones fall and society is extinguished. God, from whom all sovereignty derives, is the source of punishment too: on these two poles he established our world.'[32] The meeting upon the scaffold of these two poles might indeed engender chaos, but the phenomenon could still be categorized as a natural catastrophe, a world that turns in on and destroys itself. Robespierre, insisting that Louis's death had nothing in common with that of the English Charles I, was making precisely this point. The death of Charles I was of quite another kind, being the execution, through the mediation of the executioner, of one tyrant by another. The people, by contrast, followed no other law than that of justice and reason, enforced 'by its omnipotence' (3 December 1792). The way in which the machine supplanted the executioner thus testified to the transition from one system, from one world, to another: the Revolution avoided the spectacular convergence of the two poles of monarchic justice, and put in its place the spectacle of reason and justice made law.

The merit of the guillotine as a symbol was now reinforced by the fact that its very appearance had a representative quality. The use of a machine as the visual representative of an 'omnipotent' entity strongly suggests that reason alone was the entity's animating principle, that it was free of the uncertainty and chance attendant upon merely 'human agency'. Furthermore, the very shape of the guillotine gave substance to the principle of justice it represented – a justice humane enough, no doubt, but as inexorable as a universal axiom. The simplicity of its aesthetic impressed itself upon the visual imagination. It exhibited the three basic geometrical forms: square (in the form of a rectangle); circle; triangle. Unlike instruments of torture, which were generally more complex and meticulously designed to inflict a certain quota of pain via a specific part of the body, the guillotine had something of the simplicity and austerity of a diagram: its abstract shape was a declaration of the universal validity of the laws of geometry and gravity. The decapitating machine made public execution a celebration of the mechanical and geometrical, and so ensured the spectacular triumph of these forms of 'just' and 'reasonable' thought.

The Goncourt brothers echoed this impression in their extraordinary description of the device: 'In the guillotine, the scientific eye perceives a horizontal plane some feet above the ground on which have been erected two perpendiculars separated by a right-angled triangle falling through a circle onto a sphere which is subsequently isolated by a cutter.'[33]

The visual impact of the guillotine's geometry did not end there. By putting into motion its three fundamental geometric forms at the time of the 'greatest act of social power' (Cabanis) the guillotine set before its audience the abstract form of a law which universally governs all regular forms. It did this none the less effectively on 21 January 1793 when the body upon which it was called to act was exceptional, irregular, abnormal, having, till the guillotine was called into play, enjoyed the exorbitant privilege of sanctity and inviolability. The machine, in the instant of its action, annexed this privilege to itself. By reducing the body of the king from its monstrous sanctity to the rational norms of a universal system, it appropriated its sanctity, transforming and regenerating it according to its own laws.

This was not expected. The arguments of the delegates who voted to put the king to death testify to the fact. Though many were, in theory, opposed to the death penalty, they justified their stance by adopting Robespierre's argument concerning the universality of the Law, an argument they regarded as clinching.[34] The king's death was to be considered exceptional only to the extent that it might establish, for everyone's benefit, the rule of law underlying the Law. But the verbosity of certain delegates indicates – since 'the true republican is laconic' (Lakanal) – that things were not so clear-cut. The imagination balked at the theoretical equality with which the body royal was to be reduced to a commonplace physical person. Marat's own account of the day suggests that sacral overtones remained: 'The head of the tyrant has fallen under the broadsword of the law ... A spirit of serene joy inhabited the people; it was as though they had just attended a religious festival.'[35] The application of a law from which none was exempt was not the source of this religious fervour. The instant of the guillotine had created what we might call the '*syncope* of the sacred'; the annihilation of the previously sacred had consecrated the instrument of destruction. The reversal is the more striking in that the instant was scarcely visible. The secrecy essential to the sacred had been preserved.

Narratives

But now this invisibility concerned a paradigmatic event, *the* event *par excellence*, a historical event whose story had to be told. And the diversity of narrative that arose from the 'laconic' fact put so briefly before its audience illustrates the extraordinary effect of the guillotine's consecration.

Two narratives, written by imagined witnesses, define the boundaries within which accounts of the king's death can be ranged, the one objective, the other mystical in manner.

> Can it be the same man that I see manhandled by the executioner's four flunkeys, forced to undress, whose voice is drowned out by the drums, who is trussed to a board, still struggling, and who takes the guillotine's stroke so badly that not his neck but his occiput and jaw are horribly cut?

> Stock-still, staring fixedly, I had seen one of the headsmen cut the august victim's hair; but I did not see the head of my king fall beneath the blade of execution. A ribbon of light at that moment enfolded my dazzled orbs, and changed the instant of sacrifice into a celestial vision. I heard neither what the executioner said as he showed the head to the people, nor the solitary and sinister cry of triumph that rang out, I am told, amid the gloomy, religious silence.[36]

The mystical manner of Ballanche's narrative is no doubt encouraged by the fact that his 'eyewitness account' is part of a fictional account, *L'Homme sans nom*. The protagonist is a regicidal deputy who now repents, and in the text the invisible instant of death is replaced by a supernatural vision which articulates the meaning of the deputy's repentance. The tone of Mercier, on the other hand, is objective,[37] but posits an interrogation of the real in which objectivity itself is made to question the details it records.

These two styles define the range of all the variants, and it is the attitude ascribed to the central figure, the king, that determines which style is chosen. In the royalist version the king offers himself of his own free will as an expiatory victim. In the republican version the objective uncertainty attaching to the succession of events derives from the king's own uncertainty – his belief, maintained even on the scaffold, that his supporters will save him from death; his behaviour thus demonstrates the existence of an aristocratic plot. Between these extremes there is great narrative variety – nor should this surprise us, for we know how rarely eyewitness accounts agree. It is not therefore the variety as such that interests us, but the process of gradual 'embroidery' by which the narratives come to diverge. This process is of inherent interest, for it is closely related to the way in which 'historical narrative' of any kind comes to be written.

Even at the time, people were fully aware of this. The day after the execution the editor of *Le Patriote français* exhorted his readers thus: 'Illustrious day! Never to be forgotten day! May you come down to posterity without stain! Calumny be ever far from you! Historians, show yourselves worthy of your times! Write the truth, and nothing but the truth. Never was the truth so sacred, never so becoming to tell!' The event which took place on 21 January required a historian, a recital, but at its culminating point deployed a mechanism which allowed of none of those incidents of which narrative is made. The narrative poverty of the instant of the guillotine is replaced with a description of before and after. Since the machine cannot bear a narrative weight proportionate to its role, the 'narrative of the guillotine' deploys all the resources of narrative amplification, and does so, needless to say, in the name of historical truth.

The Impossible Objective Narrative

In the corpus of such narratives two have special status. They were written by professional and privileged witnesses, a fact that might be thought to guarantee their agreement. Not so. Their divergence can be put down to the differences between their literary genres: the first is the official report of the occasion, drawn up by civil servants allocated to this task; the second a letter from Sanson, the executioner, protesting at the falsity of an account which had been attributed to him.

Having, according to protocol, noted the administrative procedures according to which the report was drawn up, the civil servants state:

> At the same time [precisely at ten-fifteen in the morning] the column commanded by Santerre, commander-in-chief, reached the place de la Révolution. It escorted Louis Capet in a four-wheeled carriage and approached the scaffold which had been set up in the aforesaid place de la Révolution between the pedestal of the statue of the former Louis XV and the avenue des Champs-Elysées. At ten-twenty, Louis Capet, who had reached the foot of the scaffold, got out of the carriage. At ten-twenty-two, he mounted the scaffold. The execution was instantly carried out and his head was shown to the people, and we signed.[38]

The neutrality of language, befitting the genre, sets forth a minimal, administrative version of the event which is intended to convey the clockwork precision with which it unfolded.

And yet, for all its declarative sobriety, the report remains a narrative. Sanson's letter, written in response to an article that had appeared in *Le Thermomètre du jour* of 13 February, shows how the civil servants, not content with drawing a veil of silence over the events which ocurred during the two-minute delay at the foot of the scaffold and which were later to become the basis of a whole series of variants, also eliminate by their 'instantly' what we can only call 'the scaffold scene', the culminating scene of the drama:

> Here then, as I promised, is the exact truth concerning what happened. As he got out of the carriage, he was told to remove his robe; he objected to this and said he could be executed as he was. It being represented to him that this was impossible, he himself helped to remove his robe. He made the same objection when it came to tying his hands, but offered them himself when the person who was with him said that this was a last sacrifice. He then inquired whether the drums would continue to beat. He was told that no one had any idea. And this was true. He mounted the scaffold and wanted to go right to the front as if to speak. But it was made clear to him that this was impossible too. He allowed himself to be led to the place where he was bound, and here he cried very loudly: 'People, I die innocent.' Then he turned to us and said: 'Sirs, I am innocent of everything I am charged with. May my blood cement the happiness of the French people.' There, citizen, you have his last and actual words.

The little debate that took place at the foot of the scaffold hinged on his thinking it was not necessary to take off his robe or have his hands tied. He also offered to cut his own hair.

And if the truth be told, he bore all this with a calm and perseverance that astonished us all. I am firmly convinced that his perseverance was owed to the religious principles with which he seemed more than anyone impressed and imbued.

Be assured, citizen, that this is the simple truth of the matter.

Your fellow citizen, SANSON.[39]

For Sanson's contemporaries this might seem an essential document. Written by the person closest to the king, it gave the text of his last words and described the two ocurrences on which historical narrative might feed. At last, a bare and simple truth guaranteed by Sanson's letter? . . .

And yet, for all his initial 'spasm of horror' at touching 'a piece of paper over which has crawled the blood-stained hand of Sanson', baron Hyde de Neuville saw in the letter 'the last ray set upon the crown of the martyr-king'.[40] It is at first sight surprising to find Sanson, no doubt inspired by the angels, weaving Louis's immortal crown. But there is a logical explanation for this transformation. In the literature surrounding the king's death, Sanson's letter has unique status, less for the truth of his witness than for what could be made of it. Its objective manner so perfectly confirms the message of the mystical narrative that it became a key document in the royalist hagiography. It was even cited as proof of the rumour that Sanson was a fervent royalist.[41] The letter was taken as a sign of his being sent by providence to witness the king's death: 'Amidst the panic-stricken multitude, but one testimony was possible, one irrefutable! Providence allowed that he who had shed the victim's blood should become his historian.'[42]

Sanson, executioner and providential chronicler: this transformation suggests that the motives presiding over both the description and the interpretation of the event are to be studied. For, though we allow that Sanson was a historian of his victim, he was by no means the only one. By 21 February, when his letter was published in *Le Thermomètre du jour*, fourteen narratives of the execution had already been composed, for the most part variants of the two narrative styles already defined. Sanson's prestige derived partly from his status as principal witness, but also from the fact that the royalists could scarcely hope for a more authoritative confirmation of their own view than that provided by the executioner himself.

Our task is, then, not so much that of establishing what occurred on and around the scaffold, but rather to listen to the accounts given and to attempt to penetrate the motives which animate them.

The Crowd: People or Cannibals?

Le peuple is an essential character in the drama of 21 January. The king was sentenced in its name, and, as we have seen, his execution constituted a transfer of sovereignty. Not surprisingly, therefore, the attitude of the people gave rise to a wide range of interpretations.

These accounts do have one common feature: the silence that greeted the king throughout his last journey, and the calm that returned almost immediately after the excitement of the execution had passed. But the silence and the calm could be interpreted in different ways: the mystical style saw it as a manifestation of religious terror; the objective style, revealing itself as republican, saw it as the sign of an indifference or serenity 'worthy of the people'.

At first, the royalist version explained this otherwise inexcusable lack of reaction in psychological terms,[43] but the religious dimension was soon brought into play: 'With the exception of a few paid scoundrels who did the rounds of the town singing the 'Marseillaise', a gloomy silence reigned everywhere; but this was a silence like the silence of the tomb.'[44]

From the republican angle the silence is 'impressive' (*Le Patriote français*, 22 January); the republican conscience of the people oscillates between joy and a truly Roman magnanimity.[45] One account is particularly interesting for the distinctions that it draws, along republican lines, between the reactions of the different social groups. Wishing to counter the royalist account, it astonishingly blames the emotional weakness of women:

Work stopped for a moment or two, but immediately restarted, as though nothing at all had happened . . .

That evening, the citizens fraternized more than ever. In the street and in the café they would shake hands and promise, as they did so, that they would live more harmoniously than ever, now that the obstacle had been removed . . .

The women – and it would be unreasonable of us to expect them immediately to grasp the significance of political events – were, for the most part, somewhat sad; and this played a considerable part in the sullen air that Paris wore all that day. There were perhaps a few tears shed; but we know that women abound in tears. There were some reproaches also, and even some insults. All this is quite excusable in a frail and light-headed sex, which has seen the radiant last great days of a brilliant court.[46]

So casual a sexist division of the people is indicative of the paternalism which was liable to inhabit revolutionary thinking when it descended to the level of common sense. But it should be said that the author of this account, Baudrais, a municipal official, was attempting a difficult exercise – that of reconciling the two versions of 21 January, one joyful, one sullen. Since this was impossible, he simply divided political sentiment along sexual lines in a way sanctioned by tradition and stereotype alike.

The two conflicting accounts of the attitude of the people go to the heart of a highly significant political question. The overthrow of the monarchy took physical form in the destruction of the body royal, which marked the emergence of a category and image essential to republican ideology, namely the 'body of the People'. In the name of the people, its representatives had voted for the death of the king, and the people had flocked to the execution. The people's attitude could confirm or contradict the image of it created by the speeches in which it was supposed to have spoken through the voices of its representatives. The behaviour of the people should therefore corroborate the truth of Montagnard theory and rhetoric.[47] The guillotine was to muster the people, to summon it to witness the execution of the tyrant. In so doing, it would rid the people once and for all of its image as a populace of cannibals, and display it in its new dignity and unity. The guillotine symbolically transformed the very name of the people: reborn, it became, in its calm and dignity, the People.

The King's Blood

Few details in the narrative are more important than this. Popular calm was to offer a 'peremptory reply' to the 'odious insinuations' and 'slanders' which inevitably attended the behaviour of the Parisians at the foot of the scaffold. For the excitement that accompanied this birth of the People produced scenes which the republican conscience had to be able to account for 'in the name of the People'.

According to revolutionary rhetoric, the king's blood would 'seal the decree which declares France a republic';[48] it would be 'the cement of liberty'. That founding deed was still the theme of the *Révolutions de Paris* of 26 January: 'The blood of Capet, shed by the sword of the law on the 21st of January 1793, washes from us a stain thirteen hundred years old. We became republicans only on Monday the 21st, and not till then had we the right to consider ourselves a model for neighbouring countries.'

But the 'sword of the law' was a metaphor difficult to accord with the reality of the guillotine's blade, a point made by several contemporary accounts. Two opinions, two realities, were in competition in the Assembly and on the place de la Révolution, which only the skill in their telling could make coincide. For, at the moment when it was indeed shed and was slaking in very truth not the fields of the homeland but the prosaic soil of the esplanade, the tyrant's blood underwent a metamorphosis . . .

Whether in baptism of a new-born people or as proof that the soul of the king, 'freed of its terrestrial habitation, has flown into the bosom of the Almighty,'[49] the royal blood, along with the hair and clothing of the king, became the object of a collective handling which reason had neither foreseen nor predicted, and which resembled the traditional dismembering of the bodies of dead saints for the diffusion of their relics. After the cries of *Vive la Republique!* which accompanied the fall of the blade, the spectators closest to the guillotine came forward to touch the king's blood, to dip their pikestaffs or soak cloths in it. The hair of the king, which had been cropped at the foot of the scaffold, was put on sale, as were portions of his clothing which had been cut up for this purpose. It was difficult to find in this behaviour any proof of the dignity or rationality of the people. In his *Oraison funèbre de Louis Capet* Hébert therefore ascribes it to priests and pious old ladies.[50] But this is too simple; not even the republican versions follow him. The royalist accounts, far from rejoicing – as we might have expected they would, had they seen in this behaviour unequivocal proof of popular devotion to the body royal[51] – were at first extremely reserved. Slowly but surely, however, the royalist account expands to take in this theme, which is seen as proof of the barbarity of the people.[52] The episode provided the royalists with an opportunity to turn to their advantage this incontestable proof of fetishism with regard to the royal remains. Their account thus establishes a series of distinctions between the available relics – blood for the fanatics, hair for the virtuous[53] – while not ruling out the possibility that the cult of the king's blood might in some cases be inspired by reverence for the martyr:

Several people cut pieces from the clothing of the dead monarch; others endeavoured to possess themselves of locks of his hair. Wild zealots plunged their sabres in his blood, claiming that this talisman, of a kind unknown before, would render them victorious over every aristocrat and tyrant on earth. An Englishman also soaked his handkerchief in the blood, but for quite another purpose: he sent it to London, and several days later it was seen flying over the tower of that town in the form of a flag.[54]

The astonishing apparition of an English gentleman as a pious possessor of the blood royal belongs to the gradual expansion of the narrative, and is indeed a final and grandiose variant of a theme that had arisen as early as 22 January: 'Two well-dressed young men were to be seen. One of them, who looked to be a foreigner, perhaps an Englishman, gave fifteen francs to a child, requesting him to soak a very fine white handkerchief in the traces of blood that remained.'[55]

This enthusiasm for the king's blood was more difficult to incorporate into the republican version.[56] Only by stressing the religious theme of the regenerating baptism of blood could the event be satisfactorily explained. It is worth quoting Baudrais in full, for, reading between the lines of his criticism of the excessively laconic official report, we detect the requirement of a narrative worthy of the 'sovereign people'. Towards the end, Baudrais invents an improbable detail. No matter, it is for the imagination to determine the form of the narrative and make the best possible use of the dramatic potential afforded by the instrument of death:

> Jacques Roux, one of the two inhabitants of the municipality, both priests, who were appointed by the Commune to attend the execution of Louis Capet, says that citizens soaked their handkerchiefs in the blood of the king. This is true. What Jacques Roux should have added in his report to the General Council was that a great many volunteers eagerly dipped pike-heads, rifle bayonets or sabre blades in the despot's blood. The gendarmes were not slow to follow. Many officers of the Marseilles battalion and others soaked envelopes in the vile blood and then lifted these on the points of their swords, saying: 'See the blood of a tyrant.'
>
> One citizen even climbed onto the guillotine, and thrusting his bare arm deep into Capet's blood, which had flowed in abundance, took handfuls of clots and three times sprayed the watching crowd, who thronged forward under the scaffold so that each might receive a drop on the forehead. 'Brothers,' cried the citizen, 'we have been told that the blood of Louis Capet would be upon our own heads. Well, so be it! How often did he not soak his hands in our blood! Republicans, the blood of a king brings good fortune!'[57]

The worthy Baudrais was no doubt taking too literally the sacred connotations of speeches made in the Assembly, but it is also true that his version gives the episode a touch of the sublime in the contemporary sense of the word.[58] And, as we shall see, the sublime is one of the more powerful in the guillotine's repertoire of effects. Baudrais's text constitutes a fine and early example of this effect.

The republican account had in fact to take over the traditional reverence accorded to the body of a saint and reverse it so that it acquired a revolutionary sense. Thus Baudrais on another occasion attempted to justify the people's fetishistic practices:

> The priests and the devout are already seeking to place Louis XVI in their calendar of martyrs. They compare his execution to the passion of their Christ. Like the people of Jerusalem, the people of Paris tore in two Louis Capet's frock coat, *scinderunt vestimenta sua*, and everyone wanted to take home a shred. But it was out of the purity of their republican spirit: 'Do you see this piece of cloth?' grandfathers will one day say to their grandchildren. 'The last of our tyrants wore it on the day he went to the scaffold to die a traitor's death.'[59]

To eliminate any suggestion that the people might have had faith in their king, the republican version thus models itself on the royalist fiction, in which the execution is taken as a metaphor of the Crucifixion, but does so in order to exploit for its own purposes the mystical treatment accorded by the royalists to the execution as a whole. Yet, the fact remains that no royalist account ever suggested the analogy between the blood of the king and the blood of Christ. On the contrary, the taste for blood was considered the preserve of fanatics, and virtuous men confined themselves to hair. As a last paradox, the royalist accounts then offer an English variant on the theme of the blood-imbued handkerchief which becomes a flag flying over the Tower of London; it may even have been the republican newspapers which provided them with the theme . . .

The complexity of this weave of interpretations confirms at least two of the unexpected effects of the guillotine:

1. For the founders of the Republic, it was important that the people should not incur the reproach of having been turned by the guillotine into a populace of cannibals. Apprehension had already been expressed on this subject, as early as 1789, by Verninac de Saint-Maur,[60] and the term 'cannibals' was much favoured after *Thermidor* to describe the audience attending the executions.[61] It is of interest to note that the 'cannibalization' effect had been foreseen as early as 21 January 1793, despite the fact that only one execution took place on that date. The brutalization of the public had less to do with the industrial scale of

the mass decapitations of the Terror than with the type of spectacle the guillotine provided.

2. The stratagem used to appropriate the episode of the king's blood for the republican version suggests that the people, in its unvarnished reality, was not wholly consistent with the picture of it given by its representatives. Or, at least, it was not consistent yet. The republican accounts that immediately followed 21 January betray the difficulty that their authors faced in dealing with a new ideological entity – the People. The guillotine, when it was given a fully political role, was to render the definition of this entity substantially clearer.

The Scaffold Scene

Unlike the blood-of-the-king episode, where the narratives have a common factual basis but diverge as they are embroidered upon, the scaffold scene, which involved fewer protagonists, all of whom were clearly to be seen, formed the basis for the wildest inventions.

The letter by Sanson, already quoted, gives a sufficient idea of the events which took place in the two minutes timed so precisely by the official recorders. At the foot of the scaffold the king desires not to be 'prepared' for execution (by having his over-garment removed, his hair cut, and his hands tied). On the platform the king tries to speak to the people; he moves 'front stage' but is forced to retreat, and, finally, is only able to speak from the plank to which he is attached.

We are still offered two different versions, the royalist and the republican. But the difference between them takes another form, one which is in the highest degree revelatory of the issues at stake in this, the last scene of the royal drama. The republican account is embroidered with incident. For the republicans were not simply witnesses of the event; they were making history that day. The account had to show that history was made, and history is made of incident. The royalist version, by contrast, is notable for its economy of description. Incident is sometimes completely lacking, being supplanted by flights of metaphor: the imagination at work in the royalist accounts is not historical so much as religious.

The Republican Version

The earliest republican accounts are ostentatiously brief and sober. Their laconic manner is intended to mirror the magnanimity shown by the people: 'In the square and throughout the city an impressive silence reigned. Louis showed greater strength of character on the scaffold than he had on the throne. He said a few words: he spoke of his innocence, of the forgiveness which he bestowed upon all his enemies, and of the disasters that would follow his death' (*Le Patriote français*, 22 January).

But, day by day, the role of each actor became more precise, and, though the people retained its dignified indifference, the king's speech expanded.[62] The last words of Louis the Last were, indeed, to become the central subject of the scene. For the republicans they demonstrated the conflict between the desires of the king and the will of the people. The theme was touched upon by Baudrais on 26 January. His long account exploits the fertile narrative vein offered by the scaffold scene:

> He was immediately handed over to the executioner. He himself took off his robe and collar; beneath, he wore a simple undershirt of white flannel. He did not want his hair cut, and particularly objected to his hands being tied; a few words from his confessor instantly persuaded him. He mounted the scaffold and, very red in the face, walked along the left side. He considered the objects around him for some minutes, and asked if the drums would not stop beating. He attempted to step forward as if to speak, when several voices were heard shouting to the executioners, four in number, to do their duty. Even so, while the straps were being attached, he spoke clearly as follows: 'I die innocent, I pardon my enemies, and I desire that my death should serve the French people and appease the wrath of God' (*Révolutions de Paris*, 26 January).

On 20 February Sanson's letter appeared in *Le Thermomètre du jour*. It had little effect: the narrative continued to expand. Gradually, the speech of the king emerged as his last treachery, a treachery confirmed by the plot of which it was a proof. The account of Rouy l'Aîné, published in 1794 in *Le Magicien républicain*, needs to be read in its entirety. For, besides being a political reading of the scene, it enriches the dramatization remarkably, and, in particular, calls attention to the words spoken by Louis's confessor at the foot of the scaffold, words whose importance for the royalist account we shall shortly see.

> On reaching this terrible place, Louis Capet was delivered into the hands of the public executioners, who took him into their charge, cut his hair, undressed him and tied his hands behind his back. They then asked him three times if he thought he had anything further to say or to declare to his confessor. As he consistently replied that he had not, the latter embraced him and, taking leave of him, said; 'Forward, son of Saint Louis, heaven awaits you.' They then made

him go up onto the scaffold. When he got there, instead of going directly to the plank, he elbowed the executioner who was to his left and disturbed him enough to be able to go forward to the edge of the said scaffold. Here he showed signs of desiring to make a speech to the citizens present, with the hope, no doubt, that his words would make them pity his fate and win a pardon for him; or rather with the notion that had been suggested to him, and of which he was quite convinced, that his friends would be there in great number to help him, and would, for this purpose, attempt such another day of bloodshed as the tenth of August . . . He wished to begin his harangue, and gestured to the drums, which made a steady tattoo, to cease, so that he might be heard. Since there were as many as sixty, some among their number had already broken off, when a sudden agitation seized the citizen volunteers: some demanded that he be heard, and others, already irritated by the delays caused by the ceremony, said that he should not be allowed to speak. These differing opinions increased the ferment. Already an uprising was feared which could only have been disastrous, given the inevitable misfortunes which must have resulted, when the commander-in-chief, Santerre, wisely and prudently ordered the drummers to continue their tattoo and the executioners to do their duty, since the criminal had declared at the foot of the scaffold that he had nothing more to say. This order was no sooner given than carried out. The executioners seized Louis, brought him to the fatal board, on which he spoke these words in loud, clear tones, while they were attaching him: 'I am doomed, I die innocent. I pardon my enemies my death, but they shall be punished for it.' Hardly had he spoken these words when the sword of retribution fell upon his head and severed it from his body (Beaucourt, I, pp. 379–81).

It is remarkable that so much incident should have occurred in the two minutes between Louis's descending from the carriage and the descent of the blade. The significant thing from our point of view is that, in all the republican versions, the king's speech is completed, or, more exactly, a whole sentence is completed. The royalists, on the contrary, have the speech broken off: ellipses show that the guillotine also truncated the king's words, allowing free rein to the suggestive possibilities of the unspoken. The difference may seem insignificant, but it is revealing: for the republicans the guillotine fell only after a speech that was quite long enough to prove the treachery of the speaker. Thus, in the account of Rouy l'Aîné the king's little speech was enough to stir up differences of opinion, break up the grandiose unity of the people, and raise up factions. The guillotine then emerges as the instrument that, with timely intervention, thwarts the 'horrifying enchantment' worked by the king's words.

There is therefore a certain logic in Mercier's making the king's speech end with a 'terrible cry', the death cry of the monster who has struggled like a madman to avoid death:

> 'I die innocent; I forgive my enemies.' At these words, Santerre brandished his sabre. The drums in the middle set up a tattoo which made it impossible to hear. Louis stamped his foot and ordered them to cease. The general's aides-de-camp urged the executioner to do his duty. One of them, Richard, grabbed a pistol and aimed it. The executioner and his assistants brought Louis back and attached him. He talked incessantly and, at the moment when the plank tipped and brought him to the fatal 'window', he let out a terrible cry that was stifled by the fall of the blade, which took off his head.[63]

This astonishing fabrication gives pride of place to the king, and this is significant. Whereas in the earliest republican accounts the people were the real driving force of the story, the amplification of the narrative shifted attention towards the king, who, gradually regaining his monstrous status, accomplishes his death throes centre stage. Propaganda cannot explain everything: the theatre of the guillotine guarantees for the victim a leading role which can influence both the narrative and the political interpretation of the event.

The Royalist Version

In the royalist account the dramatic incidents are played down. It might be supposed that this choice was imposed by the probable lack of royalist witnesses at the execution. But there is a deeper underlying cause: for the royalists the facts count for less than the mystical interpretation that they can be given. This is clearly illustrated by the corrections which were made in the 25 January issue of the *Annales de la République française* to the factual errors in the account published on 22 January. The errors show that the editor, who was clearly not present at the execution, was loath to have the king's body touched by the executioner. These corrections made in the name of 'truth' are, however, accompanied by a noticeable increase in the mystical element of the narrative.[64] Inserted at the heart of the text, these variations also suggest that, for the royalists, the factual accuracy of the narrative was, in the last analysis, less important than its spiritual and dynastic significance. Louis himself, in a variant of Bossuet's celebrated remark that the king 'never dies', is supposed to have dissuaded Malesherbes from fomenting a plot to save him, on the grounds that (here we follow the version given in the *Mémoire* of Marie-Thérèse de France): 'The King does not die in France.'[65]

From this point of view the incidents that occurred on the scaffold have only a secondary importance for the story, and the earliest accounts leave out any anecdotal element.[66] Such restraint was unsatisfactory: it was too close to the style of an official report to elicit the desired mystical overtones. The chief text of the series is that published by Perlet in the 22 January issue of his *Journal*:

> He got out with an air of resolution. He was wearing a dark-purple robe, a white jacket, grey knee-breeches and white stockings. His hair was not untidy, and his complexion seemed unchanged. He mounted the scaffold. The executioner cut his hair; this operation caused him to shudder somewhat. He turned towards the people, or rather towards the armed forces who filled the square, and, in a very loud voice which resounded through the square, spoke these words: 'Frenchmen, I die innocent. From the height of the scaffold and about to meet my maker, I declare that this is so. I pardon my enemies; I desire that France...'
>
> Here he was interrupted by the sound of the drums, which drowned some voices shouting that he be reprieved. He himself took off his collar and presented himself to death. His head fell. It was a quarter past ten (Beaucourt, I, p. 342).

Successive narratives enlarged upon this interrupted speech. Incident is indeed introduced, but, significantly enough, it takes the form of dialogue. It is almost as if the king's speech, or perhaps we should say, the *royal word*, constituted, as transcribed by its worshippers, the true spiritual relic of the monarch, a relic all the more efficacious for being incomplete, and to which its ellipsis gave a tincture of the sublime.

The version given in *Semaines parisiennes* is the most eloquent – indeed garrulous.[67] But the preoccupation with the king's last words turns up a significant variant. A pamphlet with the revealing title *Testament de Louis XVI, dernier roi des Français, ses derniers paroles sur l'echafaud et le procès-verbal des commissaires* was dissatisfied with the silence of the last seconds, and adds this note to the narrative: '*Nota bene*: The spectators closest to the scaffold heard Louis say, in a loud voice and moving to the left-hand side of the scaffold: "Frenchmen, I die innocent. I forgive all my enemies. I wish my death to be of service to the people..." And, as he placed himself beneath the fatal blade: "I confide my soul to God."'

We have come a long way from the 'terrible cry' heard by Mercier. The mystical version of the event has its own mystical sublime. It corresponds to and answers the republican sublime, which is based on horror. That the mystical sublime is characteristic of the royalist narrative is shown by the account, published in February 1793, of *Le Véridique ou l'antidote des journaux*. The narrative is abbreviated: all reference to the interrupted speech has disappeared, along with the drama this implied. Instead, the author places the no less sublime words of the confessor directly before the fall of the blade: 'Hardly had the venerable Firmont confided these last words to the illustrious victim, "Rise, son of Saint Louis, the skies open before you", when the murderous blade fell, swift as lightning, upon the sacred head.'[68] By restricting the length of time in which the drama of the story unfolds, the author presents us with a moment of unparalleled mystical density: at the blade's edge, death and spiritual exaltation coincide with immediate accession to the kingdom of heaven. The royalist account thus manages to 'recapture' for its own purposes the mechanical instantaneousness of the machine, reversing yet again the charge of its sanctity.

The Images of History

The two variations that are introduced in *Détails authentiques sur les derniers moments de Louis XVI* are, at first sight, surprising:

> From the height of the scaffold, he addressed the following words to the people: 'I die innocent. I forgive my enemies, and I desire that France...' Here he was interrupted by the tattoo of the drums ... and the inhuman Santerre commanded the executioner to do his duty. He was attached to the board, and when the plank had reached its position he again raised his head, gazing at the multitude with a fixed stare. It was then that his confessor, leaning down towards him, in a very loud voice pronounced: 'Child of Saint Louis, you go to heaven.' At that very instant the string was cut. The head still held. Weight was applied to the blade, and the head fell.[69]

The elements of the royalist vulgate are present. But the guillotine here makes an appearance which is none the less successful for the fact that it occurs in a corpus in which its role is normally less conspicuous. This appearance is clearly designed to allow the author to combine the royalist and republican sublime. The confessor is speaking into the king's ear at the moment of decapitation, and, just as in *Le Véridique*, the rhetoric reaches its greatest intensity as the stroke of death descends. But the decapitation is divided into two stages, and the distressing hiatus that characterizes the instant of the guillotine is doubled and reinforced. In this account it reaches the peak of its ability to horrify. The author, Louis Claude Bigot de Sainte-Croix, thus gives us a version in which we recognize a supreme mastery of rhetorical effects; everything about the guillotine that speaks to the emotions is here combined in a cunning synthesis.

Bigot de Sainte-Croix's account is interesting in another respect. By placing the confessor on the scaffold, close to the king's side, he makes a welcome innovation, in which he is corroborated by the confessor himself. Abbé Edgeworth de Firmont does indeed state that he accompanied the king onto the scaffold,[70] and this privileged testimony is Bigot de Sainte-Croix's authority for having the confessor speak in the king's ear. But the expression he uses at this point and his inaccurate description of the way in which the guillotine functions suggest the true source of his inspiration: the engraving described earlier, which illustrated, prior to its construction, the *Machine proposée à l'Assemblée nationale pour le supplice des criminels par M. Guillotin*.

It will be remembered that the words accompanying the engraving said that 'the signal for Death shall be given to the Executioner by the Confessor at the moment of Absolution; the Executioner will look away and, with a stroke of his sword, cut the cord'. With the exception of certain variations dictated by the nature of the event and, in particular, the introduction of the plank, which had been meticulously represented in an English print of the king's death widely circulated at the time, Bigot de Sainte-Croix based his account on the engraving and its accompanying note, which were published before 1792. This shows that he had not seen the machine in action between April and August 1792, the date on which he left for London – the sensitive did not court the spectacle. It also suggests that if the imagination has so large a place in the narrative of history, it is partly because image and imagery are often the documentary source on which the narrative is based.

A similar phenomenon is to be encountered in the republican camp. Thus Rouy l'Aîné, in *Le Magicien républicain*, renders the joy of the people after the execution with this splendid picture:

The citizens, scarcely knowing how to express their joy at finding themselves for ever rid of the scourge of royalty, embraced one another in an outpouring of sweetest harmony and fraternal joy; after which they sang hymns to liberty and joined hands to dance in a ring around the scaffold and the entire place de la Révolution.[71]

No other account refers to this event, which could scarcely have passed unnoticed, and we are probably justified in attributing it to an engraving which does indeed show the people dancing at the foot of the scaffold. The quality of the preparatory drawing suggests that it was a preliminary sketch for a painting, and it is probably a product of David's studio.[72] If we take it that Rouy's account derives from the engraving and not vice versa, it is because dance is the most effective *visual* means of representing the joy that a narrative can simply describe.

Though these reflections are not without interest as regards the study of historiography and the history of art, what concerns us here is how well this reciprocal influence of historical narrative and image bears out the editor of the *Républicain* when he declared that the 'truth' that the historians were to record in the wake of 21 January was 'sacred' and 'becoming' to tell. The production of narrative is not so much an issue of establishing the facts beyond a shadow of a doubt, or of ascertaining the details of the disputed incidents; it is more one of drawing the spiritual, political or moral lesson in the time-honoured tradition of historical rhetoric.

3

The Political Machine

That which conduces to the welfare of society is always fearful.
Saint-Just, *Fragments*

To make France republican, happy and vigorous, a little ink and one guillotine alone would have sufficed.
Camille Desmoulins, *Le Vieux Cordelier*, III

'The French Revolution was, then, a political revolution that functioned in the manner of, and to some extent took on the complexion of, a religious revolution.' De Tocqueville's analysis is well known,[1] and we have seen the extent to which the death of the king, the founding act of the Republic, possessed strong sacral overtones. The Terror consisted very largely in the ritual repetition of this initial sacrifice, and the guillotine, 'ensign of so many a massacre', in Cabanis's words, was able to assume the status of the altar at which the new religion was celebrated.

That the daily meetings around the scaffold were 'to some extent religious' is confirmed by the notorious remark of the deputy Amar about the 'red mass' celebrated in place de la Révolution. Camille Desmoulins's irony in *Le Vieux Cordelier* provides even clearer evidence: 'I believe it was a good thing to put terror on the agenda, and to take a leaf from the Holy Book – "The fear of the Lord is the beginning of wisdom" – and from the teachings of that excellent *sans-culotte* Jesus, who said, "By will or by force, convert them all the same, *compelle eos intrare.*"'[2]

Saint-Just and Robespierre were aware that they were embarking upon an unprecedented upheaval, and it is a well-known fact that the 'holy' law which they took themselves to be founding – a law capable of saving the people of every nation – at times took on transparently religious overtones.[3] But it is Chaumette who, in his celebration of the revolutionary spirit, adopts the most biblical tone. The guillotine becomes for him the 'bulwark of eternity:

And you, oh Mountain for ever renowned in the pages of history, become the Sinai of the French! Hurl down amid bolts of lightning the decrees of Justice and the people's will! Holy Mountain, become a volcano by whose lava our enemies shall be devoured! No quarter, no pity for our enemies! Let us cast between them and ourselves the bulwark of eternity![4]

The messianic tone of the Montagnards could not help but leave its mark on the guillotine's reputation, and the philosophical machine became the object of a cult, the wording and some of the external forms of which were quite deliberately stolen from the religion of the *ancien régime*. No doubt Hébert's 'Saint Guillotine' is intended to be provocative when he furiously inveighs against profiteers whom 'Saint Guillotine seemed to have converted'.[5] But the name seems almost to have entered the Revolution's administrative terminology. The Revolutionary Committee of Angers, writing in 1793 to its representative at the Convention, refers to the *sacram sanctam Guillotinam*, and, in a letter dated 27 *Brumaire* Year II, citizen Gateau announces that in Strasbourg 'Saint Guillotine is quite wonderfully active.'[6] The expression seems to have gained popular currency. A police report of 26 *Ventôse* Year II, describes how the people of Paris reacted to the news of another plot against the Republic: 'It is only too true what they say ... that saint alone can save us.'[7]

A concomitant of the canonization of the revolutionary guillotine was, of course, the composition of litanies and songs in her honour:

Saint Guillotine, protectress of patriots, pray for us;
Saint Guillotine, terror of the aristocrats, protect us;
Kindly machine, have pity on us.
Admirable machine, have pity on us.
Saint Guillotine, deliver us from our enemies.

(*To the air of the 'Marseillaise'*)
Oh heavenly guillotine,
You cut short kings and queens.
Through your celestial might
We have reconquered all our rights. (*bis*)
Defend our nation's law
May you, O proud device
Exist for evermore
Destroying the profane.
Sharpen your razor for Pitt and his agents,
Fill your bag full of the heads of tyrants![8]

An analysis of the cult of the guillotine cannot, however, confine itself to the religious expressions used. The machine's prestige during the Revolution rests fundamentally on the political theory of the revolutionary government, and this aspect is perhaps the most disturbing from our own point of view.

From the moment it became the standard recourse of the Extraordinary Criminal Tribunal, dubbed 'Revolutionary' even before it was officially so called, the guillotine's prestige was enhanced, and it came to be regarded as the visible form of a truly revolutionary justice. The Tribunal was set up to dissuade the people from wreaking justice themselves, to avoid a repetition of the massacres of 1792, those 'bloodstained days that no true citizens can recall without lament', as Danton put it during the session of 10 March 1793: 'Let us be redoubtable lest the people become so, and let us organize a tribunal ... so that the people may know that the sword of liberty hangs over the head of its enemies.'[9] The guillotine, officially described as 'the sword of liberty', replaced summary popular justice, giving it a procedure and a form: the form of Reason. Just as the revolutionary government was the incarnation of the will of the people it represented, so the guillotine gave form to revolutionary law: the people had an instrument that fittingly represented it in the execution of its justice.[10]

The guillotine thus acquired a moral value and it could be sullied by being employed on those unworthy of it. Camille Desmoulins expresses this notion clearly, angered that the guillotine would be dishonoured by its use upon Bretons, who made the following plea to the Commissary of the Republic: 'Please have me guillotined soon, so that I can come back to life in three days' time.'[11] It might have been thought that, at a later stage, after he had proposed the Committee for Clemency – an idea that would result in his being sent to the guillotine himself – Desmoulins would have revised his opinion. But no. On the contrary, he saw the guillotine as honouring those it unjustly struck down: 'What is the guillotine but a sabre blow, a blow most glorious to a deputy who dies the victim of his own courage and republicanism?'[12] At this stage, clearly, the guillotine had long ceased to be an auxiliary of justice, but actually *represented* justice in all its moral and political glory.

In her *Considérations sur la Révolution française*, Madame de Staël compares the machine with the form of the revolutionary government: 'The machine of terror, which events had wound to this pitch, was alone all powerful. The government resembled the horrific, deathdealing machine: one saw rather the blade than the hand that moved it.'[13] The point is well made, and the resemblance is not simply the effect of a casual analogy; the way the guillotine worked did indeed illustrate a principle of government and came thereby to have a didactic function which was an almost didactic and strictly political role.

The Machine for Government

For the guillotine's contemporaries there was no doubt about its political effectiveness. As early as Year V, an understandably anonymous pamphlet had stressed the need for revolutions to have in their midst the 'mainstay of Terror'.[14]

It was in fact on 5 September 1793 that the Convention decided that the Terror should be 'on the agenda' till the advent of peace; from *Frimaire* (21 November – 21 December) Year II the number of those condemned soared until in *Ventôse* (February – March 1794) it began to exceed the number of acquittals. The guillotine had ceased to be the instrument of an egalitarian system of justice and had become a veritable machine of government. Its repetitive violence expressed, in Saint-Just's words, 'the vehemence of a pure government' which wanted to 'reinforce equality'.[15]

The Goncourts were, no doubt, exaggerating when they called the guillotine the 'Prime Minister' of the Revolution.[16] But in October 1793, Saint-Just criticized the Ministry, referring to it as just a 'world of paper', and in his *Rapport sur la nécessité de déclarer le gouvernement révolutionnaire* he expressed the view that the 'sword must everywhere be found alongside the misdeed, so that everything may be free in the Republic'.[17] Pétion, the former Mayor of Paris, considered that crimes such as the massacres of September were 'morally odious' but 'politically advantageous'; in June 1794, he admitted reluctantly that the 'current legislators' had made the guillotine the 'mainspring of their government'.[18]

Government itself being now conceived in mechanical terms, the prestige of the guillotine derived from the fact that the terminology of the one might be applied to the other. Saint-Just took this comparison to an extreme. The Terror was, in his view, an individual machine within the central government of France, and the government of France could not be accomplished without normal institutions: 'The Terror can rid us of monarchy and aristocracy; but who shall deliver us from corruption? Institutions. But no one has any inkling of this; they think that, once we have a machine for government, nothing further remains to be done.'[19] The image has a historical origin: towards the end of the eighteenth century, the concept of 'machine' had attained a status which meant that it could be widely applied as a theoretical model.[20]

Thus, the guillotine could indeed serve as a metaphor for a type of government: it was a machine and at the service of the Terror; and the Terror was a machine *for* government that was, till peace allowed the formation of institutions, to guarantee the correct functioning of the machine *of* government.[21]

Metaphorically, metonymically, the guillotine represented this form of government, and homage could be paid to it in public ceremonies such as those organized by Schneider's 'Propaganda' in Strasbourg, in which the 'capuchin of Cologne' directly addressed the guillotine as a symbol of the revolutionary government.[22] The machine could serve as a symbol in this way because it accorded so well with the principles of government set out by Robespierre and Saint-Just. These principles were to culminate in the law of 22 *Prairial* (10 June 1794) which reorganized the Revolutionary Tribunal.

The guillotine is little more today than the image of an outmoded system of justice, and it is difficult to conceive how the Jacobins could have seen in it an exemplary instrument of democratic justice and an expression of revolutionary government. But one has not far to look in the writings of Saint-Just and Robespierre to find precisely this sentiment.

Unlike the constitutional government, which aimed to conserve the Republic and retained a concern for civil liberty, the revolutionary government was on a war footing and aspired to found the Republic; as such it 'owed its enemies nothing but death' (Robespierre). 'There is nothing in common between the people and its enemies but the sword. Those who will not be ruled by justice must be ruled by the sword: the tyrants must be oppressed' (Saint-Just).[23] Revolutionary justice is 'severity' and not 'mercy' (Saint-Just, 26 February 1794); the 'sword of the law' must 'everywhere move with fell swiftness' (Saint-Just, 10 October 1793), for 'the mainspring of popular government in revolution is both virtue and terror ... Terror is nothing other than prompt, severe, inflexible justice; it is, therefore, an emanation of virtue' (Robespierre, 5 February 1794). A 'shining sword in the hands of the heroes of liberty' (idem), the guillotine closely resembled the government whose justice it served, and, 'striking like lightning', it stood as an example to those authorities whose laws were 'not sufficiently expeditious' (idem).

This is not all. The relation of the guillotine to the bodies of its victims mirrored the surgical operation that the revolutionary government was performing upon the body politic in order to regenerate it. Camille Desmoulins superbly formulated the revolutionary image of the guillotine as the instrument by which the purification of the body politic should be completed. The coherence of his medical and physi-ological metaphor confirms the almost organic relation that rev-olutionary thought took to hold between the guillotine and the health of the body politic which it helped to govern:

> With every passing year the national representation grows purer ... The purge effected by the fourth election will no doubt leave the Assembly with a permanent and unwavering majority for the friends of liberty and equality ... The infection was in the blood. The purging out of the venom by the emigration of Dumouriez and his henchmen has gone more than halfway to saving the body politic; and the amputations of the Revolutionary Tribunal ... the vomiting forth of the Brissotins from the midst of the Convention will finally ensure a healthy constitution for that body.[24]

Impressive as this chain of metaphors is, it does little more than register an extreme variant of a metaphor by now banal – that of the body of the nation: with the Terror, the guillotine had become the instrument by which the people was to be regenerated in its collective body. Amputations perfected the work of successive elections, and the scaffold became the locus of a unique confrontation – that of the individual body of the condemned man and the fictive body of the nation. Unmasked, guillotined, the criminal was seen to be one of the many parasites whose extirpation was to regenerate the body politic.

'Tremble, ye leeches on the body of the people: its axe is raised to strike you down!' *Le Père Duchesne*[25] is more heated, but the metaphor it uses in relation to the place de la Révolution had already been used by Robespierre in the Assembly in December 1790.[26] But when the blood flowed for real upon the square, its impurity too had ceased to be a metaphor. For, with an efficiency that was as fearsome as it was magical, by purging the body of the people of the leeches that were sucking its blood, the guillotine gave substance to a rhetorical meta-phor: *the body of the People*. The people gathered upon the place de la Révolution to see itself purged of its parasites, and the guillotine had an important part to play in this process of regeneration. It gave substance to the rhetoric of the Revolution. By its operation the rhetoric became reality, and, after destroying the monstrous and mystical body royal, the guillotine modelled the fictive body of the people, the body of a colossus in rude health. It could do so all the more effectively in that this body was present in the guise of the assembled crowd. The people *en masse* attended the surgical operation by which it came into existence, and simultaneously regained its health, and the liberating cry that greeted every head that fell – *Vive la République! Vive la nation!* – testified to the success of the treatment. We might almost say, remembering the dictum that gave Guillotin 'the executioner for midwife', that the People of the Republic had 'the guillotine for midwife'.

It is at all events difficult to understand in any other terms what good republicans found so entirely objectionable about the proposal made by the editor of *La Gazette de Paris*, Durosoy, who, condemned to death for his part in the tenth of August, philosophically offered his blood for experiments in transfusion. The suggestion was rejected with horror, and regarded as a trap, an attempt to diffuse tainted blood and infest with it the blood of the people – an operation precisely contrary to the one effected by the guillotine. Durosoy, in these terms, was a veritable monster, who, not content with the impurity of his own blood, wished to infect the blood of the collective body of the nation.[27]

It was not, therefore, the people that was cannibalistic or blood-thirsty, but only these monsters, who by infecting it, could make it so. Excision was an urgent necessity, and the work of the machine indisputably revolutionary in tendency. The point is reasserted in the pamphlet *Des causes de la Révolution et de ses résultats*: 'Eighteen months was enough to root out of the people customs centuries old, and to implant others that several centuries would scarcely have sufficed to establish. The violence of the Terror made of it a new people.'[28] This is not so far removed from the ideas of Saint-Just himself. In his *Rapport* of 15 April 1794 he stresses the need to 'mould a public conscience', to implant a *civic spirit* in the individual heart which would form a public conscience 'consisting in the inclination of the people towards the public good'. The severity of revolutionary justice was saving the Republic: 'We have matched sword with sword, and liberty has been established. It was born out of the heart of the tempest. It shares this origin with the world, which was born of chaos, and with man, who is born in tears.'[29]

Later we shall have something to say about the sublime tone of this rhetoric. For the time being, we should note how the guillotine made of these images a reality: on the place de la Révolution, the Republic in the throes of revolution stated the birth of its own body politic.

Guillotine and Democracy

Elevated to the status of a machine for government, the guillotine was made to work for the foundation of a true democracy, one in which the people was effectively sovereign. A closer definition of the guillotine's political significance in this role is necessary. The birth of the people which it helped to effect combined two attributes which were no less significant for being, at first sight, mutually exclusive. Each 'extirpation' was individual, particularized, but each was also serialized, its effect determined by the series to which it belonged, and its place in the series emphasized by the identical repetition of each phase of the execution. The coincidence of these two attributes, serialization and particularization, broadens and defines the connotations of the political machine.

The point is best illustrated by the failure of the attempt to construct 'accelerated' guillotines. The monoplace guillotine was sometimes criticized for being too slow relative to the number of heads awaiting removal. In February 1794 Parisian police reports indicated that the people would like to see the process speeded up.[30] A first step might have been to have several guillotines functioning at once, and several Parisian sections requested this in 1794. Another possibility was to multiply the number of windows and blades. There was a strong rumour that experiment had been made in Paris with a five-windowed machine – the number quickly became eight, nine and even thirty. There was no technical obstacle to this improvement, and a guillotine with four windows was successfully constructed in Bordeaux at the request of the President of the Military Committee governing that town.[31] It was, however, never used. It is true that it was ready only in July 1794, in *Thermidor*, and so a little late ... But the hostility that the multiple guillotine encountered was much more deep-seated. As the Surveillance Committee of Bordeaux observed in January 1795, a machine of this kind was 'contrary to all revolutionary laws, and in defiance of those of justice and humanity'.[32] That the guillotine should have but a single window was an issue of principle: the principles involved were those of humanity, still traditionally appealed to regarding the machine, but also those of revolutionary law. The 'accelerated' guillotine notably offended against the principle of the individuality of the victim; 'humanity' required that this be respected, and revolutionary law required it for the declarative act of execution.

Let us state the point clearly: in eradicating the parasites on the body of the people, the guillotine plucked out each and every individual will that opposed the general will of the people constituted as a political body. In the sense in which the Committee for Public Safety understood government by the people, the guillotine was democratic, and its functioning a spectacular illustration of a particular theory of 'popular democracy'.

But here we must return to our sources. Robespierre, adapting Rousseau, again and again emphasizes that government by the people is exclusive of all expression of individual will; the virtue with which the people is imbued consists precisely in the 'sublime sentiment [that] prefers the public interest to all private interests'.[33] The revolutionary government must be severe with itself but show confidence in the people, for – the point is a fundamental one – the people and individuals are different in kind: 'It is in the nature of things that each body, like each individual, has its own will, distinct from the general will, and that it should seek to make this will prevail.'[34] But 'to love justice and equality the people has no need of great virtue; it need only love itself'.[35] For the people to be restored to an awareness of its own natural virtue, then, its general will had to be revived by annihilating all private interests and by eliminating all those internal barriers that formed the divisive inner structure of the society of the *ancien régime*.[36]

The violence of the revolutionary rhetoric in regard to factions must be understood in this context. Factions were selfish splinter groups: they were distinct from the general will, and therefore contrary to it, as it expressed itself in the consensus of its representatives in the Assembly. The dispassionate intransigence of law and guillotine was the only possible reaction.[37] The depth of this revolutionary hostility to the selfishness of private interests is attested to by its recurring in the words of Charlotte Corday, whom we need not otherwise suspect of favouring Robespierre: just as Robespierre, seeking to consolidate the Republic, exalted 'all that tends to kindle love of the homeland, to purify morals, elevate the mind, channel the passions of the human heart towards the public interest', and wished to repress 'the baseness of the individual self',[38] so also Charlotte Corday, in prison, awaiting the fate of Brutus: 'Today there are few patriots willing to lay down their lives for their country; selfishness is all, or almost all. This is a pitiful people with which to build a republic.'[39] This unexpected agreement illustrates the widespread enthusiasm of the 'heroes of the Revolution' for their common cause: the People. In the minds of those who made it, the Revolution was indeed a moral one, and its primary virtue was the sacrifice of private interests to the general will.

The fate of Camille Desmoulins, Robespierre's friend, who went to the guillotine on 5 April 1794, is in this regard instructive. His fall was caused by his betrayal of the fundamental revolutionary principle of the indivisibility of the general will; he had become one of the 'tolerant' who were prepared to countenance 'unlimited freedom of opinion', that is to say, the expression of a fragmenting of the general will. Not only had he, in *Le Vieux Cordelier*, cited the military victories in favour of clemency, when these were clearly not the peace whose advent was to mark the end of revolutionary government, but also he saw in the

Terror nothing more than 'an equality of fear, the abasement of courage, and the reduction of the noblest souls to the level of the most vulgar'.[40] Finally – a worse sin in the political context – he asserted the right to diversity of opinion, grounding his assertion in a traditional national spirit. This was clearly at odds with the regeneration to which the Revolution aspired, and which justified both its intransigence and its annihilation of all opposition.[41] Thus, it was of no avail to suggest that 'all these parties, all these little circles, will always be contained within the larger circle of good citizens who will never tolerate the restoration of tyranny', nor that 'leniency should be shown to the *ultra* and the *citra* on condition that they do not disturb the *intra* or the great mass of the allies of the one and indivisible Republic'.[42] Robespierre had in December 1793 announced that the foundation of the Republic could not stem from 'caprice or inattention, nor from the chance result of the choices of each individual claim and each revolutionary element'.[43] A revolutionary must necessarily be transported with hatred at any precedence of the particular over the general – regionalism not least – gained at the expense of the single, central, indivisible will. De Toqueville, once again, makes explicit in the very words that he uses the enemy against which the Jacobin Revolution was struggling at this point: it was *individualism* in the collective form that it had assumed.[44]

In 1793 individualism was anti-revolutionary because a revolutionary state could allow of only one entity into which each individual had to be subsumed, and this entity was the State. Saint-Just articulates this argument clearly. In his opposition to federalism he states that 'no one should be allowed to stand apart'; but as regards the relations between France and its neighbours, on the contrary, isolation is the goal: 'States are hardly ever disturbed except by neighbouring governments. To be happy, one should isolate oneself as much as possible.'[45]

This transfer of individuality to the collective – that is, to the State – was one of the root elements of the revolutionary consciousness, and – here we have come full circle – the inevitable consequence of this transfer was a pitiless application of the guillotine: 'You must punish not merely the traitors, but even those who are indifferent; you must punish anyone who is passive in the Republic and does nothing for it. From the moment in which the will of the French people is clear, anything that opposes it stands outside the sovereign sway, and he that stands without is the enemy.'[46]

The guillotine acquired from this standpoint considerable representative force, since its working exemplified the very principle of revolutionary democracy: it emphasized the individuality of each of its victims the better to annihilate it – more exactly, to deny this individuality by the mechanical process with which the victim was destroyed.

By decapitating its victims one by one, by having them mount the scaffold one by one, by repeating for each one of them each phase of the execution, the guillotine demonstrated that the enemy to be struck down was none other than the individual who had chosen to prefer his own individual will to that of the collective.[47] One is tempted to see in the basket in which the decapitated heads were gathered the ballot box in which the, as it were, negative votes of the general will were recorded in the 'electoral purges'. Saint-Just defined the general will as 'the majority of the wills of individuals, collected one by one';[48] the basket is the mirror image of the election, and collects one by one the minority of individual wills which have set themselves apart from the singular, general will. The guillotine visibly confirmed in its democratic operation the terrifying omnipotence of universal suffrage.

It did so the more effectively in that its mechanical operation denied the individuality that it destroyed. Its mechanically egalitarian working reduced the uniqueness of individual death to a uniformity measurable simply as a lapse of time. This production-line effect was all the more striking when the heads that fell were famous.[49] The twenty-one Girondins were 'dispatched in twenty-six minutes'. This made an impression on people – the virtuosity with which the Parisian executioners processed their material was admirable.[50] Differences or any signs of individuality only occurred as a result of accidents. The expression 'game for the guillotine' (*gibier à guillotine*), used by one of the jurors on the Revolutionary Tribunal, can also be taken fairly literally. The systematic use of the guillotine turned the *patient* referred to by Dr Louis into the most mechanical of corpses, and the report on a day's work did indeed resemble the register of a day's shoot. The moral was drawn by Dumas, the President of the Tribunal: 'Man lives by virtue alone; crime exists only in the corpse . . . We may contemplate without fear the register of the traitors we have punished.'[51]

This denial of individuality may also help to explain the use of *amalgames* – a practice which consisted in sentencing at a single sitting, and executing in a single batch, persons who had nothing in common but their appearing on the same bill of indictment. The logic of the guillotine did not encourage detail in the indictment, which would amount to sentencing, according to category, an enemy of the people and/or an aristocrat and/or an agent of a foreign power and/or etc.[52] At a Jacobin meeting on 10 April the President of the Revolutionary Tribunal articulated the principle involved:

The goal of every conspiracy is the same: they all seek to enslave the people ... They are all of the same kind ... They all have the same source ... They all share the same methods ... One has but to consider how Hébert, Vincent, Ronsin and their accomplices, and Fabre d'Eglantine, Danton, Lacroix, Chabot and their accomplices have served the foreign interest. These men, apparently at odds, were united in their purposes. Their methods, though at opposite extremes, are indistinguishable in their results. We should not perceive the full horror of their crimes if we did not see in them a single grand design.[53]

It is, therefore, incorrect to regard the increasing numbers of executions in the nine months prior to *Thermidor* as the processes of the Terror run horribly out of control, or as executions cynically and deliberately carried out 'in error'. Precisely because the military victories, without restoring peace, encouraged the reappearance of possible divergences and personal opinions within the Convention, revolutionary logic required that the guillotine work harder than ever to crush the forces eroding the national consensus. This is confirmed by the records. The guillotine was a matter of concern to the government only in so far as there were doubts about its cost-effectiveness. In March 1794 Fouquier-Tinville notified the Committee for Public Safety that 'despite the zeal shown by the Tribunal, cases are building up to such an extent that it is difficult, if not indeed impossible, for all the conspirators brought before the Tribunal to suffer the stroke of the law, as all good and true republicans wish and must wish they should'.[54] As early as January, Fouquier-Tinville had pointed out, in relation to the 110 bourgeois sent to Paris from Nantes by Carrier, that the simultaneous execution of 110 persons would inevitably present certain difficulties. His 'doubts', he specified, were 'of a purely political kind': 'Should the criminal lives of the guilty be ended by the usual instrument of death, since they are so many and, at a time of revolution, inhabitants of a rebel area?'[55] Fouquier-Tinville favoured a firing-squad, which was more expeditious and proper in the case of a military tribunal. The case shows clearly that the 'purely political' success of these production-line executions was the sole consideration.

In short, individual considerations took second place to the problems of nigh-industrial scale posed by the use of the guillotine. The egalitarianism that produced the machine had become, in revolutionary times, a version of political equality whose visible sign was production-line uniformity of execution. This democratization of death did not end with the death of Robespierre, but in 1797, when a military commission was set up to try *émigrés* who had returned too soon, and the death that awaited them was no longer the guillotine but a firing-squad. By reintroducing a distinction in the methods of political execution the Directory effectively terminated the symbolic institution of political death established by the Montagnard-dominated Convention, which had made the guillotine the sole instrument of justice sanctioning the combined notions of democracy and the general will.

Chateaubriand wrote: 'One cannot deny [the Jacobins] this appalling merit: they were consistent in their beliefs.'[56] The form in which the decapitating machine most definitively symbolizes the Jacobin revolution is as the instrument (of justice) of a political system founded on the functioning of an 'apparatus' of government, indeed on a 'government by apparatus'[57] Montagnard ideology required that those in power be merely spokesmen, the products of a political mechanism by the mediation of which it was the people that was said to govern.

'Robespierre had acquired the reputation for a high degree of democratic virtue; he was thought incapable of holding a personal view.'[58] Robespierre's strength consisted precisely in his having destroyed in himself the 'baseness of the individual self'; he therefore appeared never to defend personal interest, never to possess an individual will. He was a channel of expression for the general will. When he claimed to be inspired only by the 'selfishness of those who are not degraded', which consisted of a 'tender, imperious, irresistible passion..., that deep revulsion of tyranny..., that sacred love of the homeland, that sublimer holier love of humanity, without which a great revolution is nothing more than one spectacular crime which destroys another',[59] he was claiming nothing other than that he was the embodiment of Jacobin ideology; he was but the representative, the mouthpiece through which the people spoke, the man who, on the evening of this, his last speech, read it out at a Jacobin meeting in order to submit it for its direct approval.

The Assembly could not be wholly Montagnard, as Desmoulins, before his outbreak of 'indulgence', had hoped; and not until the fourth electoral purge did it become so. But the Jacobins organized a 'party apparatus' which functioned as the all-powerful body where a consensus was worked out and superintended; this consensus was none other than the will of the people, which its delegates represented. The political strength and value of the guillotine derived from the fact that the scaffold was the ultimate and sublime manifestation of the omnipotence of the people, but the subordination of the individual to the opinion of the collective was inherent in the Jacobin system – in the meetings of the club and sections, where, more effectively than in the Assembly, the People could meet its representatives.

PART III
The Theatre of the Guillotine

When [under the influence of the theatre] the crowd is transformed and becomes the people, what a great mystery is there!

Victor Hugo,
Littérature et philosophie mêlées

His death was a sort of carnival . . . Carts, benches, scaffolding, all kinds of preparations were made for a view of this pleasant spectacle. The square had become a theatre.

Michelet,
Histoire de la Révolution française,
XVII, 3

At the hour when the setting sun left the town wreathed in shadow, at the hour when the firmament is stained with red, amid the clatter of iron and the gallop of the horses the great sacrificial throng emerged onto the place de la Révolution.

On the square, around the eminence of the guillotine, around the plaster statue of Liberty already tinged with the fumes of blood, thousands of red-bonneted heads undulated like a field of poppies. They watched one and all; clusters of men clung onto the base of the statue of Louis XV and watched; from the Tuileries and Champs-Elysées the pleasured classes watched; flung wide, the windows of the Garde-Meuble were watching.[1]

The Goncourts' hyperbole stresses the degree of spectacle with which the Terror had invested execution by guillotine – spectacle certainly, and, more precisely, theatricality. A backdrop, actors and a public: all were present, and the execution was meticulously staged. Contemporary authors frequently reiterate the point: the place de la Révolution was a vast theatre. One of the most striking eyewitness accounts is the narrative of Danton's death by Antoine Vincent Arnault – we can recognize the stylistic mastery of the dramatist whose *Marius à Minthurnes* had been staged in 1791, and in whose *Lucrèce* (staged 1792) a very republican Brutus had appeared:

Danton was the last to appear upon this stage that was running with the blood of his colleagues. Night was drawing on. At the foot of the hideous statue whose bulk loomed huge against the sky I saw the form of the tribune stand like some Dantesque shade; half lit by the dying light, he seemed rather to rise from the tomb than ready himself to enter it. Nothing so bold as the countenance of the athlete of the Revolution; nothing more formidable than the set of that profile which defied the axe, than the expression upon that head, which, doomed to fall so soon, seemed yet to dictate the law. Horrifying dumb show! The memory of it is undimmed by time.[2]

The death of Danton, punctuated by epigrams and last words all the more memorable for the fact that their author was, apparently, speechless, was one of the most successful performances of the place de la Révolution theatre. But the executions of 5 April 1794 formed part of a series of performances which were already exceedingly popular, and a major part of whose success was due to the entirely novel role played by the machine in this theatre – it was no papier-mâché mock-up. The fourth issue of *Le Vieux Cordelier* commented that 'those who frequented the spectacle' despised 'the habitués of opera or tragedy', who saw nothing more than 'cardboard daggers' and actors feigning death.[3] The special thing about the theatre of the guillotine was that the deaths were real, and for each actor there could be but the single performance. Camille Desmoulins emphasized how attractive to the public this revolution in theatrical convention was: 'It was not the love of the Republic that each day drew so many to the place de la Révolution, but curiosity, and the new play that could have but a single performance.'[4]

So successful was the machine that it became part of the machinery of traditional theatre; it was used in puppet-shows to guillotine Punchinello,[5] and in 1793 it took the leading role in a play to be presented at the Théâtre du Lycée, whose very title was expected to attract huge audiences: *La Guillotine d'amour*.[6]

Only much later did the guillotine begin to conceal its work; for the time being, it was the centre of a popular entertainment celebrating the Republic. One might indeed say that executions provided the most frequent and popular of revolutionary festivals, and a major concern for the organizers was to maintain the quality of the spectacle:

> I wouldn't want you having those rascals accompanied with the drum. Make it a trumpet; it's a better way to announce the justice of the people. The guillotine is too quick for people to be really thrilled; you have to make up for that by the way you bring the enemies of the people up to the guillotine. It's got to be a sort of spectacle for them. The singing and dancing have to prove to the aristocrats that the people take nothing but pleasure in their deaths. Also, you have to make sure there's a big crowd of people to go with them to the scaffold.[7]

This proposal definitely would not do. For the organizers the spectacle did indeed have to be a good one, but it had, above all, to be grand. Though some compensation was required for the speed of the guillotine, this could only consist in the spectacle of the majesty of the Law as it revealed itself in history. The series of visual operations accompanying the functioning of the guillotine *per se* constituted a ritual, and for the religious ritual of the *ancien régime* the Terror substituted that of Reason, the bearer of just retribution.

Three characteristics marked the deaths inflicted by the *ancien régime*: the production of a certain quantity of suffering; a juridical codification of the suffering to be produced; and the incorporation of the suffering into a 'punitive liturgy'.[8] The guillotine in its philosophical aspect eliminated the first two of these characteristics. The Terror made use of the 'simple mechanism' to lay emphasis on the third, though in a simplified and highly philosophical way. The guillotine perfectly satisfied the conditions laid down by Michel Foucault for such a punitive liturgy: that it should be stigmatizing [*marquant*] for the victim, and spectacular [*éclatant*] as regards the system of justice which imposes it. Mechanical decapitation removed all trace of social differentiation in the production of suffering; but the ceremony that surrounded the decapitation was most certainly 'a ritual organized in order to stigmatize the victims and manifest the power that punishes. It is not the action of justice provoked beyond endurance and losing all restraint in the loss of its principles. In the 'excesses' of [death by] torture there is to be found a complete economy of power.'[9] And so with the guillotine during the Terror: its 'excesses' consisted in replacing the individual quota of suffering by a quantity of painless deaths, whose cumulative effect was to deprive each individual will of its particularity.

We have seen that this substitution was the hallmark of the Jacobin Revolution. But we should note, too, that the fall of the blade was only one in a carefully planned series of effects comprising the ritual. Even the cry of '*Vive la République! Vive la Nation!*' that greeted the death was a lay version of the *Salve Regina* intoned by the crowd, under the *ancien régime*, before the executioner commenced the public torture.

The fall of the blade was the last episode of the second phase of a ritual spectacle comprising three phases. The first was the procession from place of detention to place of execution; the sudden change of rhythm at the end of this slow, preliminary procession added to the production-line effect.[10] The third phase testified to the moral and political efficiency of the spectacle. The people shouted, whereupon the executioner picked up the detached head and held it up to the crowd. The gesture consecrated the sacrifice and marked the end of the ritual.

The rite could be allegorized by being given a setting that functioned like a theatrical backdrop. In Paris the executions took place at the foot of a statue of Liberty, which had aptly been substituted for the statue of Louis XV. In Brest a pyramid covered with papier-mâché rocks was constructed opposite the scaffold as an emblem of the *Montagne*. In Orange the situation of the town made such a décor unnecessary, as a letter from the public prosecutor indicates: 'You know the position of Orange. The guillotine stands in front of the mountain. It is as though each head that falls, in doing so pays to the *Montagne* the homage it deserves: an allegory dear to the hearts of all true friends of liberty.'[11]

The spectacle of revolutionary execution had to be *sublime* because, in the view of its authors, the Revolution was a sublime venture. Camille Desmoulins makes this clear: to wish to 'make humanity happy and free' was to attempt a 'sublime experiment'.[12] Robespierre frequently recurs to this point in his *Rapport sur les principes de Morale politique qui doivent guider la Convention*.[13] After the death of the king and the two visions of the sublime, royalist and republican, that this event gave rise to, the Terror set out, by ritually repeating the initial sacrifice, to create in the public consciousness a sense of the sublimity of the Revolution. Like the Kantian spectator of a violent storm, the spectator of the Terror shuddered at the *terribilitas* of what he saw, yet enjoyed the knowledge that it could do him no harm. The Revolution broke 'upon the wicked like a thunderclap', and the Terror which 'passes like a storm' (Saint-Just) was indeed pregnant with a feeling which the age described as 'sublime'. In his *A Philosophical Enquiry into the Origin of our Ideas of the Sublime and the Beautiful*, Burke writes:

> Whatever is fitted in any sort to excite the ideas of pain, and danger, that is to say, whatever is in any sort terrible, or is conversant about terrible objects, or operates in a manner analogous to terror, is a source of the sublime ... In this case the mind is so entirely filled with its object, that it cannot entertain any other, or by consequence reason on that object which employs it. Hence arises the great power of the sublime, that ... hurries us on by an irresistible force ... the inferior effects are admiration, reverence and respect.[14]

But with the guillotine, this effect could not be counted upon; it is one of the more revealing facts about the theatre of the guillotine. The physical reality of blood and death undermined the sentiment of 'sublime astonishment', while the spectators were that other actor in the drama, the people. The nature of the stage and the reality of the spectacle invested it with a horror that, for many, made participation incompatible with the least self-respect.[15] As early as 1789 it had been feared that the novelty of the machine might 'excite the horrible curiosity of the people,[16] and the most awkward problem posed by the political theatre of the guillotine was that of its audience. The image of the people regenerated by the catharsis of the scaffold sat rather ill with the behaviour of the crowds, who did not merely attend but took an active part in the rite of execution. In the last analysis the *People* which the guillotine was supposed to engender never arose – the material from which it was to be created proved too refractory to political ideology.

It follows that in any analysis of the theatrical apparatus of the revolutionary guillotine, the people occupies an important place. Both spectator and actor, omnipresent, its role altered with the different physical location and changing uses made of the scaffold-stage. Formless and polymorphous, its reactions varying between detachment and participation, its behaviour ranging between the 'cannibalistic' and the sublime dignity of the citizen, the people, for whom, and in the name of whom, the spectacle was presented, was undoubtedly its leading actor.

So constant a factor is the people that it receives in what follows no individual treatment. It is present on every page. Our concern here is to analyse the theatrical effects involving the *machine*, that other star of this theatre. Only the executioner merits a similar spotlight: he too is unique, indeed doubly so, for not only is he the master of his craft, surrounded by his assistants, but, having no less of a solo role than the victim, he has also the inestimable privilege of performing it more than once.

1

The Procession

The theatre of the guillotine resembled any other theatrical activity in appropriating to itself a finite space; it occupied a portion of space in the urban fabric at the heart of which its performances were held. And just as theatrical activity does not necessarily imply either a physical enclosure or any separation between audience and 'stage', so the setting of the theatre of the guillotine was spread or rather strung out in a spatial disposition that called forth two quite different kinds of spectacle: a slow-moving procession and the sudden fixity of the scaffold's location.

The scaffold was only the final backdrop, the rudimentary stage. The spectacle that finished there had in each case begun long before at the gates of the prison, and extended along the route across the city from prison to scaffold. It was the longest part of the ceremony; it lasted in general between one and a half and two hours. It was also that part of the performance about which police reports were most forthcoming. The route had, if the procession was to participate in the spectacle, to be stable and clearly defined.

One long police report details the complaints that were made whenever the itinerary of the procession leading from the Conciergerie to the place de la Révolution was changed. The principal complaint seems to have been that uncertainty as to the route made a consistent delimitation of the theatrical scene impossible, and, when a well-known itinerary was changed, citizens who had no desire to witness the procession could not help but do so.

The report should be cited in its entirety; it gives a very good idea of the disquiet that surrounded the use of the guillotine, a disquiet which could easily be exploited for propaganda purposes. It lent itself, too, to the reappearance of the most primeval fears – proving, yet again, the extent to which the 'philosophical machine' defied its sponsors' intentions. Having noted in a first report that 'it is requested that the executioner's tumbril always take the same route, so that the weak-hearted may keep away', the police spy Perrière reiterates the point:

93

I return to the recommendation made in yesterday's report that the executioner's tumbril should be given a single invariable route. First, because it represents the feeling of several well-intentioned people who are astonished that its previously stable route should now vary between rue Saint-Honoré and the quais and the quais and rue Saint-Honoré. Secondly, because aristocrats, adept at turning any incident to political advantage, make use of accidents such as the one I reported yesterday[1] to draw the people's attention to the number of executions, and, wherever possible, to move it to pity the fate of its enemies, inciting hatred for those who prepare the people's triumph. 'We cannot so much as go out,' they say, 'without coming upon the guillotine and those who are being taken to it. Children are becoming cruel and it is to be feared that pregnant women will bear progeny marked at the neck or motionless as statues in consequence of the disturbing impression made upon them by these dismal sights.' The people perceiving nothing in these remarks but humanity and good faith, reacts to them with an air of profound thought which may call forth ideas and feelings quite the contrary to those it should have.[2]

How far these reactions are from the effects desired by the 'father' of the machine, Guillotin, whose own birth was supposedly affected by his mother's shock at the cries of a man being broken on the wheel! The significant point here is that the excessively frequent spectacle of the guillotine was alienating the people from the opinions 'it should have' – the guillotine's educational effect had clearly not sufficed, in *Ventôse* Year II, to instil the 'public conscience' expected of it.

The route of the procession normally followed the long, narrow rue Saint-Honoré. The pace was slow, the horses proceeding at walking pace, and the tumbrils were open. Quite unlike the galloping progress described by the Goncourts, the procession was intended to *display* the victim to the public before that distant and abrupt event, his execution. The condemned were most visible at this point – more dramatically visible than those punished by being displayed on the scaffold in the place de Grève; for the procession that displayed these prisoners brought them to their deaths.

The 'humanity' of the legislators brought no attenuation of this long and terrible process. It was not until 1832 that the Prefect of the Seine decided that 'for reasons of humanity, these places [of execution] should be chosen to be as close as possible to the place where the condemned are imprisoned'.[3] The procession through the city remained for the time being the first phase in the ceremony of the infliction of death, as it had been under the *ancien régime*.

The procession was a great attraction. 'At the sound of the tumbrils everyone rushes to the windows.' So wrote baron de Frémilly on 20 April 1794, and he went on to give a detailed account of the spectacle which took place on 5 April:

It was in rue Saint-Honoré. Three red-painted tumbrils, each drawn by two horses and escorted by five or six gendarmes, moved at walking pace through a vast crowd ... In each tumbril five or six condemned prisoners. I can remember only the first clearly: I was dumbfounded and horrified at the sight of two faces. The first was that of Danton, Pompey to Robespierre's Octavian, the greatest of the victims of the day. He wore an expression of impudence on his huge, round head, and stared proudly down at the gaping crowd; the smile on his lips was a grimace of fury and indignation. The other was ... Hérault de Séchelles, dejected, broken, shame and despair written on the brow he bent almost to his knees. His black hair was short and dishevelled, his collar undone, and he was half dressed in a shoddy brown dressing-gown. I had a sudden vision of him as he had been in *parlement* when he had admitted me to the Bar: young, elegant, exquisite in every refinement of costume and coiffure.'[4]

Baron de Frémilly had caught one of the stars of the Revolution in transit to the guillotine. But he had missed by just a few days one of the most popular processions of the time. On 25 March, a bare twelve days before Danton and his supporters, Hébert and the Hébertistes had passed the same way: 'Everyone wanted at least to see them go by, to judge the impression it made on their criminal souls to see the mass of the people indignant at their crime, and thus to anticipate the death they were about to suffer. And so the crowd of onlookers, gathered for their passage or present at their execution, was innumerable.'[5] Hébert's procession shows how the people was, at this stage of the spectacle, no mere audience; it was an actor in the procession, and determined to make a success of the spectacle: 'The *sans-culottes* mainly had it in for Hébert, and shouted insults at him. "He's damn well furious," said one, "they've gone and broken all his pipe-bowls..." Others had brought pipes and bowls and held them up for Père Duchesne to see.'[6]

Perrière's report is noticeably different: 'The French people, good and great-hearted as ever, confined itself to shouting '*Vive la République!*' when he who had so cruelly and criminally deceived passed by.'[7] Perrière is a good republican, and as such seeks to exaggerate the magnanimity and dignity of the people; he respects and strengthens the colouring that this episode ought to have had in accordance with its political role and intent. A secular equivalent of the processions of penitents that accompanied the condemned to their death under the *ancien régime*, the procession of the people that followed Sanson's tumbrils was intended to give the ceremony a certain grandeur.[8] The people, who founded the Republic, was to demonstrate, by its majestic attitude towards the passing criminals, its 'philosophical' and 'humane' character.

This was the lesson that the procession was supposed to impart, and the ideal had been realized in the procession of Louis XVI. *Le Magicien républicain* gives a republican account of it which is instructive:

> Never, never has the world seen so impressive a spectacle. The order and harmony, which everywhere prevailed, elicited surprise and admiration in all who witnessed them. Not a single voice was raised; on the contrary, a gloomy, religious silence was observed by everyone, and this, in combination with the weather, which was calm, though dull and misty, produced an effect as surprising as any that mortal man may see: no other sound but that of trumpet and drum made itself heard throughout the time taken by the procession to reach its destination.[9]

The passage dates from 1794, and, with hindsight, the majesty of the king's procession would come to seem unique. The people was not generally so restrained, and the police reports as a whole suggest that the 'philosophy' of the people was honoured more in the breach than in the observance. Moreover, the sublimity of the spectacle, since the sublime depends upon fear and astonishment, could only be attentuated by repetition.

The distance covered by the procession was also the source of a considerable diversity of theatrical effect. Its duration and inherent drama gave rise to incidents of a kind that the scaffold's brevity debarred. Relative to the performance as a whole, the procession constituted the duration of the drama – at times indeed of the melodrama – and the procession's route was its 'stage'. Between prison and scaffold the most intense confrontation occurred between the two categories, people and victim, whose proximity worked a sort of fusion that made of both categories a single company of players.

The incidents that arose were sometimes touching and might offer some last consolation to the victims in the form of the sympathy of a few isolated people in the crowd. More often hatred or a vindictive joy were spontaneously and openly expressed. Thus, level with the Oratoire, a mother held up in the air a child of the same age as the Dauphin so that he should blow a kiss to Marie-Antoinette; but on the square in front of Saint-Roch, a woman tried to spit on the queen.[10] Robespierre's procession stopped by the house where he had lived for many years. There was dancing around the tumbril, while brooms dipped in ox-blood were used to spatter the walls of the house with blood.[11] Bailly, who got down from a tumbril overloaded with beams that had been added at the last moment, was thrown down in the mud and his robe torn to pieces. No sooner had he been put back in the tumbril under the protection of the gendarmes than a hail of projectiles assailed him.[12]

Though the *Mémoires de Sanson*, in which this last scene is described at length, is apocryphal, the police reports are there to testify to the violence of such incidents. The people-as-actor got carried away on occasion, and the sublimity of the spectacle suffered in consequence.[13] Immediately after the first political executions in August 1792 improvements to both the machine and the organization of the procession were suggested on humanitarian and philosophical grounds,[14] and the terms in which *Révolutions de Paris* returned to the point on 27 April are revealing:

> The ceremonial of execution should also be improved and everything in it that derives from the *ancien régime* should be eliminated: the tumbril in which the condemned man is placed, and which Capet was spared; the hands tied behind the back, which force the convict to adopt an awkward and servile posture; the black robe that the confessor is still allowed to get himself up in, in spite of the decree banning ecclesiastical dress. This ceremonial does not bear the hall-mark of a humane, enlightened and free nation.

The recommendations were ignored. The 'props' of the procession formed the theatrical location which had to mirror 'the image men have of the spatial relations prevailing in the society in which they live, and of the conflicts underlying these relations'.[15] The cropped hair, the hands tied behind the back, the tumbril – these were neither gratuitous nor simply convenient. They bore a weight of meaning: they symbolized the ignominious nature of the ceremonial, which reached a culmination in the prone position of the condemned man beneath the impending blade – as opposed to the noble kneeling position of the *ancien régime*. And since, as we have seen, all those sentenced were necessarily accomplices of the aristocracy, the ceremony of execution had the additional merit of standing on its head the privilege formerly attached to the use of horse or carriage; this was most vividly exemplified by the royal progress through the city, in which the magnificence of the turn-out was an illustration of the social hierarchy. Sanson's tumbril revived the 'tumbril of infamy' of medieval times, into which Lancelot had been willing to mount even though Gawain refused the 'disgrace of exchanging . . . a horse for a cart'. The hierarchical emblem had its significance inverted by the humiliating theatre of the procession, and the pleasure felt by the people at this spectacle demonstrates how well it worked: the people 'was happy' to follow the procession.[16]

Contrasting and even contradictory accounts of the behaviour of the people are not an obstacle to our analysis; on the contrary, they allow us to distinguish the different kinds of pleasure the procession provided. The real feelings of the condemned counted for less than the way in which they were seen by the people to fulfil their role – the theatrical manifestation of their humiliation. In the pleasure of the people three different nuances are observable: the vindictive; the sublime; and the revolutionary.

Vindictive Pleasure

Vindictive pleasure replaced whatever pity the spectacle of a humiliated adversary might elicit in the spectator. When the condemned man was unable to perform his role in the manner dictated by the ideology of the spectacle, when his humiliation was mirrored by his state and his performance constituted, relative to the dramatic situation, a pleonasm, then there was no pity for him. By acting thus, he prevented the sublimation of the emotions of his audience, whose passions could not attain to sublimity, could not exult in the omnipotence of the People and its Justice. The victim refused to internalize the morality that his role prescribed, he refused to find in it 'a shining example of the respect owed to the law', and the people was, in consequence, deprived of any opportunity to demonstrate its magnanimity. In this situation the only pleasure to be taken was that of vengeance, a double vengeance that found pleasure equally in punishing the traitor and rebuking the actor who had failed in his role.

It is not surprising that this reaction was particularly prominent in the case of Hébert. *Le Père Duchesne* had claimed to be, stylistically and otherwise, the voice of the people. Hébert's proven treachery was therefore all the more scandalous: his physical and mental collapse during the procession tainted the image of the people he had claimed to represent. The collapse of the spokesman-victim constituted an indictment of the writer. In accounts of the people's reaction, then, the vindictive unsurprisingly prevails: 'Everyone tried to interpret the expressions of the victims, in order to relish, as it were, the pain they were inwardly feeling; it was a sort of revenge that people took pleasure in.' 'After the execution, everyone was talking about the conspirators. People would say: "They died like cravens." Others said: "You'd have thought Hébert would have shown more courage, but he died like a knave."'[17]

The close examination of faces still alive, still capable of expression – and thus of acting – minutes before their expressions froze in death, the triumphant fascination that lay in attempting to work out their emotions from their faces as though from a painting, the exploration of the psyche of the *moriturus* – these were undoubtedly among the most intense of the pleasures denied by the scaffold and permitted by the procession.

The Pleasure of the Sublime

The pleasure of the sublime was much rarer. It occurred when the condemned man's performance was of a kind that allowed the procession to attain its proper symbolic function, that of manifesting the omnipotence of the People. By internalizing the exemplary lesson that his death was supposed to give and by exhibiting his acceptance in equally exemplary conduct, the condemned man allowed his audience to sublimate its passions. For the procession to realize this balance between the performance of the victim and the participation of the audience was very rare, and it made for a *nec plus ultra* of mortuary theatre. For the noble and heroic performer met with a degree of astonishment in his audience, and we have seen that Burke defined this astonishment as the principal source of the sublime.[18]

But, for the spectacle to attain the sublime, certain conditions had to be fulfilled, and they go far to suggest how fragile an effect it was. The pleasure of the sublime could, in this context, take two forms.

The first might arise where the condemned spontaneously sang the praises of the Revolution, offering it up as a model shared by both audience and victim. Such was the case with the revolutionaries who went to the scaffold singing their *chanson de guillotine*, verses they had written specially to sing on this expedition. Their sublimity was more or less guaranteed by the quite sumptuous rarity that literary endeavour acquired under the circumstances. The song was a genuine swan-song, and the guillotine followed afterwards to wring the neck of its eloquence. Its content was of less significance than its theatricality. The theme of the Revolution went one last time upon the boards, offering a final communication between the singer and the audience. The songs were an undeniable attraction; not only did many of them survive in writing, but certain of them went on to become popular hymns after being, where necessary, completed by other people. Thus the song of Girey-Dupré, the Girondin editor of *Le Patriote français*, who was guillotined on 29 November 1793, formed the basis of the hymn 'Mourir pour la patrie!', and Charles Maurice notes in his journal that 'its memory was long preserved by street-singers'.[19]

The second pleasure of the sublime was provided by what we might call the Roman style of death, in which the actor gives a performance of stoical heroism. This was the model preferred by Charlotte Corday, as is shown by the tone of her last letters from prison: 'I am to be sentenced tomorrow at eight, probably by midday I shall have lived, as the Romans say ... I do not know how my last moments will be, and the end is the crown of all endeavour ... I am as yet wholly without fear of death. I valued life only for the use to which it could be put.'[20] The defence offered by her lawyer was of a brevity remarkable in a case of such importance. He confined himself to a 'single observation': the solitary attenuating circumstance in her case was the sublimity of her attitude, which was positively unnatural.[21] That afternoon, Charlotte Corday's procession showed that the plea had been accepted, and the People was sublime in its magnanimity.[22]

The procession of Madame Roland, on 8 November 1793, was certainly among the most sublime. 'Her appearance was unimpaired. Her eyes sparkled, on her lips a charming smile came and went, and yet she was serious and did not make light of her death.'[23] She had a foil; she was accompanied in the tumbril by Simon François Lamarche, who was so 'overwhelmed with terror that his head seemed almost to come off with every jolt of the cart'[24] comically anticipating the moment of decapitation. In this company, Madame Roland's performance had the desired effect; admiration; silence; the sublime.[25]

Such cases were exceptional. The daily-repeated voyage of the tumbrils from prison to scaffold inhibited the propagation of the sublime. Not only were there too many victims for all of them to be impassive, but their numbers were such as to eliminate the element of surprise which the sublime requires. Moreover, the people were drawn into the theatre of the procession, and, failing to maintain the distance of an audience, ceased to have that impassive dignity by which the 'grandeur' of the People was expressed.

The surprise of the sublime was also at risk from another source. The emotion elicited by the performance might easily be transformed into one of hostility, and the boundary was a very narrow one. If, for example, the audience interpreted the dignity of the victim as hostile, it was received in quite another spirit, and, instead of showing an admirable self-mastery, the condemned man was regarded as showing nothing but pride and audacity – in a word, a 'Roman insolence' full of contempt for the people, 'those poor wretches ... that Roman insolence terms proletarian'.[26] The victim, instead of testifying to the omnipotence of the People by the resignation with which he or she accepted the humiliation inflicted, might seem, by a display of criminal arrogance, to dispute this omnipotence. At this point the people's pleasure became revolutionary pleasure.[27] The extreme fragility of the sublime goes far to explain why it is not always possible to distinguish the pleasure of the sublime from revolutionary pleasure, and why the pleasure of the sublime remained exceptional even though it was ideologically the most desirable.

The Revolutionary Pleasure

Revolutionary pleasure occurred when the anger of the people was provoked by the arrogance – real or supposed, the distinction counted for little – of the victim, who made use of his position centre stage to subvert the spectacle's significance. In such cases, the people showed that it too could act, and spoke up to reaffirm its invincible power even before the scaffold's inevitable vindication thereof.

Marie-Antoinette remained impassive throughout the procession, and Rougyff expresses his regret that the people did not do the same.[28] Not only was the Austrian-born queen the object of a fierce and widely shared hatred, but her calm was seen as haughtiness, and the most appropriate response was the most basic. The letter of a citizen of Argentan to her committee is an example of this attitude:

> The bitch went to her end as good as that pig of Godille's, he's the local butcher, she was incredibly calm as she went to the Scat Fold [*sic*] ... She crossed the whole of Paris looking at everyone with contempt and Disdain ... The rogue went to the Scat Fold without flinching.[29]

Even the spelling is important here; it is a first indicator of the social issues that conflict expresses, and of the popular sentiment to which Hébert attempted to give literary form by a sort of 'zero degree' of style:

> What's more, the bitch was audacious and insolent to the last. But her legs weren't any good to her when she was on the plank to play at clap-hand ... Her head was finally taken off her long, scraggy neck and the air re-echoed with shouts of '*Vive la République*', buggeration.[30]

The contempt is answered with baseness, and both parties are confirmed in their social roles: the people plays up to Marie-Antoinette's expectations because Marie-Antoinette plays up to the people's expectations, and vice versa.

ꞮThis pleasure is rightly termed revolutionary, for what is staged is quite simply the political and class conflict that the Revolution was an attempt to solve. The political utility of the procession lay in its demonstration that the solution could only be a violent one, thus justifying the sentences of death handed down by the Revolutionary Tribunal.[31]

The incident to which this revolutionary anger gave rise naturally made for the most dramatic of processions. Spontaneous dialogue broke out as the people reasserted its position as the architect of history: 'A condemned man before he mounts the scaffold says to those present: "Farewell, starvelings!" An indignant citizen replies: "We may have no bread, but we have a blade, as you will soon find out."'[32] Of all the forms of behaviour recorded, the most puzzling from our perspective is no doubt the indifference of the condemned and their occasional laughter. This derision of the grandeur of revolutionary justice caused considerable indignation. Police reports cite many cases of the condemned dancing on the tumbril (28 *Ventôse* Year II), indulging in practical jokes (22 *Ventôse*), laughing among themselves and making fun of the audience:

> Today five people sentenced by the Revolutionary Tribunal got into the executioner's carriage, including one very tall woman who looked foreign. When he gave her his hand to help her up, she grasped it in both hands and hugged it to her. Then she started to laugh. Three of the others were talking and exchanging glances, and they laughed when the people shouted 'To the guillotine!' One of them said: 'Go on with you, it'll be your turn soon.' 'Maybe tomorrow,' said the other, who is said to be an army supplier. They have robbed the army and no one is sorry to see them punished.[33]

Even the *chansons de guillotine* were an excuse for jokes. The people's reactions to Danton's were not recorded:

> We are brought to our deaths
> By criminals; this
> Is a sorrow we cannot deny.
> But the moment will come
> When they too shall succumb,
> Which gladdens our hearts as we die.

One may also wonder what effect was produced by the songs written by Louis Bernard Magnier, an agent of the Committee for Public Safety, who was brought before the Military Commission in *Prairial* Year III:

> (*to the tune of 'Ports à la mode'*)
> Tomorrow, Sanson, with a foolish air
> Will tell me 'I must cut your hair.'
> Thanks friend, but kindly terrorize
> The inhabitants of paradise.

> (*to the tune of 'Bonsoir la compagnie'*)
> It is my consolation
> That this my immolation
> Is for my country's sake:
> I hear the headsman's call,
> I go a willing thrall.
> Pleasures and pains I leave behind:
> Goodnight to one and all![34]

At all events, and whichever of the three modes the procession assumed, its spectacle served to inculcate in the people an awareness of its omnipotence and its historical role. Vindictive pleasure did indeed humiliate the victim, as the people searched his expression for indications of this. The pleasure of the sublime celebrated a noble compliance with the law, and revolutionary anger reinforced the righteous indignation felt by the people for those by whom it had been betrayed. The people was not always equal to the role of *People*, was not always sublime and magnanimous. But it showed its enthusiasm, was always present, and, taking its cue from the victim's performance, played out its own role.

After the Empire, after the Restoration, it was the July Monarchy that marked the conclusion of the revolutionary chapter. The guillotine lost all political significance, and became the humanitarian instrument that Guillotin had intended. The new dispensation took documentary form in the grounds advanced by the Prefect of the Seine when he had the guillotine removed from the place de Grève. From its position outside the Hôtel de Ville and at the heart of the city, he had it moved to the gate of the city closest to the prison, in order to minimize not only the distance between prison and guillotine but also the number of spectators at the execution.

Given that the place de Grève can no longer be used as a place of execution since loyal citizens have nobly shed their blood there for the national cause;

Given that it is necessary to designate only places that are distant from the centre of Paris and are of easy access;

Given the further consideration, that for humanitarian reasons, these places should be chosen as close as possible to the prison where the condemned men are held . . .[35]

The Prefect invoked the memory of the citizens who fell during the July Revolution in the overthrow of Charles X, but the fact was that the bourgeoisie and its monarchy were removing the instrument of revolutionary justice from sight. The guillotine, clearly, was being depoliticized – it was going middle class.

2

The Scaffold

On reaching the stage, he repeated the same words: 'Yes, that's what I say! Fuck the Republic and long live the king!' and then, turning to the executioner: 'Now, guillotine me!'

Le Thermomètre du jour, 7 May 1793

Dominating the square, with its own height surmounted by '*la guillotine debout*', the scaffold is the final destination of the procession's twists and turns, its inevitable terminus, the immobile setting of its last act. On arrival, the performance is suddenly transformed: its sense and rhythms change. In cinematic terms, we cut from a lingering close-up tracking shot (the procession) to a static long shot of the scaffold. The function of the spectacle and the rules governing its presentation alter. The stage is used in a completely different fashion, and a new relationship between public and victim is established.

The location of the scaffold and the history of its movements around Paris tell their own story. Whereas the guillotine for common-law crime remained in the place de Grève, the political guillotine very quickly acquired its own site. Only after the fall of Robespierre was this distinction abolished and the place de Grève used for both categories. The distinction confirms, if further confirmation were required, the specificity with which the Jacobins wished to invest their executions; a site had to be found which had never previously been used for this purpose. The machine's capacity to render death banal was still operative, but against a background of connotations meticulously calculated by the authorities.

The scaffold was moved to the place du Carrousel (which was then the place de la Réunion) after the very first series of political executions – those that followed the tenth of August. On 17 August a special tribunal was set up to try the crimes of that historic day. Thirty-two cases came before it, and it had handed down fifteen acquittals and seventeen death sentences before being dissolved on 19 September. The inauguration of the ordinary guillotine had proved a disappointment to the public, but the inauguration of the political guillotine was a great success. The difference, needless to say, lay not in the spectacle but in the new political dimension.[1]

The first execution took place on 21 August, and it was decided, as of 23 August, that the scaffold would remain permanently in the place du Carrousel, 'the cutter excepted, which the public executioner will be authorized to remove after each execution'.[2] The decision was entirely pragmatic; but its effect was none the less significant. Though the two guillotines in their different locations might now function simultaneously, the political guillotine was guaranteed an infinitely greater prestige; even without its blade, the chassis of the machine was on permanent display and served to illustrate the immutable principles underlying the justice of the Revolution. Similarly, after the massacres that had occurred in the prisons from 2–5 September, the guillotine's performance was a visible reminder to the people that it had to have confidence in the Assembly and rely upon the justice of Reason rather than indulge in summary executions which sullied its reputation.

Moreover, by explicitly locating the guillotine on 'the scene of the crime', and making it the 'scene of expiation',[3] the Assembly emphasized that the place du Carrousel had become a theatre of justice. Each subsequent removal also had a specific meaning.

The guillotine remained in the place du Carrousel for eight and a half months, until 10 May 1793. It was only moved twice during that time: on 11 November to the Champ-de-Mars for the execution of Bailly, and on 21 January to the place de la Révolution, for the execution of the king.

In the second case, the move was motivated by a concern for security. There were rumours that the royalists would attempt to rescue Louis by main force. An official request for guards was made. It was forbidden to show oneself at a window, and the decision was taken to avoid the twisting, narrow roads around the place du Carrousel. From the Temple, where the king was imprisoned, there was a much safer route via the rue du Temple, the boulevards and the rue Royale. But these choices were not made on exclusively pragmatic grounds. The place de la Révolution had previously been called place Louis XV, and the monarch's equestrian statue had already been pulled down: the great size of the square would allow a large crowd to witness the transition from the symbolic destruction of the monarchy to the very real death of Louis the Last.

The scene of the crime was again the theatre of expiation on 11 November, in the Champ-de-Mars, where Bailly was executed for the massacre of 17 July 1791. For this execution there was a special ceremony. The armed forces had fired without warning, as martial law provided that they might. In this case a red flag, as a symbol of martial law, was to be 'attached to the back of the carriage, and dragged to the place of execution'. It was then to be burnt under Bailly's eyes before he was decapitated. Politics here took unusual precedence over the humanitarian principle that the execution should not be long drawn out.[4]

Political reasons also determined that the guillotine should leave the place du Carrousel, which it did on 17 May 1793, and take up residence in the place de la Révolution, where it remained for a little over a year, until 9 June 1794.

The deputies had moved into the salle des Machines in the Tuileries. The departure of that other machine, the guillotine, was directly linked to this fact. On their first day in these premises the deputies had been forced to witness two successive decapitations. A decree was immediately passed that removed the machine from their view, placing the length of the Tuileries gardens between the Assembly and the place of execution.[5] Their decision illustrates the divergent attitudes towards the guillotine held, respectively, by the people's representatives, the people and the *People*. The spectacle that attracted the common man proved intolerable for his representative, and the people was to be metamorphosed into the *People*, at the behest of its representatives, by a spectacle that the latter could not bring themselves to watch. What are we to say of a representative act of national justice which the representatives of the nation could not bear to witness?

In June 1794 the scaffold left the place de la Révolution at the western edge of the city, and, in two short jumps, reached the eastern edge. On 9 June it was set up in the place Saint-Antoine (now place de la Bastille). It stayed there just three days, before being erected on 13 June at the Barrière du Trône Renversé, now place de la Nation.

The reasons for this whistle-stop tour are revealing. The political implication of the alternative sites was thought to be self-evident,[6] but there was a further and more deep-seated reason: the revolutionaries were having difficulty dealing with a machine whose impact on the imagination had been so profound. The first transfer was motivated by the failure of the Terror to merge the two contradictory forms of its sublime. The second transfer, which came so quickly after the first, casts light on the growing divergence between the decisions of the Assembly and the actions or reactions of the people.

The scaffold left the place de la Révolution on 9 June 1794. The date was not chosen at random: it was 21 *Prairial* Year II, the day after the Festival of the Supreme Being had been celebrated on that same place de la Révolution; the day before the Assembly had passed the famous law of 22 *Prairial* dealing with the reform of the Revolutionary Tribunal. The coincidence of thse dates clearly shows the difficulty of reconciling the sublime spectacle presented, on 20 *Prairial*, by the united 'first people of the world', with that same people exulting at the streams of blood (impure blood, let it be said) which were shed in its name.

Robespierre had extolled the Festival of the Supreme Being in the following terms: 'That day made upon the nation a profound impression of calm, happiness, wisdom and goodness. At the sight of this sublime gathering of the first people in the world, who could believe that crime still existed on earth?'[7] And who, in that case, could have understood why an instrument for the punishment of crime remained upon the very same spot? The regeneration of the people had been successfully completed, and the Festival of the Supreme Being was the proof of this. But the law of 22 *Prairial* gave the guillotine even more work to do, and to prevent the soil consecrated by the Mass of the Supreme Being being further slaked with criminal blood, on 21 *Prairial* the guillotine was moved. For, there were monsters unwilling to participate in the communion of the people; their 'private vices', exemplified in each new victim,[8] were to be eradicated definitively and expeditiously. The surgery had to become all the more radical now that the people were halfway to the status of *People*. But the sublimity of the surgical guillotine was decidedly antithetical to the touching sincerity of the communion; so the sword of liberty decamped.

Three days later the machine left the place Saint-Antoine for the Barrière du Trône Renversé. Place Saint-Antoine had seemed politically suitable, but the reasons for this second retreat were different: they had to do with the problems unexpectedly posed by the quantity of blood flowing onto the square.

❧ The law of 22 *Prairial* caused a sudden increase in the number of executions at a time when they were already increasing sharply. In *Germinal*, there had been 155 convictions and 59 acquittals; in *Floréal*, the proportion was 354 convictions to 155 acquittals; in *Prairial*, though the law took effect only in the last days of the month, 509 to 164; in *Messidor*, 796 to 208; and in the first nine days of *Thermidor*, 342 to 84. The numerous acquittals pronounced by the Revolutionary Tribunal are, perhaps, too easily forgotten, but the fact remains that the number of executions per day increased dramatically: an average of 5 a day in *Germinal*, 17 in *Prairial*, over 26 in *Messidor*, and 38 in *Thermidor*. During the guillotine's three days in the place Saint-Antoine 63 people were decapitated.[9]

These figures radically altered the nature of the spectacle and stirred up unexpected opposition. The guillotine could hardly be expected to remain sublime when the regularity of the spectacle had eliminated the surprise of a singular and grandiose event. The only surprise available now was surprise at the rapidity of the executions and even this was attenuated by daily repetition. The flood of executions was too constant to be very frightening.

Camille Desmoulins had predicted this danger as early as 1790. Marat had heralded the mechanical process that was later to characterize the Terror: 'Six months ago, five or six hundred heads might have been enough to save you from the abyss. Now that you have stupidly allowed your implacable enemies to gather their strength, it may be that five or six thousand will have to be struck down. But, were it necessary to strike down twenty thousand, we need hesitate not a moment.'[10] Desmoulins immediately retorted: 'Monsieur Marat ... you are the dramatist of journalism; the Danaids, the Barmecides are nothing to your tragedies. You cut the throat of every character in your play, even that of the prompter. Are you unaware that hyperbole in tragedy is a bore?'[11] We are reminded of Saint-Just's famous remark that 'The workings of the Terror have made people indifferent to crime just as strong liqueurs blunt the palate.'[12] But, after *Prairial,* the *spectator* could not be other than indifferent – unless he was the proverbial 'cannibal' by temperament, and so in any case immune to the purpose of the spectacle.[13]

The 'batch' executions of the Terror might seem analogous to other famous historical massacres, such as that of Saint Bartholomew's day. But they were very different: the Saint Bartholomew's day massacre more closely resembles the September massacres. The batch executions were by no means a frenzied outburst of killing; they were a colourless processing, a regular production of death, in which the reliability of the machine was placed at the service of industrialized capital punishment that could execute identically and indefinitely. The machine confirmed the technical prowess of Dr Louis, but it undoubtedly lost a great deal of prestige in doing so, and its removal to the Barrière du Trône Renversé was directly connected with this degradation.

A parallel can be drawn with the slow process by which the guillotine was finally withdrawn from the public eye. In 1832 the procession was made as short as possible; in 1851 it was decided that the scaffold should be set up directly at the gates of the prison; in 1872 the scaffold was abandoned altogether and the guillotine placed on the ground, which considerably reduced its visibility for all but the front row of spectators. In 1899 a campaign began in favour of all executions taking place within the prison walls so that the 'unwholesome curiosity' of the spectator might not encourage the kind of 'terminal play-acting'[14] some convicts went in for. It was only in 1939, after the much-photographed execution of Weidmann, that the Ministry of Justice decided to exclude the public entirely from executions.

This decision gravely undermined the well-worn argument concerning the exemplary nature of the penalty and still more so that of execution. But it was in line with the concepts of bourgeois justice that slowly evolved during the nineteenth century, and which tended to replace the ideology of atonement and example with that of surveillance and punishment. Stripped of the 'great theatrical ritual' in which the Revolution had clothed it, the guillotine at last became 'the machinery of quick, discreet death'.[15]

These developments have a certain logic in the context of bourgeois thought, and look forward to the abolition pure and simple of the death penalty, but their appearance at the height of the Terror is somewhat paradoxical. The guillotine's removal to the Barrière du Trône Renversé is perhaps our surest indication of the discord that was emerging between political requirements and the increasing pressure exerted by society.[16]

For it was society which demanded that the guillotine should leave place Saint-Antoine. The inhabitants objected to it mainly on the grounds of hygiene. The quantity of blood spilt was much too great for it to be quickly absorbed by the ground, and it was feared that its 'noxious stench' might cause an epidemic.[17] But this was not the only matter for concern, as is attested by the reluctance of the population to allow neighbouring cemeteries to be used for the burial of the decapitated.[18] Given the number of bodies involved and the rather unsatisfactory burial they were accorded, this reluctance too might have stemmed from health considerations. But there was more to it than that: for example, the protests of those who lived close to the Errancis cemetery (now parc Monceau) occurred only after they had been informed that the decapitated bodies had been put in the Madeleine before before being transported by night to the cemetery.

The guillotine of the Revolution populated the scaffold with ghosts. Superstition influenced the public mind in ways which ran counter to the political purposes that the guillotine was supposed to serve. During the last two months of the Jacobin Terror, it became increasingly clear that the theatre of the scaffold contradicted its own purposes, for the people at its foot could hardly be other than cannibalistic or superstitious. With the loss of the cathartic dimension of the sublime, the scaffold was in grave danger of eliciting no other reaction from the assiduous spectator than that ferocious and cannibalistic joy that was in any case the primary ideological threat hanging over the head of the people, reducing it again to the status of contemptible *hoi polloi*. The problem had already been discussed in traditional terms as early as 1789.[20] Prudhomme took up the question in April 1793 in terms strikingly similar, though newly enriched with experience.[21] But in April 1793 there had been only nine decapitations in the place du Carrousel ... What did Prudhomme think in June 1794? What would he have written if *Révolutions de Paris* had not prudently ceased publication on 28 February of the same year? What would he have said of a time when the very executioners were complaining that they had frequently to replace their clothes because these were ruined by the blood with which they were inundated each day?[22] And what would he have said of the 'spectacle of blood' that remained even after the tumbril full of corpses had left? For 'the blood of the dead remains on the square where it was shed ... Dogs come and sate their thirst with it and ... a crowd of men feed their eyes on this sight that inspires ferocity.'[23]

This 'industrial' use of the guillotine gave rise to kinds of behaviour directly contrary to those which the theatre of the guillotine was supposed to instil. The culmination of this process had been reached when the guillotine awakened beliefs supposedly long extinct, occasioning superstition in its spectators:

> Popular superstitions. Apparently not all of them have been eradicated and some people even encourage them. Yesterday a citizen was telling the group around the guillotine how he had been unable to persuade a friend of his to come near the site where the scaffold was set up: the friend had been told that several of those executed returned to haunt the spot.[24]

In political debate, in the Assembly, the guillotine was still considered in the light of its grandiose functions, but conversation around the scaffold or in the taverns gave a completely different picture. Between these two different images stood the spectacle, and the little that could be seen, the much that could be imagined, formed a complex pattern from which narrative and anecdote were woven.

Stage Direction

Despite the height of the scaffold, despite the geometrical clarity of the space through which the blade fell, despite the warning of the imminence of the spectacle constituted by the condemned man's being strapped to the board, most spectators of the guillotine saw nothing more of the decapitation than a spurt of blood accompanied by the hollow sound of the blade striking the support after cutting off the head.[25] But a public execution should be edifying. The theatre of the guillotine therefore necessitated a degree of stage direction to compensate for the machine's insufficiently spectacular performance. Not only was the final episode too rapid to be perceived, but the position of the actors on stage left much to be desired, with the victim prone and the two executioners standing on either side of him and blocking the view.[26] Opera-glasses and platforms on which seats could be rented gave better visibility. But at times something more was called for, and, if the victim was worth the trouble, the mechanical succession of events could be modified.

The lightning stroke of the guillotine could, at such times, be slowed down or stopped. At the request of the people the executioner could draw out the moment of decapitation and for a short while imitate the protracted deaths of the executions of the *ancien régime*. To interfere in this way with the working of the machine was against the law. It was therefore very rarely practised, and occurred only when the 'avenging fury' of the people demanded its own particular satisfaction.

In at least one case this effect was obtained by an ingenious manipulation of the mechanism of the guillotine itself. That Hébert was the victim should be no surprise – his treachery was all the more criminal for his having pretended to the role of spokesman of the people. The people would seem to have contrived for him an abominable (and premonitory) variation on the theme: 'O time! Suspend thy flight!' Sanson's humanity being one of the themes of his apocryphal *Mémoires*, we turn to Perrière for a description which suggests how easy it was to subvert the guillotine's humanitarian speed:

> Hébert was kept till last. The executioners placed his head in the fatal ring, and responded to the will of the people, who had expressed the desire that the great conspirator meet with a harsher death than that of the guillotine, by suspending the blade over his criminal neck for a few seconds, and while doing so whirling their hats triumphantly around him and assailing him with piercing cries of 'Long live this Republic' that he had wished to destroy.[27]

This vengeance upon the scaffold prolonged the vindictive pleasure that had accompanied Hébert on his procession: the people's violence is the more exemplary in that, as we shall see, on other occasions when the first blow was not fatal public indignation followed.

But Hébert's case was necessarily exceptional: the instantaneousness of execution was an article of law. For this reason, the compensation for the too rapid instant came before or after. The *before* was the province of the leading actor, who, raised to the dignity of the scaffold, could use this vantage-point to 'have the last word'; the *after* was the province of the executioner, who picked up the head, and, in a gesture full of significance, showed it to the people.

Several 'stars' of the Revolution uttered famous last words. Danton's are perhaps the most celebrated. He contrived to participate in the aftermath of his presence with the sublime remark: 'But do not forget, do not forget to show my head to the people: it is worth seeing.'[28] It is less well known that the remark 'Oh Liberty, how many are the crimes committed in thy name!' was made by Madame Roland to the plaster statue of Liberty that had replaced the equestrian statue of Louis XV. Few indeed are those who know that Olympe de Gouges allegedly looked off towards the trees of the Champs-Elysées as she murmured 'Oh fatal aspiration to fame! I wanted to be a somebody!'[29]

Our concern here is not to draw up a list of these famous last words, nor to demonstrate their authenticity; it is simply to note how necessary they were felt to be by both actors and audience. For it is clear that most of these remarks were not heard and have therefore been fathered upon their supposed authors. This is indeed suggested by Arnault's account of Danton's death: '. . . his last words, terrible words that I myself could not hear, but which were repeated with shudders of horror and admiration: "But do not forget, do not forget . . ."' Who, after all, could have heard his *penultimate* words, spoken at the foot of the scaffold? A gendarme wished to interrupt Danton as he gave a farewell embrace to a comrade, and Danton riposted: 'You won't prevent our heads from kissing in the basket, I hope?'[30]

The remark was no doubt fathered upon him; but though the paternity is doubtful, the child was welcome. The 'last word' answered to a deeply felt need of the revolutionary imagination; it was a further instance of the sublime, this time in rhetorical form. Indeed, the last word represents the height of the revolutionary sublime, a rhetoric born of that 'instant of the guillotine' which proscribes all further remark and cuts off all rhetoric in mid flow. The last word is all the more effective for conforming to the first rule of revolutionary rhetoric; by constraining any expression to the even greater tersity of silence, the guillotine demonstrated the fundamental rhetorical principle of a true revolutionary government: as Saint-Just said, 'It is impossible to rule without laconicism.'[31]

It would be perfect if the last word of the victim might be truncated by the blade itself. Rhetoric would reach a peak at which, in a 'dying fall', it was cut off at the point it made; the sublimity of the ellipsis . . .

Such indeed was the sublimity of the royalist account of Louis XVI's last words. In the republican account we find instead the howl of the monster who refuses to die.[32] So we should not be surprised to find this cry echoing through the death of Robespierre, who had himself become, in the natural course of things, a monstrous and blood-thirsty tyrant: 'The executioner strapped him to the board and, before pivoting the plank abruptly, tore the bandage off his wound. He gave a roar like a dying tiger that was audible in the furthest corners of the square.'[33] In the roar of the tiger we hear a denial of the eloquence, the silence of the sublime.

The effect of the last word was enhanced by what followed – the enforced silence of the victim whose head the executioner then showed to the people. An executioner's reputation depended on his flair in this gesture, which was a considerable addition to the repertoire of the theatre of the guillotine. To the cries of an audience greeting the success of the operation and of the performance – the cries differing very little from the applause that follows the last note of a concert or opera – the last gesture of the executioner was to pick up the truncated head and lift up this now speechless object for the audience to inspect. He gave them something to see. Gloriously nullifying the fall of the monstrous head, its 'monstrance' was the concluding incident of the execution, fixing the fatal moment and reversing it visually and symbolically.

The political significance of this theatrical gesture is evinced by its place in the iconography of the revolutionary print. Royalist engravings linger affectionately on the last moments of the condemned man, and so, for the most part, on his last words. The revolutionary prints repeatedly show the gesture with which the head was displayed. It was among the favourite themes of the edifying imagery of the new regime. True, the gesture was easy to show, whereas, of the other episodes of the execution, the death was invisible and the instant before decapitation was difficult to represent because of the prone position of the condemned. Decapitations under the *ancien régime* generally showed the latter moment, with the victim on his knees and the executioner's sword raised over him. But the choice of this gesture for the revolutionary print was no doubt also influenced by its existence in the wider field of iconography. The decapitated head held out by the 'executioner' has its own tradition, one that confirms the resonance of the 'monstrousness of the monster': it is the well-known gesture of Perseus holding out the head of Medusa to petrify the tyrant Polydectes. The gesture freezes, the image fixes the 'petrifying' conclusion of a theatrical rite addressed to anyone who felt 'nostalgic for tyranny'.[34]

The most effective way of compensating for the guillotine's unspectacular denouement was to produce a narrative in which there might appear not only what the narrator saw, but also what he had seen incompletely or not at all. The guillotine was therefore a fertile source of narratives without documentary value, but revealing in their fiction. Of those dealing directly with the events on the scaffold, the most informative are those which recount clearly impossible events. The more fantastical the invention the more indicative, for what is revealed is the pressures at work upon the imagination. The narrative takes up these pressures and, by giving them expression, give them reality. This goes some way to explaining the extraordinary success of the anecdote concerning Charlotte Corday, which won credence even from the medical profession. The anecdote, it will be remembered, concerned the blush of indignation that suffused the cheeks of Charlotte Corday's severed head when it was slapped by the executioner. By staging, as it were, 'live', the fascinating theme of the death lived out by the severed head, the narrative acquired a force of conviction which was proof not only against medical scepticism, but also against the common sense displayed the day after the execution in a letter explaining the incident: 'The executioner's hands were covered in blood; he left traces of this on the cheeks of the dead person.'[35]

Two other accounts also serve to exemplify the rules governing the composition of such narratives. Both accounts fly in the face of the facts, and in both the flight of fantasy is rewarded with a spectacular surprise. The function of this surprise is to restore, to a death otherwise quite scandalously banal, the unheard of, the unique, the incredible.

Lafont d'Aussone, a most irreproachable royalist, had no scruples about protecting the death of Marie-Antoinette from the taint of the guillotine and the soiling touch of the headsman. There could be no altering the ineluctable succession of events that culminated in her appearance on the scaffold. He therefore invented an admirable *coup de théâtre* which, even in the context of the royalist accounts, turned the death of the queen into a monstrously inhuman event.

> At the sight of the scaffold, Marie-Antoinette's eyes closed, her face grew mortally pale, and her head fell upon her breast. She was no more. A fulminating apoplexy had made an end of the life of the queen, and it was not herself but her pitiful corpse that the republicans carried onto the scaffold.[36]

Lafont d'Aussone exploits a detail given in *Le Magicien républicain*'s account:

> As she arrived in the place de la Révolution, she turned her eyes upon the château des Tuileries with some emotion. Her confessor, who sat beside her, spoke to her, but she seemed neither to listen nor to hear.[37]

Lafont d'Aussone's ridiculous invention enlarges upon this moment of distraction, but it is at the price of the facts of the execution, which did honour to Marie-Antoinette.[38] But for a dyed-in-wool royalist the sacred inviolability of the nation's sovereign body had to survive her death, even if this meant the loss of an opportunity to praise the queen's courage – courage being in any case expected of royalty.

The death of Madame Roland, in which actor and audience combined for a performance consistently sublime, supplied the background for a particularly brilliant narrative variation, one in which the solitary feature visible at *every* execution – the gout of blood spurting from the truncated neck – is quite simply denied. According to this narrator, the blood which spurted from the neck of Madame Roland was in itself unusual:

> When the blade had cut off her head, two huge jets of blood shot forth from the mutilated trunk, a thing not often seen: usually the head that fell was pale, and the blood, which the emotion of that terrible instant had driven back towards the heart, came forth rather feebly, drop by drop.[39]

Bertin's fanciful account kills two birds with one stone. On the one hand, his invention evokes the terror with which the prospective victim was filled (and on this point we need not disbelieve him) by inventing a physical phenomenon whose very impossibility emphasizes the monstrous character of the event; on the other, he makes Madame Roland's death, which would otherwise have been banal, exceptional in its gory horror.

There is, however, another kind of account, which constitutes an elaborate theatrical response to the visually unsatisfactory denouement of the spectacle and the unreliable interpretation the public might give of it: these are the popular songs handed out after the execution. They were an excellent method of inculcating the lessons of the Revolution. Written by specialists, they were intended for the people and attempted to adopt the language of the people. Their simple style pointed to a clear political moral to be drawn from the execution, and thus corrected false impressions that the event itself might give rise to.

The death of Hébert occasioned one such exercise in interpretation, and '*l'Impromptu sur le raccourcissement du Père Duchesne et de ses*

Illustrated Neapolitan chronicle (late fifteenth century), *Scaffold for the Execution of G. A. Petrucci*, 11 December 1498 (Pierpont Morgan Library, New York)

Georg Pencz, *The Sacrifice of Titus Manlius* (Bibliothèque nationale, Paris)

After Lucas Cranach, *The Martyrdom of Saint Matthew* (Bibliothèque nationale, Paris)

The Maiden (1564) (Royal
Museum of Scotland,
Edinburgh)

Machine proposée à l'Assemblée Nationale.
Pour le Supplice des Criminels par M. Guillotin

Les exécutions se feront hors de la Ville dans un endroit destiné à cet effet la Machine sera environné de
Barrieres pour empecher le Peuple d'approcher, l'intérieur de ces Barrieres sera gardé par des Soldats
portant les armes basses, et le Signal de la mort sera donné au Boureau par le Confesseur dans l'instant de
l'absolution, le Boureau detournant les yeux coupera d'un coup de sabre la corde apres laquelle sera
suspendu un mouton armé d'une hache   N.º Une semblable Machine a servi au supplice de Titus Manlius romain.

*Machine proposed to the National Assembly by Monsieur Guillotin for the
execution of criminals* (musée Carnavalet, Paris)

Execution by means of the guillotine, anonymous German engraving
(Bibliothèque nationale, Paris)

Frontispiece of the General
List of all the conspirators
sentenced to death by the
Revolutionary Tribunal,
Paris, 1794, anonymous
woodcut (musée Carnavalet,
Paris)

Vorstellung der Hinrichtung Ludwigs des XVI. Königs v. Frankreich, den 21 Jenu 1793.
1. der Schloß Plaß. Carousel. 2. die Kutsche. 3. wie Er ausgestiegen. 4 wie Er sich aus Kleidet 5 wie Er niederkniedt
6 wie Ihm der Henker das Haar abschneid. 7. wie Er in der Guillotine gerichtet wird. 8. die Soldaten u. Tampor.
9. das Blutgerießt. 10. die Zuschauer. 11. sein Beicht Vater 12. das Kopf herumtragen.13. der Karren mit dem Korb.

Execution of Louis XVI King of France, 21 January 1793, anonymous
German engraving (Bibliothèque nationale, Paris)

LE GUILLOTINE.

The Guillotine, anonymous
English etching (Bibliothèque
nationale, Paris)

Guillotine, élevée en Place du Carousel, le 13 aoust 1

vant à punir les conspirateurs et ennemis de la Patrie.

The Guillotine erected in the Place du Carrousel, 13 August 1792, being used to punish conspirators and enemies of the homeland (musée Carnavalet, Paris)

LA VERITABLE GUILLOTINE ORDINAERE.
HA LE BON SOUTIEN POUR LA LIBERTÉ !

LEFT: *The genuine working guillotine*, anonymous engraving, (musée Carnavalet, Paris)

BELOW: *The death of Louis Capet, 16th of that name*, 21 January 1793, anonymous engraving (musée Carnavalet, Paris)

MORT DE LOUIS CAPET 16.ᵉ DU NOM LE 21 JANVIER 1793.

Cruikshank, *The Martyrdom of Louis XVI King of France* (musée de la révolution française, château de Vizille)

Unschuldige Hinrichtung Ludewigs des XVI
König von Franckreich den 21. Januar 1793.
Dieses Schnur haut der Scharfrichter auf den Ihm gegeben Winck. Zwischen a. und b. durch.

Execution of Louis XVI, King of France, 21 January 1793, anonymous German engraving (musée Carnavalet, Paris)

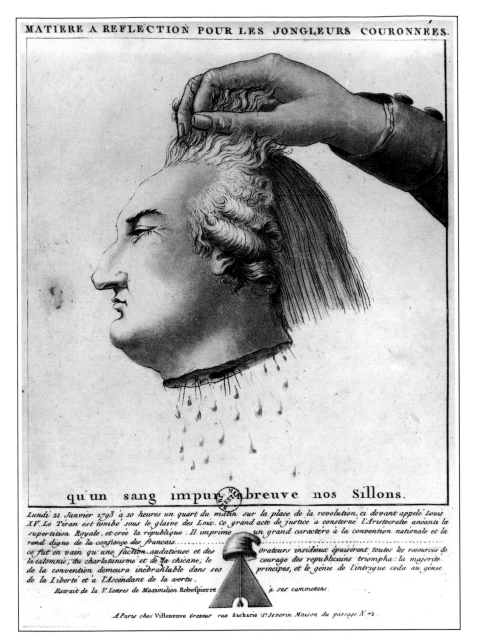

Villeneuve, *A Matter for crowned mountebanks to consider*, engraving (musée Carnavalet, Paris)

Cruikshank, *The Martyrdom of Marie Antoinette Queen of France*, 16 October 1793, engraving (musée Carnavalet, Paris)

Act of justice of 9 and 10 **Thermidor**, anonymous engraving after Viller (musée
Carnavalet, Paris)

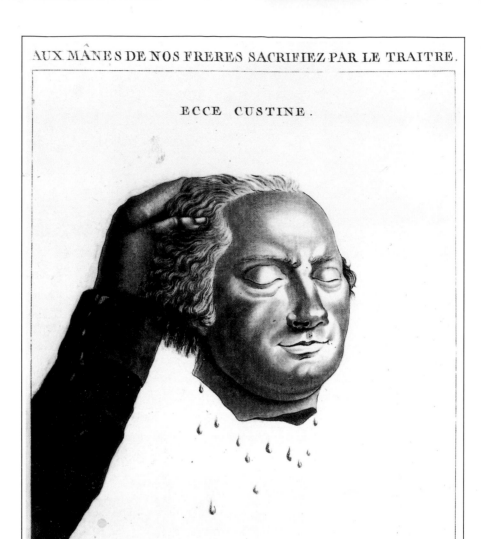

Villeneuve, *Ecce Custine*, engraving (musée Carnavalet, Paris)

complices' to be sung to the tune of 'Cadet Roussel', is a perfect example of its kind:

> Père Duchesne has been condemned
> To the guillotine, by God.
> How he blinds and swears and shouts
> To see his head come off!
> Oh dear, really,
> He's not a happy man . . .
>
> His sneaking bloody newspaper
> Half bleeding did us in.
> Stick him on the guillotine
> With all his tricky friends.
> Oh dear, really,
> Guillotine them quick!
>
> Père Duchesne, he would have gone
> And starved us all to death.
> He held supplies up everywhere.
> His crimes'd fill a book.
> Still, as you can see
> We guillotined the sod.
>
> Père Duchesne was a Norman,
> Not so far from Caen.
> He said he was a *sans-culotte*,
> But this seeming patriot
> Went the way of others
> Onto Guillotin's machine.[40]

Songs like this concluded the spectacle. It was opened, in Hébert's and other cases, by life histories which were hawked on the square while people were awaiting the arrival of the procession. Perrière's account shows very clearly the purpose of these pre-execution narratives, whose themes were reiterated by the songs. They had a theatrical and a political function:

> Further on, readers were preparing the people for the execution of the notorious hypocrite, who had craftily inveigled his way into its confidence and esteem. They were preparing the people by telling the story of his private life, lest the gigantic patriotic reputation he had built up in the minds of the citizens should, at the moment of his execution, seem at odds with the sentence imposed.[41]

The guillotine was not afraid of work. Though it so cleanly 'wrung' the neck of counter-revolutionary eloquence, it transformed the excessive brevity of the puppet-show played out on the scaffold into texts written, read, recited and sung. Paradoxical that the decapitating machine should set the scene for these modes of discourse . . .

3

The Executioner

*What a man this Sanson is! He comes and goes just like anyone else.
Sometimes he goes to the Théâtre du Vaudeville. He laughs, he looks at me.*
Mercier, *Le Nouveau Paris*

*'Where have you been, young misses?' 'Mummy, we went to see a guillotining:
oh, my goodness, how that poor executioner suffered!'*
J. Joubert, *Carnets*, 30 July 1804.

The sacrifice is about to begin ... the executioner and his assistants
ascend and get things ready. The former puts a blood-red outer
garment over his clothes. He positions himself on the left, to the
west, with his assistants on the right, the east, facing Vincennes. The
tall one is admired in particular and praised by the cannibals for his
competent air, his air of *deliberation*, as they say.[1]

In the theatre of the guillotine the executioner has a special role. He is
the first on stage and the last to exit. He opens the spectacle and marks
out the area of the stage. He is more than one, since the guillotine,
unlike the sword, requires more than one operator; but he is also the
actor to whom least attention is paid, though he frequently obstructs the
audience's view. Half actor, half stage-hand and walker-on, of all those
who go upon the boards of the scaffold, he is the one whom accounts
least mention, though he is the only permanent member of the company,
the only player for whom the 'tragedy' has more than one performance.

So we should consider him separately. Not because he is that
'extraordinary' being celebrated in Joseph de Maistre's description,[2]
for the machine leaves him little to do but trigger an impersonal
mechanism. There is no bodily contact, and the guillotine's blade
severs the terrible bonding of victim/executioner, ending their uneasy
relationship. Yet the union of guillotine and Sanson seems at first sight
to be a meeting of irreconcilables – of the banality of the mechanical
with a person who is strange, out of the ordinary, in some sense 'sacred'.
What becomes of the executioner when the guillotine is top of the bill?
How were the old and new theatres of death to be reconciled?

The Difficulty of being Ordinary

It would seem, then, that the executioner and his assistants had only a minor part; they were at most operatives or *exécutants*, to use Desmoulins's word, and it was their duty to pass unnoticed. Indeed, it required exceptional circumstances for the reactions of the audience, or indeed of the other actors, to be addressed to the executioner. Invariably present, the executioner had to be invisible and generally was. The anecdotes in which he is mentioned are few and far between.

To this end the law and the machine had been introduced. The headsman could not become the mere executioner – as the bureaucracy now referred to him – until he ceased to be held in awe; he was now to be a man like any other, and only his professional functions were to be other than ordinary.

This had been the theme of the debates, which had begun as early as 1789, well before the construction of the guillotine, as to whether the executioner should be entitled to stand for election to the Assembly. The traditional arguments were put by Abbé Maury, who was bitterly opposed to the Revolution.[3] Those who argued that the executioner should be eligible pointed out the paradox of refusing citizen's rights to a man whose responsibility it was to apply the law. Sanson's advocate, Maton de La Varenne, at this stage wrote a *Mémoire* which is of great interest to us in that it suggests that an executioner who was well liked might enjoy considerable prestige.[4] But the most remarkable contribution to the argument was that of the comte de Clermont-Tonnerre. His succinct argument clearly explained the new standing of the executioner:

> Professions are either harmful or not. Those that are constitute a habitual infraction that the law should prohibit. Where they are not, the law must be consistent with justice, on which it is based ... We have simply to overcome a prejudice ... Whatever the law requires is good. It requires the death of a criminal. The executioner simply obeys the law. It is absurd that the law should say to a man: do that, and if you do it, you will be abhorrent to your fellow men.[5]

The neutral tone is significant: enlightened rationality thought it possible to 'stage-manage' the character of the executioner, to have him seem an ordinary person. But on the theatre of the scaffold the divergence of character and person was sufficient to defy the legislator's good intentions, and to do so in several different ways.

The executioner was finally allowed to stand for election, and in 1792 the use of the guillotine should have confirmed his ordinariness. He was required to show his skill at a single point of the execution – strapping the victim to the board – and his speed in performing this was the only criterion by which he could be judged on humanitarian grounds. As the numbers to be executed grew, the victims ceased to be bound; this speeded up the operation and avoided a cruelly extended delay for those sentenced. Strength, decisiveness, and agility were the only qualities necessary in the executioner at this stage as at least one account shows:

> When all was ready, the old man went up with the help of the executioners. The principal executioner took him by the left arm, the senior assistant by the right arm, the second by the legs: in a flash he was lying face down, his severed head and fully clothed body tossed into a huge tumbril where everything was swimming in blood. And each time the same. What butchery![6]

This casts some light on the admiration felt for the 'art of the guillotine' that Sanson and his team had apparently achieved. The good executioner had become an accomplished butcher, and thereby lost some of the prestige of the *carnifex*, but gained the great advantage of ordinariness: he had become a full citizen, almost a civil servant like any other. When he failed to discharge himself correctly of his minimal responsibility, he was taken to task for it in just this spirit. This happened to Jean-Denis Peyrussan, who made a horrendous mess of an execution in Bordeaux on 4 June 1794, and had to drop the blade several times on each of the four condemned. He was summoned before a military commission whose president reminded him of the new principles by which he was professionally bound:

> Under the *ancien régime* the august function that you exercise had become odious, and one had to be a savage to perform it! This is no longer the case today; in every employment, one can show oneself humane and sensitive. A humane man can now practise your fearful profession . . . You should thank the Lord for the Revolution, which has restored your position in society and made honourable citizens of you. You should have shown yourself humane. He who strikes in the name of the law may do this.[7]

A humane man. The paradox of the near tautology testifies to the progress the guillotine had made: it had eliminated the only inhuman man who might perhaps have survived into the society of equality and sensitivity.

Yet at its birth the Republic had shown little trust in its executioner. This is clear from the scandal that erupted when, in late 1789, *Révolutions de Paris* discovered private presses used by the aristocracy in Sanson's house. The affair was the talk of the town, and Desmoulins's paper carried a reference to it.[8] The 'savage' executioner of the *ancien régime* might well have seemed a royalist at heart. He inherited a post that had been all but dynastic since his ancestor Charles was named executioner in 1688 by a letter of appointment signed by Louis XIV. Charles Henri was the third in a line of descent in which the forenames succeeded one another with the regularity of a monarchic dynasty: Charles Sanson called Longval (1688–1707); Charles II (1707–26), Charles Jean-Baptiste (1726–78); Charles Henri (1778–95 resigned). The status of this dynasty was also held in a certain awe, but it was of a negative kind: they were not ordinary people.[9] But Sanson, now an ordinary citizen, exercised his right as a citizen, and his enemies were convicted of slander in open court. This amounted almost to a certificate of republicanism, and the only relations thereafter held by the government with its executioner were of a financial and administrative order. The executioner was just one of its employees, responsible for the 'timbers of justice' [*bois de justice*].

Two details in the correspondence necessitated by these relations do, however, suggest that the process of turning the executioner into an ordinary citizen was not perfectly smooth. The first is that, though executioner and execution were now to enter the commonplace, the machine apparently did not. The government did not provide for its maintenance, but left this task to the executioner by continuing to pay the traditional 'maintenance fee', a lump sum the executioner received annually in addition to his wages.[10] The second is the popular resistance the government encountered when it tried to transfer executioners from one *département* to another, as it did with other employees. The law of 13 June 1793 had provided that there be one executioner for every *département*, and the South lacked executioners at a time when the North was full of them. Transfers were therefore arranged, but, when the Northern executioners came to exercise their profession in the South, there were objections. The situation was indicative of the difference between the logic of the administration and the realities of a given locality. Most of the surviving correspondence dealing with executioners concerns this difficulty, and the question was not resolved for some time.[11] It was not enough simply to introduce new regulations. That much is clear from the terms in which the Minister of Justice, Duport-Dutertre, in 1792 entered an appeal in favour of the executioners whom the new law would make redundant. He declares his 'rather strong sympathy' for the executioners, given the 'great horror' of crime that their profession inspired in them, but nevertheless referred to the popular prejudice against executioners as a 'natural feeling'.[12]

There was, then, a fierce contradiction between the desire to make scaffold and headsman commonplace, and that natural feeling which the laws were unable to combat precisely because it *was* only a feeling. One philosophical executioner noted this, not without dignity, when deciding to give up his profession: 'The mind of the people is not in every respect on a par with its principles, and I know from experience that I would still be subject to those remnants of prejudice that philosophy has not yet eradicated.'[13]

Popular Reactions

The people could indeed be disgusted by the savagery of the executioner, but its indignation was generally reserved for those cases where the executioner failed to work the machine correctly and made of the easy death required by the law a variant of the torture it replaced.

The first such incident seems to have occurred in Paris in July 1792. The ropes that held up the blade became tangled; the blade was slowed down in the final stage of its fall, and had to be dropped a second time.[14] The rope was later replaced by a mechanical trigger. But inattention, emotion or inexperience could all cause the executioner to transform the spectacle.

Chalier, who had terrorized the bourgeoisie of Lyons with his threats, was, during the town's insurrection, sentenced to die by the instrument with which he had threatened his insufficiently republican compatriots. But the machine, which was new, had not been properly set up, and the blade slid slowly down onto the victim's neck, three successive efforts doing little more than deepen the gash. The head had to be cut off with a knife. And as if this were not enough, in order to show the head to the people, executioner Ripert had to hold it by the ears: Chalier was bald. This grotesque and macabre death scene led to the execution of the executioner and his assistant when republican repression battened on the town. Chalier's head became, by contrast, a relic of the Republic, and was solemnly offered to the City of Paris by Collot d'Herbois. who demanded that the martyr be honoured with a place in the Panthéon.

The recurrence of incidents of this kind inspired the royalist author of the *Conspiration de Robespierre* to the most extravagant fancies; the guillotine was used, he says, at a quite literally hellish rate: 'The number of those executed rose considerably. The strength of the executioners was exhausted; their arms grew weak. The fatal knife itself grew blunt and the last victims who received its stroke suffered a long and painful death, crying out shrilly.' Guillotin would have been horrified.

A hitherto unpublished account, which describes a bungled execution, is worth quoting here. Although the execution in question did not occur until 1806, the very precise description gives an excellent idea of the reaction elicited by such departures from the norms of the theatre of death:

> I am pleased to inform your Excellency that on 14 April sentence of death was carried out on four individuals.
>
> Among these individuals was a young girl of twenty-two years old, whose beauty, youth, and misfortunes had attracted the sympathy of the assembled spectators. They were not the less inclined to pity her for her spontaneously falling to her knees after mounting the scaffold and asking the forgiveness of the public for the scandalous impression her dissolute life had caused.
>
> When the moment of her execution had come, the executioner failed to tie her legs to the board and left on her head a bonnet in which her hair was gathered up. He had also omitted to cut her hair, and the movements of her head caused some of her locks to fall onto the back of her neck. When the blade fell it did not cut off her head, which remained full of life. She was horribly convulsed and her legs fell off the board leaving her in an indecent position.
>
> The executioner raised the blade a second time, but it proved unable to detach her head, until, finally, at the third stroke it was detached from the body.
>
> This horrific scene so animated the public against the executioner that shouts were heard on all sides urging that the executioner be stoned, and perhaps only the armed force that I had exceptionally requested by way of precaution prevented this from occurring. One man was arrested and taken to prison . . .
>
> I should add that the executioner is an aged man, German by birth, formerly executioner at Forbach, in the *département* of Moselle, who speaks neither French nor Flemish, and consequently he can communicate neither with the officers responsible for overseeing executions, nor with the condemned, nor with the public.[15]

This account makes it clear that the machine's reliability was by then taken for granted, and that any malfunction was to be ascribed to the executioner alone; but it also suggests that public indignation did not stem only from pity. In Chalier's case the Lyonnais audience had remained silent, and, for Hébert, the people had spontaneously demanded a refinement which was more or less indistinguishable from that involuntarily produced by the senile executioner of Bruges. This apparent contradiction suggests two thoughts:

First, the use of the guillotine had indeed changed the expectations of the public concerning the spectacle offered by capital punishment. Fifteen years before the same audience would have been fascinated by the spectacle of death by torture (for instance, breaking on the wheel), which lasted much longer and caused even greater suffering to the victim. Fifteen years later the guillotine's failure to make a theatrical unity of time and action was unacceptable. The decapitating machine had undoubtedly transformed people's expectations and, in this respect at least, had fulfilled the ambitions of Guillotin and his successors.

Secondly, popular indignation against the executioner was reserved for cases involving common-law convicts. We may infer that such anger was not simply an expression of pity for the victim, but a resurgence of sympathy that the people had traditionally, if only occasionally, felt for condemned men, and which the authorities were sufficiently well aware of to guard against.[16] The provision in 1789 of a location outside the town, of the fences around the scaffold and of soldiers with their arms ready to keep the people at a distance from the machine clearly had the same purpose, and it is interesting that this precaution was thought to be necessary even under the *ancien régime*. In 1789 no political executions were envisaged. The precautions were to prevent the crowd from showing in regard to common-law convicts a sympathy we may perhaps attribute to 'class solidarity'. The people relished the special death that was reserved for Hébert, but it is no coincidence that, in the only case of a man being rescued from the scaffold during the Revolution, the motive was not pity but solidarity. This was the famous episode of 3 *Prairial* Year III (22 May 1795). Jean Tinel, one of the ringleaders of the popular insurrection of 1 *Prairial*, the goal of which had been a return to the Constitution of 1793, was snatched off the tumbril at the foot of the scaffold and hidden in the Saint-Antoine quarter. Three days later, rather than allow himself to be recaptured, he threw himself off a roof-top.[17]

The guillotine failed to forge the public conscience wished for by Saint-Just. But the theatre of the guillotine did radically alter people's expectations of the spectacle of capital punishment, and the people consented to its political use as long as they were convinced that this use served their interests.

Thermidorian Reaction

After *Thermidor* the two most visible agents of the Terror, the guillotine and the executioner, suffered a rapid eclipse. In 1794 it was suggested that the guillotine be hidden after each execution. In 1806 it was proposed that the executioner should be provided with a uniform to reassure 'honest folk' and to avoid the executioner's disguising his identity or passing himself off as someone else.[18] In his *Second Discours sur Louis Capet* Robespierre had vented his sarcasm on these 'honest folk', calling them the 'schemers of the Republic'. There can be no doubt that this formal rejection of the executioner and his theatre by honest folk derived from their perception of agent and machine as the creature and prop of the Jacobin Terror.

If, however, the executioner so quickly regained, for some at least, his previous and monstrous status, it was also because the law preserved at least one moment when the executioner departed from his role of conscientious technician. This was the gesture by which, momentarily restored to his leading role, he showed the victim's head to the people. Here his profession obliged him to soak his hands in the blood of his fellow man and again become that 'unimaginable' being, the need for whose existence the machine had been intended to eliminate. The law was the more responsible for this awakening of the ancient horror, in that the blood fever of the scaffold could inspire in the executioner extravagant behaviour in which people were quick to recognize atavistic savagery or 'cannibalism'.[19] The desire to make political capital of the guillotine was itself a factor in the re-emergence of the monster that Law and Reason had conspired to eliminate.

The Executioner as Man of Sensibility

However, if the Terror had denied a human face to the executioner, his position afterwards was an exceedingly complex one. It is not enough to say that with *Thermidor* the old prejudices again broke out, for the executioner came out of the Terror with a reputation that we could hardly have predicted. For the first time in the history of his profession he had acquired, paradoxically, a reputation for humanity and even *sensitivity*.

Accounts tend to emphasize not the executioner's barbarity, but his humanity towards his victims. In this way, the Terror improved the reputation of its executioners.

It has to be said that, whether out of a sense of humanity, or from habit and a desire to be finished as soon as possible, the suffering of the condemned was greatly alleviated by the [executioners'] expeditiousness – by the attention they showed in helping the condemned down and placing them with their backs to the scaffold so that they could not see anything. I was grateful to them for this, as I was for the decorum they maintained and their consistently serious manner, which was wholly without mockery or insult for the victims.[20]

The marquise de la Tour du Pin confirms this sentiment in her journal, and contrasts the humanity of the executioner with the monstrous novelties that the cruelty of the judges had seen fit to add to the spectacle. In the eyes of the marquise, the real villains of the piece were the revolutionaries themselves.

This army of torturers, who brought the guillotine with them, was already at La Réole, where it had carried out several executions. I will cite a single example ... The husband was condemned to death and, while he was executed, his wife was placed opposite the guillotine in an iron collar, with her two sons tied close beside her. The executioner, more humane than the judges, positioned himself in front of her so that she would not see the fatal blade descend.[21]

The executioner was not merely more humane than his masters; he was also capable of showing touching signs of sensitivity when circumstances caused him to abandon the strict neutrality required of him by law. On 27 August 1792, well before the Terror, the audience was struck by the sight of the executioner crying on the scaffold. The tears were inspired not by one of his victims, but by one of his assistants, perhaps his son, who, careless or over-excited, had fallen to his death while showing a victim's head to the people. An accident of this kind was most unusual in itself, but what all the different accounts found still more remarkable was the executioner's tears and the intense emotion which he did not know how to hide.[22] The tears were no doubt real enough, but the important point is that the sensitivity of the executioner had been established as a fertile theme for fiction, its potential guaranteed by its offering a locus for the debates that raged around the revolutionary guillotine.

The royalists could not deny that the executioner had killed their king. But they could and did restate the magical and sacred link between monarch and executioner, such as it had existed under the *ancien régime* and such as de Maistre had so eloquently defined it. Thus the royalist account removes one executioner from the scaffold for every Royal

Highness who mounted it, and the guillotining of royalty seems to have cost almost as many Sansons as monarchs. A new legend of the executioner was born, whose definitive expression is to be found in the apocryphal *Mémoires de Sanson*: it is the legend of the humane and royalist executioner.

If it was indeed the son of the executioner who died on the place de Grève in August 1792, reducing his father to tears, the death of the king was to have even more serious consequences, for the 'horrid spectacle' was to bring the executioner to his grave.[23] The execution of Marie-Antoinette caused the disappearance of another executioner. This one did not die from the horror of his sacrilegious act; he simply retired, overwhelmed with remorse: 'The young man, the son of Louis XVI's executioner, refused ever again to mount the scaffold, and left his sinister work to other hands: the head of Marie-Antoinette was the last he ever struck off.'[24] Nineteenth-century historians were left wondering who had executed whom. For the son of Sanson who fell off the scaffold in 1792 cannot have executed the queen in 1793, and yet one of Sanson's sons was certainly alive in 1795, since he officially succeeded to Sanson's post upon his resignation. We know, moreover, that Charles Henri Sanson survived the execution of Louis XVI. But the remark concerning the youth of the executioner who guillotined Marie-Antoinette is disturbing if we compare it with that of Abbé Carrichon who on 4 *Thermidor* noted that the master executioner stood out from his two assistants 'by his youth and his dandyish costume and airs' . . . Something had indeed occurred on the stage of the scaffold, something that excited people's imagination. This something was that the official executioner of the Republic, Sanson, had others to stand in for him, whether his sons or assistants, at the most significant moment of the execution – the release of the blade. Sanson the elder was not anxious to appear in the role of master executioner where the guillotine was concerned. But it does not necessarily follow that he objected to it . . .

These are simply legends. Execution having become a collective operation, it was of little importance to know who exactly triggered the mechanism. Even for historians the matter is not a significant one. But its legendary aspect is of considerable importance to our history of the guillotine's impact on the imagination, and the notion of the headsman whose excessive sensitivity inhibits him in his duties is a piquant one. It could hardly be better illustrated than by the anecdote Joubert indignantly noted in his *Carnets*: '"Where have you been, young misses?" "Mummy, we went to see a guillotining; oh, my goodness, how that poor executioner suffered." This horrifically displaced pity defines our century, in which everything has become its opposite.'[25]

The Executioner as Jacobin Citizen

Remarkable as it may seem, it is only in accounts hostile to Jacobinism – and these are for the most part royalist – that such attention is paid to the sensibilities of the executioner. Republican accounts generally do not mention them, and confine themselves to remarking on his efficient neutrality, much as though he were a part of the machine he operated.

The paradox is only apparent. For the Jacobin republican the virtue of an executioner was invisibility, his capacity to perform his role without attracting attention, without singularity. For the royalist or the moderate republican it was precisely this anonymous efficiency which constituted the horror and fascination of the Jacobin executioner: his neutrality was something incomprehensible, unimaginable, which defined him as both monstrous and monstrously modern.

Unlike Joseph de Maistre's executioner, the executioner who worked the guillotine was not a torturer, and what was frightening about him was simply his machine-like indifference. In 1795 Louis Sébastien Mercier wrote for his *Nouveau Paris* a description which is, all things considered, even more interesting than de Maistre's. Mercier takes no account of the traditional aura attaching to the executioner. He considers the monstrousness of the executioner's role in the light of his new, mechanistic role:

> I should love to know what goes on in that head of his, and whether he considers his appalling duties simply as a profession . . . How does he sleep after receiving the last words and the last glances of all those severed heads? . . . He sleeps well enough, we are told, and it may well be that his conscience is untroubled . . . It is said that the queen apologized to him when, on the scaffold, she accidentally placed the tip of her foot on his. What were his thoughts then? The coins of the royal treasury were for a long time his living. What a man this Sanson is! He comes and goes just like anyone else. Sometimes he goes to the Théâtre du Vaudeville. He laughs, he looks at me. My head is still attached to my neck; he doesn't recognize it.[26]

Mercier does not answer his own questions. The unimaginable cannot be imagined. But his questions suggest what exactly is monstrous about the modern executioner. It is something quite different from that of the torturer of the *ancien régime*. It is the fact that the modern executioner exercises his profession with the neutrality of a civil servant who is willing to provide his services to all administrations in order to ensure the continuity of government. This indifference is what is now unimaginable.

The consequences are far-reaching. This ability, in Robespierre's words, to strip oneself of all individuality, this denial of personality for the sake of the law and the good of the People, is the Jacobin ideal of citizenship, and the executioner might be taken to exemplify this 'form of socialization whose principle is that its members must, in order to perform their role in it, cast off their every real difference, their everyday social existence'.[27]

The executioner brings together even more perfectly the two sides, social and individual, of the Jacobin ideal, for it is his social existence that requires him to shed all true individuality. There is a very real logic in the way in which the republican accounts pass over the executioner in silence; he has, in the last analysis, nothing in particular to say.

The invention of this new protagonist, the neutral executioner, is highly significant. The opponents of Jacobinism found his neutrality monstrous, to such an unimaginable extent that they created for him a fictitious humanity. But that neutrality marked the successful incarnation of the Jacobin citizen at the heart of a spectacle, in which the People (that is in this case, a group of people each of whom has surrendered his own individuality) attended the sacrifice of individual wills that were too individual and too wilful to be able spontaneously to divest themselves of their all too real differences. The executioner on the scaffold – or rather he and his team, his collective – were the ideological delegates of the People, which invested him from below with the power to execute. Sanson, under the Terror, showed that it was possible to subject one's social being to one's political being. At the other extreme of the exercise of power, when the members of the Revolutionary Tribunal were tried, they identified themselves with 'the axe', and were at pains to point out that one does not punish an axe;[28] this is the same ideology put to the contrary use. Robespierre himself, as we have seen, enjoyed that ineffable sweetness, that sublime sentiment of selflessness, by which his self was fused into the higher, collective entity of the People and its general will.

The Jacobin Terror thus created a situation whose rich harvest of meaning was steadily updated. *Thermidor* was the occasion for a re-evaluation of the social and a downgrading of the political. The executioner was gradually to become the neutral instrument of a purely social justice, and the guillotine the instrument of a class-orientated justice.

Three things confirm this:

1. In 1840 the grandson of Charles Henri Sanson was interviewed by the *Gazette des Tribunaux*. The impression conveyed is rather of some necessary cog in the social machine than of a monster or savage.

> What I saw of the residence of Monsieur Sanson is furnished with an austere simplicity befitting such a place . . . The present executioner is a very different man from his father. When he speaks of his profession and the details thereof, he has none of that embarrassment, that awkwardness and uneasiness that afflicted his predecessor. Thoroughly convinced of the utility of his work and of the service that he renders to society, he considers himself no different from a bailiff who executes a sentence, and he talks of his duties with remarkable confidence and fluency.[29]

Henri Clément Sanson was not his grandfather's equal in moral character, and his conviction that his was merely a job like any other was so deep-rooted that he was willing in 1847 to give the guillotine as a security to creditors who had had him imprisoned for debt. This seemed to the authorities to be taking the social integration of the instruments of justice too far, and the last of the Sanson line was dismissed.[30] The anecdote is nevertheless indicative of the degree to which the executioner had become an ordinary member of society, and of the reputation he enjoyed in the bourgeois society of the mid nineteenth century.

2. In April 1871 the Commune publicly burnt the guillotine 'at the foot of the statue of the defender of Sirven and Calas, the apostle of humanity, the harbinger of the French Revolution – at the foot of the statue of Voltaire'. This was an explicitly political act.

> Citizens, following our discovery that a new guillotine was even now in construction, a more portable guillotine capable of more rapid operation, ordered and paid for by the odious government that we have overthrown, the sub-committee of the 11th *arrondissement* has decreed the confiscation of these servile instruments of monarchic domination and has voted that they be destroyed once and for all. Accordingly, they will be publicly burnt on the square in front of the town hall for the purification of the *arrondissement* and the consecration of liberty.[31]

There is something surprising about the abrupt transformation of the guillotine into the servile instrument of 'monarchic domination', but what the Commune in fact here denounces is the supposed neutrality of the decapitating machine. Its 'servility' lay in its being the instrument of law, and the law, though it purported to exist for the good of the public at large, was in fact in the hands of the bourgeoisie. By its public destruction of this symbol of class domination, the revolution of 1871 reaffirmed the lesson of 1793 – that in its eyes the social and the political were one and the same.

3. In 1870 Adolphe Crémieux, the Minister of Justice of the provisional government, ordered that the use of the scaffold be discontinued. Executions were to take place at ground-level. This measure was a product of the desire of the government to enhance what we might call the 'spectator morality' of capital punishment. Villiers de L'Isle-Adam immediately pointed out that the scaffold's absence would undermine the theatre of the guillotine. It was a further step in the process of the social integration of capital punishment – its assimilation into the natural order of things.

> This trivializing informality, this exaggerated down-to-earth attitude towards the instrument of justice, is here grossly inappropriate … The steps of the scaffold are the rightful *property* of any person condemned to death. By removing them we deprive him of an illusion which is none the less *sacred*, and take from him the opportunity (should he desire it) to save his unfortunate memory, through our witness, from extra and undeserved humiliation.[32]

Another author refers more directly to the spirit in which this measure was decreed, seeing in it nothing more than 'the hypocritical and bureaucratic guillotine taking over from the guillotine of scandal'.[33] And it is true that the abolition of the scaffold, that stage of the guillotine's theatre, was accompanied by an immediate and considerable increase in the executioner's salary. By contrast, the Second Republic had not merely abolished the death penalty for political matters, but had systematically reduced over two years the number and remuneration of executioners.[34] The executioners' pay-rise and the abolition of the scaffold were, then, symptomatic of the desire of the bourgeoisie of the Third Republic (as it was soon to become) to neutralize the guillotine and make of its operator an ordinary citizen. It was the final victory of the bourgeoisie over a justice that the Terror had sought to politicize.

Conclusion:

The Guillotine
and Portraiture

It repeats mechanically what can never again be repeated existentially.
Roland Barthes,
La Chambre Claire.
Note sur la photographie

The guillotine focuses our attention not upon the body as a whole, but upon the head. The organic unity through which the blade passes is divided into two parts, and of these it is the head that attracts both attention and comment. The Jacobin ideology sought by decapitation to put to death a representation of the body politic in which the head (of state) incarnated the nation in his own body. The guillotine separated this head from its body, and by exhibiting it in all its regal solitude systematically deprived it of its representative value.

But by removing the head from the body to set it before the spectator's eyes, the guillotine springs one last surprise. It becomes a sort of portraitist, a veritable, indeed a terrifying, 'portrait machine'. As early as 1793 an Englishman had written: 'This destructive instrument is in the form of a painter's easel'. The comparison is apt: between the uprights of this massive easel something is indeed depicted, something we should, by way of conclusion, take a closer look at.

To say that the guillotine is a portrait machine is merely to record one of the customs that prevailed during the Terror. Of the various kinds of revolutionary engraving, the *portrait de guillotiné* is certainly one of the best established genres (in the sense this term has in the theory of classical painting). In it, the economy of the image is the product of a specific iconographic purpose, and subject to a clearly defined code of interpretation.

Against the neutral background of the paper on which the engraving is printed, in a space geometrically delineated by an internal frame, a head is outlined in full or three-quarter profile. Two iconographical motifs make it clear at a glance that the head has been guillotined, so avoiding confusion with a bust or portrait: the drops of blood that fall from the cleanly severed neck are drawn upon the blank lower part of the page; a dark forearm holding the head up by the hair to exhibit it to the spectators evokes the final gesture of the theatrical rite of execution. This portrait is accompanied by a standard text: 'His impure blood slaked our soil.' The words explain the meaning of the drops of blood not in relation to anecdote or event, but iconographically, in that the motif (the drops of blood) represents a theme (the impure blood of the traitor).[1] Set either above or below the image, other, much more variable inscriptions specify the allegorical content of the image, which may vary with the individual represented.

The image is thus quite distinct from the revolutionary engravings that show the moment preceding decapitation. It is not documentary; it is a *guillotine portrait* (portrait of a guillotined person), an image whose elements are as well defined as those of the royal portraiture of the *ancien régime*, and quite as susceptible of precise theoretical analysis. The consistency of the genre is demonstrated by the fact that the portrait of 'Robespierre guillotined' receives the same iconographic treatment as the portrait of 'Louis XVI guillotined'. The political use of the machine gave rise to a type of image whose various connotations repay close analysis.

A first notable characteristic: the body is not depicted – neither the executioner's nor the victim's – and this in itself defines the essence of the guillotine portrait. By excluding the body from the pictorial space and concentrating on two fragments, the forearm and the head, which are depicted in contrasting fashion, the image accurately represents the revolution that was taking place in power relations at the time. The severed head, generally given a rictus and expression that the convention of the engraving would have us believe is 'taken from life', belongs or belonged to a man whose immolation tended towards the abolition of a system of power, that system of power whose incarnation was the singular and extraordinary unity of the body royal. By contrast, the forearm, generally anonymous and without any form of characterization, belongs not to a particular executioner, but to that neutral personage, the representative of the executive power to whom the People had delegated the responsibility of enforcing its law.

Removed from the hurly-burly of events, the image represents the new order. On the scaffold, at the height of the ritual, the gesture of the executioner evoked that of Perseus presenting the head of Medusa to Polydectes. In the image, and at the heart of what one might call the iconographical corpus of this theme, the gesture acquires a further connotation that is religious in origin. The gesture appears in an engraving among the illustrations of an emblem book by the Dutchman Jacob Cats. The book was well known in the eighteenth century. The engraving shows a decapitation scene featuring one of the guillotine's many forerunners. The hand of the executioner holds the victim's head under the blade, but from a cloud descend the forearm and hand of God, which cuts the thread by which the blade is suspended. The action of the divine hand is consistent with the title of the poem to which this emblem refers: *Le Cercueil pour les vivants ou Emblèmes tirés de la parole de Dieu* [The coffin of the living or Emblems drawn from the word of God].[2] By relating the gesture of the divine hand to the hand of an abstract executioner, we arrive at one of the most fundamental meanings attached by Jacobin mysticism to its executioner's gesture: the guillotine *laicizes* the hand of God, and the hand of the executioner *socializes* it. For the imagination the social power that thus replaces the hand of God gathers to itself the attributes of divinity, and is, as Robespierre repeatedly claimed, deified.

This context gives the proper resonance to one of the genre's most sophisticated exemplars, the portrait of 'Custine guillotined'. Inside the frame, above the severed head, an inscription proclaims in capitals: ECCE CUSTINE. Without going too far into the possibly contradictory resonances that this reference to the Passion of Christ might elicit we can see how the image exploits the religious echo of the formula, replacing *Ecce homo* with *Ecce Custine*. The parody shows the triumph of secular (but none the less sacred) law and makes use of the ostensive evangelical formula to depict and demonstrate the treachery of the traitor by exhibiting his head (see illustration).

The guillotined head appears, moreover, at the centre of a network of inscriptions whose interaction generates meanings the more precise for their being the product of a system of transformations. The various titles used are based on the ideological relations between singular and plural, which reflect, on the lexical plane, the very fundamental political distinction between individual and *People*. The two main inscriptions outside the frame of the image relate chiastically through their plurals and singulars: 'To the shades of our brothers sacrificed by the traitor' and 'So perish traitors to the homeland.' Plural and singular are here representative of the new ideological structure of the body politic: the traitor has sacrificed the brothers; the traitors will be sacrificed to the homeland. The transformation that occurs between the two singulars, traitor and homeland, guarantees the triumph of the Republic, since the singular traitor is an individual, whereas the singular homeland is a collective, that of the general will and the People. Finally, within the frame, within the field of the image, the possessive adjectives again take up the theme and relate the theory to its figuration (his blood/our soil), while the reference to the future national anthem in 'his blood slaked our soil' matches the allusive style of the parody of the Gospel in *Ecce Custine*. But even here a change has occurred, and the present tense of the *Ecce Custine*, that present of the head held up to the gaze of the spectator by the forearm of the executioner, has, transforming the optative of the 'Marseillaise' ('May impure blood slake our soil'), become the past 'slaked', a past in which the triumph of the homeland over the traitor is historic.

The portrait of 'Custine guillotined' is certainly one of the most successful of its kind. At the foot of the page is another inscription, in cursive script, which gives the details, '28 August 1793, Year II of the one and indivisible Republic, ten-thirty in the morning'. The image is thus supposed to derive directly from the event. The face it portrays is 'taken from life' or, to use the legal term, a face 'taken' at that redoubtable instant when 'death supervenes'. The inscription testifies to the image's likeness to the face of the traitor at that instant. It thus enjoys the prestige that belongs to the portrait in general, the prestige that belongs to the genre in its function of representing the human face. The term 'portrait', unlike 'effigy', implies that painter and model have shared the same time and space. In the traditional portrait it is indeed this here-and-now quality of model and painter which gives the painting its 'all but divine'[3] strength. If the portrait is 'lifelike', it is because the artist was able, through the magic of his art, to capture the life of the model and transfer some portion of it onto the canvas. It is important to note that the guillotine portrait, faithful to its genre, claims a part in this traditional prestige. It claims to have been painted at the time of the event and in the presence of the model, or, at the very least, what it shows claims to be a particular and specific form of the here-and-now nature that underlies all portraiture.

This fact sheds some light on the motives that drew such consistently large crowds to the spectacle of the guillotine. We have said that the spectator was unlikely to see much of the event; the distance, the obstacles in the way, the executioners on the scaffold who masked the action, all of these things prevented him from seeing clearly. Yet the crowd was always there, and this was probably because people sought less to see clearly than just to be there, to share the place and time of the execution, to be present at the sacrifice and thereby to receive some benefit, by means of an osmosis in which the Christian theme of benediction receives a further secular transposition.

Moreover, by referring to the here-and-now of the event, the guillotine portrait has the incomparable merit of showing in close-up what could not be seen from a distance, that is, the ultimate expression of the guillotined person. It allows the spectator to scrutinize it uninterruptedly, to seek in the lineaments of the face any trace of 'intimate hurt', of suffering, of a last thought.

This is not all. The last portrait of the monster is also his *true* portrait, as the designation *Ecce Custine* suggests. The truth of the portrait is owed to the very process by which it is produced. The technique of engraving eliminates the potentially deceptive charm and rhetoric of colour. The art of engraving is that of line, and draughts-manship is, in Ingres's words, the 'honesty of art'. But the expression of the face thus represented expresses no intention, and is wholly free of hypocrisy. The model cannot influence the representation any more than the artist, and the hazards of interpretation and distortion are removed. The guillotine does away with the unreliable 'human agent', and produces yet another of its mechanical effects, this face in which the traitor is depicted and acknowledged.

Imitation here is doubly laconic; the deforming rhetorics of both artist and sitter are excluded. The guillotine portrait thus becomes a sort of revolutionary variation of the Holy Shroud, the veil of St Veronica through which, miraculously and without human agency, the true face of Christ was imprinted – his true portrait, his *vera icona*, compared to which any painted image of Christ is only an imitation more or less distant from the truth.

The position in which the guillotine-easel places the sacrificial victim is, on reflection, strangely rich in overtones. The head passes through the 'window' of the guillotine and, isolated from the body, appears in front of the transparent canvas formed by the frame of the machine ... And the last expression, taken from life, is printed on the very face, which stands revealed in its ultimate and most intimate truth. Here then is Custine; here is the true image of the true Custine, transcribed as truthfully as possible by a neutral line incised on the copper plate and immediately and mechanically printed upon the page.

This doubly mechanical provenance, which ideologically precludes the artist's ego coming between model and spectator, gives the engraved guillotine portrait a title to even greater truthfulness than that of the painted portrait. In this, it is reminiscent of the perfect imitation of painting of which Fénelon dreamt in 1690, a painting without a painter, an art of painting in which 'the pictorial operator' (Démoris) was eliminated in favour of an almost photographic fixing of the features of the sitter on the image.

> There was not a painter to be found anywhere in the country; but when one wanted to obtain the portrait of a friend ... one put water in great basins of gold or silver, and set this water before the thing one wanted to portray. Soon the water froze, became like the glass of a mirror, in which the image of the object remained indelible.[4]

By reducing the 'exposure time' to instantaneousness and fixing the expression of the face by a 'technique' as neutral as it is irrefutable, the guillotine produces something like the ideal of the classical portrait.

For, in its classical form, the successful portrait is the synthesis of two things: the traces left by history on the model's face, and the essence of the self inhabiting that face as expressed in its 'physiognomy' – the face's underlying and immutable structure.[5] The most complete portrait, that which best exhibits the person as a whole, must therefore be the last, in which, at the hour of death, history is summed up in the traces that it has left. For the portrait always points to death, be it only in recording the moment in which *I was*, there and then, in the here and now of the portrait before us, and the guillotine, therefore, produces the ideal of the portrait. By fixing the last expression of the face it puts before us the *mask* that concentrates and summarizes the totality of its history and its meaning.

The term 'mask' is particularly appropriate to the type of image the guillotine portrait represents. For it was possible to make the portraits from death masks taken from the head before it and the body were thrown together into the communal grave.[6] But the term introduces a further and especially fertile theme, whose fascination lies in the nexus formed by the three terms 'mask', '*figure*' (face and also figure in the sense of having been drawn), and face. The guillotine portrait is thus seen as a *figure* in which mask and face coincide.

'Thus there are in the world many celebrated *figures* about which no one knows anything. What is famous is the mask; the face itself is not generally known.'[7] Robert de La Sizeranne, author of *Les masques et les visages à Florence et au musée du Louvre*, a work which has fallen into well-merited oblivion, here comes very close to an idea whose current formulation has it that the mask is 'what makes a face the product of a society and its history'.[8] Laying bare the essence of what it represents, the mask excludes the detail of personal and contingent singularity to become the 'meaning in so far as it is absolutely pure', such as the portrait of a black man 'born into slavery' that shows 'the essence of slavery laid bare'.[9] Shall we not say the same of the guillotine portrait, whose mask does no other than unmask the traitor, so as to show him in the absolute transparency of his meaning, clearly labelled by the inscriptions that interpret the image. These inscriptions, however, are scarcely necessary, for the configuration of the image makes its meaning *absolutely pure*. The guillotine portrait unmasks the traitor in his death mask – the true face of the traitor and the only one he deserves, for, in Robespierre's words, the 'mask of patriotism' strives to 'disfigure by insolent parody the sublime drama of the Revolution'.[10]

As a genre the guillotine portrait here coincides with photography. So it is not surprising to discover that the term 'guillotine' also refers to a kind of shutter (the drop shutter) found in nineteenth-century cameras; its mechanism is distinct from that of the 'diaphragm' shutter and was chiefly used for portraiture. Nor is it surprising that, by way of reciprocation, the technical term for the executioner who stands in front of the uprights and whose job it is to place the victim's head in the 'little hole' that closes around the neck, a hole thus thoroughly 'shuttered', is called the 'photographer'.[11] The black humour of the designation hits the nail on the head. Nor is it simply a coincidence if one of the processes of photography is described by Roland Barthes in terms very similar to those that describe the placing of the victim beneath the blade: '. . . that instant, however brief, in which a real thing stood motionless before the eye . . . In the photograph something *has posed* before the little hole and has remained there for ever.' Nor is it coincidental if the potential horror of photography corresponds to the horror that the guillotine inspires: 'Photographing corpses . . . if it makes photography horrific, it is because it certifies, as it were, that the corpse is alive, *as corpse*.'[12] Photography revives the fascination of the dying head, that living and already dead head which the perverse iconography of the guillotine portrait presents: 28 August, ten-thirty in the morning . . .

Guillotine and photography are related in that both of them guarantee, in their portraits 'taken from life', that 'this has been'.[13] Still more than the photographic portrait, the guillotine portrait claims to certify a double authenticity. *Ecce Custine* does not merely designate this image *as* Custine – Custine who was guillotined at ten-thirty in the morning; it is also Custine *tel qu'en lui même* (such as in himself) he was. The image makes visible his status as traitor, whose mask, thanks to the guillotine, now allows truth to transpire.

The meeting of guillotine and photography was by no means a purely theoretical one; the fruits of their union are to be found in social history and the history of law enforcement. From the moment photography acquired its own status, like that of the guillotine, as an instrument for the control and supervision of society, the two mechanisms established a sort of complicity, indeed a veritable collaboration.

When, in the late nineteenth century, guillotined heads were photographed, the purpose was no longer to strip off the mask of the traitor, but to identify the mask of the true criminal, the social monster, and, by building up a collection of faces/masks, to record their inmost characters and thus reveal the truth, the hidden law which they were thought to embody. Portraits of criminals, portraits of guillotine victims (sometimes even in the form of the cranium scraped clean after autopsy), portraits of the ill, portraits of hysterics – the nineteenth century went in for extended series of heads cut off and cut up, of which the most striking common element was the repetitive, cumulative, production-line character of the procedure and research. The purpose behind this obsessional practice was to uncover the general laws of physiognomy of which every face would be only a particular example – a mask capable of being unmasked simply by visual observation, and shown to conceal some sickness or inbred criminal tendency. The attempt to define these laws was the task of the new 'science of the image'. Charcot in his *Iconographie de la Salpêtrière* (1875), Lombroso in his *Atlas de l'homme criminel* (1878), Galton in his *Inquiries into Human Faculties* (1883) and, finally, Bertillon, whose work on forensic photography laid the basis for modern anthropometry (1890–3), were working towards similar goals on the basis of a shared premiss: that in the mask of a face, 'classified according to casts of feature',[14] one might detect the anthropometric laws of appearance, establishing an identification code that would allow the common facial features of criminality to be recognized, and perceiving in every face the potential 'mugshot'.[15]

I The word *anthropométrie* made its debut in French around 1750. In 1792 it still referred to the study of the proportions of the human body. It was not until 1871, when the Commune set fire to the guillotine and the people of Versailles had an improved model built, that the term came to mean a specific technique of measurement which was soon to distinguish itself in its forensic capacity.

The history of the French language thus suffices to show that the decapitating machine, that paradigm of the instrument of criminal justice, stands at the point at which the aesthetic science of proportions is transmuted into the forensic science of identification. It was not Guillotin's machine that prepared the way for this transformation, but the 'Jacobin machine', which, with its production-line methods, contributed to the production of the series of images that served as its 'proofs' or prints. From the outset the political guillotine was the instrument that sorted the good from the bad, while the series of guillotine portraits already suggests the idea of a diffuse resemblance among the features thus represented, among these masks whose sentence guaranteed that they belonged to a single series – that of traitors and monsters.

That there was a criminological motive at work in the iconography of the guillotine portrait is attested as early as 1793 by Charlotte Corday's last letter. She desired, while in prison, to have her portrait painted, and gave two reasons for this extraordinary but highly significant request. The first is the traditional motive for portraiture, the desire to leave some record of herself to her friends. The second is a more modern and complex one, and reflects the circumstances of the Revolution: she wanted to provide study material for those who were curious about the physiognomy of criminals.[16] This letter by Charlotte Corday testifies to the pre-scientific prestige enjoyed by physiognomy as a tool that allowed the expressive value of the more permanent features of the face to be deciphered.

Charlotte Corday's regard for both the social premises of criminality and the private motives of friendship prefigures the 'publicizing of the private' that Roland Barthes so strongly objected to in photography. Describing his resistance to it as 'necessary', he desired that the 'divide between public and private' be reconstituted in order to 'articulate inwardness without betraying the intimate'.[17] The guillotine had already made public that most private moment when each individual has only himself to rely on – the moment of death. In Oelsner's words it prostituted the victim to 'the gaze of the populace', offering to the public the most inalienable instance of a face – its appearance at the moment of death.

There is a certain logic in the guillotine's being at the root of this 'publicizing of the private'. One of the fundamental points of the Jacobin morality was, as we have seen, that the private be sacrificed to the public, and that the singularity of the individual be sacrificed to the prescription of law. Political before it became social, the guillotine contributed to moulding the imagery and rules of an inaccessible ideal of democracy that was later to become the index of bourgeois health: conformity.

In the last analysis what emerges from these considerations is the extraordinary 'informative capacity' of the guillotine. Just as it 'deforms' the physical body by suddenly and brutally imparting a divided form, so it 'informs' us about the latent meanings of the new image of the civil or political body that it helps to mould.

Perhaps the most general of the ideological issues raised by the guillotine – that which allows us the greatest insight into the reactions and associations of which the guillotine has been the locus – is a concept whose current sense only emerged in the last quarter of the eighteenth century: *banalité*. Under the *ancien régime* it referred to the people's obligation to acknowledge the status of the suzerain by monetary tribute. But shortly before the Revolution the concept took on the opposite meaning: it came to refer to what was very common, common to the greatest number and wholly without privilege. This semantic reversal prefigured one of the most basic aims of the Revolution, that of transferring the rule of a single being and a particular caste to the *banalité* of the greatest number: the people.

It may even be imagined that the guillotine's profound impact on the imagination ultimately derives from the fact that it reduces death and bodies to instances of a law. At the moment of death its effect is to implant in the soul of each individual a conviction of their true finality, as unbearable as it is irrefutable: the ultimate banality.

Notes

INTRODUCTION

1. The term is to be understood in the sense given by Pierre Francastel in *La Réalité figurative*, Paris, 1965, p. 107.

2. Diderot had previously suggested that if the condemned man survived, he should be allowed to live on. *Encyclopédie*, article on 'Anatomy', Livourne edition, 1770, I, p. 402.

3. Quoted in A. Soubiran and J. Théoridès, 'Guillotin et la rage: un mémoire inédit' in *Histoire des sciences médicales*, 1982, XVI, 4. I should like to thank G. Didier-Hubermann for pointing out this little-known text to me.

4. Victor Hugo, *Littérature et philosophie mêlées*, Paris, 1976, 1, p. 259 (December 1820).

INTRODUCTION TO PART I

1. cf. L. Bridel, '*Le Conservateur suisse*, 15 September 1796: 'There is one just like theirs [like the French guillotine] in a picture of the bridge of Lucerne which shows Christians being martyred under one Hirtacus; the picture was painted well before Monsieur Guillotin was born. Another of these machines, which are these days all too familiar or at least all too active, is to be seen in a wood engraving, by Salvatore Rosa if I am not mistaken. The engraving shows the death of the son of Brutus.' On the forerunners of 'Guillotin's machine', see below and D. Arrasse and V. Rousseau-Lagarde, *La Guillotine de la Terreur*, Florence, 1986, I.

PART I, CHAPTER 1

1. Robespierre 'Discours sur les peines infamantes', *Oeuvres complètes*, Paris, 1910, I, p. 44. Cf. J. Goulet, 'Robespierre, la peine de mort et la Terreur' in *Annales historiques de la Révolution française*, 1981, 2, pp. 219ff.

2. J.-P. Marat, *Plan de législation criminelle*, quoted in J. Delarue, *Le Métier de bourreau*, Paris, 1979, p. 19.

3. M. Foucault, *Surveiller et punir*, Paris, 1975, p. 38.

4. Abbé de La Porte, *Voyageur français*, XIX, p. 317.

5. cf. J. Delarue, op. cit., pp. 151ff.

6. Two of these accounts suffice to show the twofold nature of this ancient machine: aristocratic élitism and mechanical efficiency. In 1507 Demetrio Giustiniani organized in Genoa the revolt against Louis XII; he was executed on 13 May. 'The executioner blindfolded him. Then he of his own volition knelt and stretched his neck over the frame. The executioner took a cord, to which had been attached a large block, armed with a very sharp axe-blade, fixed into the block, and falling from above between two posts; the executioner pulled the said cord, so that the armed block fell between the head and the shoulders of the Genoan, such that the head went one way and the body fell the other.' (Jean d'Auton, *Chronique de Louis XII*, quoted in A. G. de Manet, 'La Guillotine et ses ancêtres' in *Le Mois littéraire et pittoresque*, Paris, p. 356.) In 1632 duc Henri II de Montmorency, Marshal of France, was decapitated for having, with Gaston d'Orléans, taken up arms against Richelieu. The *Mémoires* of Jacques de Chastenet describe the execution: 'Then he turned to the executioner and said: "Do your duty." He had a rope thrown around his arms and went to his scaffold. He reached this by going through a window which had been opened and led to the said scaffold. This was set up in the courtyard of the town hall, and on it there was a block on which he was made to rest his head. In that part of the world an axe is used which is fixed between two pieces of wood. When the head is on the block, the cord is released and the axe descends and separates the head from the body. When he placed his head on the block, the wound he had received in the neck caused him pain, and he moved and said: "I am not moving because I am afraid. My wound hurts." Father Arnoul was close to him and did not abandon him. The cord that was attached to the axe was released, and the head was separated from the body. The head fell on one side of the blade and the body on the other.' (Quoted in de Manet, ibid.)

7. Thus, having given an account of Guillotin's speech, the *Journal des Etats généraux* notes that 'the legislators of the eighteenth century are all inclined to soften the penal code; but some among them seemed disgusted that there should be no nuance of difference between the death of a parricide, a regicide and a homicide. The Abbé Maury, Target and a great many other members requested that these questions be considered at some later date, so that they might make a well-

informed decision.' (Quoted in Soubiran, *Ce bon docteur Guillotin*, Paris, 1962, p. 160.)

8. One such song is as follows: '(To the tune of "Quand la mer rouge apparut") The blow has come down/Before you know it/You scarcely notice it/You don't see a thing/A hidden spring/Is suddenly released/Off it comes, comes, comes,/Off it flies, flies, flies/Off jumps/Off flies the head,/It is a much much better way (Quoted in E. and J. Goncourt, *Histoire de la société française pendant la Révolution*, Paris, 1918, p. 428).

9. ibid., pp. 428–9.

10. H. Bergson, *Le Rire*, Paris, 1918, p. 39.

PART I, CHAPTER 2

1. cf. Marcel Normand, *La Peine de mort*, Paris, 1980, p. 20. In his famous speech of 30 May 1791 Robespierre emphasized the fact that in the Russia of Catherine, despite the prevailing despotism, the death penalty had been abolished: 'Has Russia been thrown into confusion since the despot who governs it has entirely abolished the death penalty, as if she intended by this act of humanity and philosophy to expiate the crime of maintaining thousands of men under the yoke of absolute power?' (Robespierre, *Oeuvres complètes*, Paris, 1950, VII, p. 439.)

2. The most illuminating comment is without doubt that made in the *Courrier de Provence*: 'Monsieur Prugnon favoured the maintaining of the death penalty; Monsieur Robespierre demanded its abolition. The former dealt with this dire subject with the tact and grace of a witty conversationalist; the latter with the sensibility of a philosopher imbued with the grim importance of his subject-matter.' (Cf. Robespierre, *Oeuvres complètes*, Paris, 1950, VII, p. 441.)

3. A comparison of *Journal de Louis XVI et son peuple* and Marat's *L'Ami du peuple* (cf. Robespierre, op. cit., p. 445) sheds light on contemporary views: 'The democrat, Robespierre, spoke at length against the death penalty which he considers unworthy of a free people. His discourse is the merest philosophy, supported by some historical examples, but is without political sense and has still less the profundity that characterizes the able legislator.' (*Journal de Louis XVI.*) '... the Assembly rightly decreed, although to no avail, that the death penalty should be reserved for the gravest crimes: on this question Messieurs Pétion and Roberspierre [*sic*] set out an opinion which does great honour to their sensitivity, but is attended by drawbacks too serious to be adopted. Society's right to inflict the death penalty derives from the same source as the right of every individual to inflict death, that is,

the need to defend one's own life. Now, if each penalty is to be commensurate with the crime, the punishment for murder and poisoning must be capital, and *a fortiori* that for conspiracy and arson.' (*L'Ami du peuple.*)

4. *Rapport de Charles Henri Sanson au ministre de la Justice sur le mode de décapitation.* See Appendix 1.

5. Since the law cares to see in the death penalty nothing more than the 'deprivation of life', 'it follows from the observations which the executioners have made that, in relation to the sort of concerns that the Constituent Assembly has been considering, death by decapitation will be horrible for the spectators. Either it will show that the spectators are blood-thirsty, or the executioner, himself intimidated, will be exposed to the plots of the people.' (Quoted in L. Pichon *Code de la guillotine*, Paris, 1910.) Cf. J. Delarue, op. cit., p. 121; Soubiran, op. cit., p. 17.

6. See Appendix 2.

7. 'Decree of emergency. The National Assembly, considering that the uncertainty as to the method of execution of article 3 of the first title of the Penal Code suspends the punishment of several criminals who have been sentenced to death; that it is necessary that these uncertainties be speedily resolved, as they may otherwise give rise to seditious movements; that humanity requires that the death penalty be as painless as possible in its application, decrees an emergency.' 'Definitive decree. The National Assembly, having decreed an emergency, decrees that article 3 of the first title of the Penal Code shall be applied in the manner specified and the method adopted in the consultative document signed by the Permanent Secretary of the Academy of Surgery, which is to be annexed to this decree. The Assembly consequently authorizes the executive to make whatever expense is necessary to implement this method of execution and to ensure that it is uniform throughout the country.' (Quoted in Soubiran, op. cit., p. 179.)

8. This specification differed from the final product in two respects: the shape of the blade, which was, as his *Avis motivé* had announced, convex; and the position of the condemned man: 'The condemned man shall place his head on a block of wood eight inches high, four inches thick, and one foot wide ... Lying on his stomach, he will raise his chest on his elbows, and his neck will rest comfortably in the opening in the block. When everything is properly arranged, the executioner, standing behind the machine, shall bring together the ends of the rope that holds up the axe-blade. These he shall let go of simultaneously, and the blade, falling from above, by its weight and the acceleration of

its momentum will separate the head from the trunk in the twinkling of an eye.' (Quoted in Delarue, op. cit., p. 125).

9. cf. Soubiran, op. cit., p. 186.

10. ibid., p. 187.

11. Quoted in G. Lenotre, *La Guillotine et les exécuteurs des arrêts criminels pendant la Révolution*, Paris, 1920, pp. 230–31.

12. cf. Delarue, op. cit., p. 127.

13. cf. Soubiran, op. cit., p. 183.

14. Quoted by Delarue, op. cit., p. 169.

15, cf. comte Beugnot, *Mémoires*, quoted in Delarue, op. cit., p. 136: 'This poor man was a philanthropist, generous, and both erudite and clever, but the misfortune of the fatal machine being named after him made his life a bitter one.'

16. cf. Beugnot, ibid.: 'He was willing for our sake to deprive his machine of custom.'

17. Bonneville and Quénard, *Portrait des personnages historiques de la Révolution française*, Paris, 1796.

18. cf. Delarue, op. cit., p. 144.

19. ibid., p. 147.

PART I, CHAPTER 3

1. Quoted in G. Lenotre, op. cit., pp. 233–4.

2. cf. Delarue, op. cit., p. 28.

3. *Journal de la France*, quoted in Soubiran, op. cit. Cf. also *Chronique de Paris*: 'The people, moreover, were not satisfied; they had seen nothing; the thing was too quick. They dispersed disappointed, and to console themselves for their disappointment sang a song about it: "Give me back my wooden gibbet,/Give me back my forks!"' Quoted in Lenotre, op. cit., p. 235.

4. cf. Delarue, op. cit., p. 156. Strictly speaking, the first political guillotining took place in the spring of 1792; nine *émigrés* who had been captured weapons in hand were decapitated in the place de Grève. The execution was therefore an ordinary one; but the prestige conferred by its political dimension is suggested by the fact that it was the first decapitation by guillotine to be illustrated in the *Révolutions de Paris*.

5. Without going as far as Chateaubriand, who, in *Mémoires d'Outre-Tombe* (Paris, 1946, I, book IX, 3, p. 295), expresses the opinion that 'the machine can be considered the executioner', it is undoubtedly true that henceforth it played the leading part. Verninac de Saint-Maur had predicted this in 1789; in his letter, already cited, to *Le Modérateur* he expressed his hostility to the machine in the following terms: 'The

novelty of the machine and its admirable efficiency would undoubtedly excite the horrible curiosity of the people to come and view it. Diverted by the bloody lesson taking place before their eyes, the people would clap their hands at the *coup de théâtre*. More: things would come to such a pitch of immorality that they would desire that these terrible performances be often repeated.' (Cf. Goncourt, op. cit. p. 436.) This prediction was not so profound. Verninac de Saint-Maur does no more than suggest that the admiration accorded under the *ancien régime* to the virtuoso executioner might be transferred to the machine. Thus, at the decapitation of Beaulieu de Montigny, in 1737, the executioner's skill had been triumphantly applauded: 'He then showed [the head] to the people on all sides, put it down again and bowed to the public, who applauded his skill with a storm of clapping.' (Cf. Delarue, op. cit., p. 231.)

6. The death of Foullon was particularly dramatic: the rope with which he was hanged on the notorious Lanterne (streetlamp) which stood opposite the Hôtel de Ville broke twice, and the hanging was successful only on the third attempt. Their heads, paraded through Paris, passed beneath Chateaubriand's windows: 'Everyone stood back from the windows; I remained. The murderers stopped in front of me and held up their pikes, singing and gambolling and jumping so that the pale effigies came level with my face. An eye from one of these heads had come out of its socket and hung down over the dark face of the dead man. The pike-head had come through the open mouth and the teeth were clenched on the blade ... These heads and others I came across soon after changed my political tendencies.' (*Mémoires d'Outre-Tombe*, Paris, 1946, I, book V, 89, p. 171.)

7. ibid. *Plaintes de l'exécuteur de la Haute Justice contre ceux qui ont exercé sa profession sans être reçus maîtres.* See Appendix 3.

8. And this success, the extreme rapidity of the result, could elicit enthusiasm. A letter written by the king's commissioner in Falaise to the Minister of Justice on 8 June 1792 testifies to this: 'I had ordered the construction of the machine used to execute Duval-Bertin. I was pleased to inform you in my letter of 17 May of the incalculable rapidity with which Duval-Bertin's head was separated from his body. This was the speed of lightning, the lightning that is the herald or harbinger of thunder. In the twinkling of an eye the head leaps to some 17 or 18 inches from the trunk ... Ten necks piled one on top of another could not escape the power precipitated by the speed of this instrument, which, having produced the intended effect, sank its blade up to the hilt in a piece of wood.' (Quoted in E. Seligman, *La Justice pendant la Révolution*, Paris, 1901, I, p. 464.) The phenomenon of the 'leaping'

head recurred during the execution of the Girondins. On this occasion a police report noted that 'the execution was performed so vigorously that several heads leapt right off the scaffold'. Cf. Caron, *Paris pendant la Terreur*, Paris, 1943, VI, p. 273.

9. This appeal was a feature of the execution of Damiens for example; cf. Foucault, op. cit., p. 9.

10. See illustration.

11. This concern was an old one, as the story of the death of Beatrice Cenci in Rome in 1599 bears witness. As is well known, the 'Beauteous Parricide' was decapitated in her twenty-second year by a *mannaja*, a 'sort of guillotine' as Stendhal describes it in the *Chroniques italiennes* which narrates the story of the Cenci: '... having mounted the scaffold, she nimbly put one leg over the plank, placed her neck under the *mannaja*, and perfectly positioned herself of her own accord so as to avoid being touched by the executioner. By her quickness she was able to avoid the public seeing her shoulders and breast when the taffeta veil she was wearing was removed. A difficulty arose and the blow was long in coming.' Stendhal explains this 'cruel' delay in a note that brings us directly back to the issues of 1789 – the simultaneousness of decapitation and absolution, delivered, in this case, from a distance: 'Clement VII was most anxious about the salvation of Beatrice's soul; as he knew that she had been unjustly convicted, he feared a gesture of impatience. When she placed her head on the *mannaja*, a cannon was fired in the Castello Sant' Angelo from which the *mannaja* was clearly visible. The Pope, who was praying at Monte Cavallo in expectation of this signal, immediately gave the young girl perfect absolution *in articulo mortis*. Whence the delay at that cruel moment of which the chronicler speaks.' (Cf. Stendhal, *Chroniques italiennes*, in *Romans et nouvelles*, Paris, 1982, II, pp. 706–7.)

INTRODUCTION TO PART II

1. 'The Republic, the sacred object of all our wishes, of all our hopes, must eradicate, along with all signs of royalty, those of a tyranny darker and more fearsome – though fortunately by its very nature more unstable and precarious – which seemed to make of the guillotine its ensign' (Cabanis, *Note sur le supplice de la guillotine*, in *Oeuvres complètes*, Paris, 1823, II, p. 181).

2. Chateaubriand *Mémoires d'Outre-Tombe*, Paris 1946, I, book IX, 3, p. 295.

[PART II, CHAPTER 1]

1. René-Georges Gastellier: *Que penser enfin du supplice de la guillotine?*, Paris, Year IV, p. 11.
2. Cabanis, op. cit., p. 171.
3. The machine could be described when still, but its action remained indescribable. The prints published during the Terror confirm the impossibility of representing the act of the guillotine, whose invisibility in action was a part of its 'sublimity'. Many engravings show 'the death' of distinguished victims, but they never show the moment of decapitation. The event is represented in two distinctly different ways. The royalist prints emphasize what preceded the 'fatal instant', and develop at length the theme of 'last moments', during which the victim speaks his last words and gives one last lesson in morality or piety; they often portray the 'martyr' as making oratorical gestures which there was in truth no time to make, but whose presence is motivated by the need to expand on the moments which preceded execution. The revolutionary engravings give pride of place to the moments subsequent to the execution. As mechanically as the machine repeats its action, they repeat the gesture of the executioner presenting the head to the people. On these images, cf. D. Arasse and V. Rousseau-Lagarde, op. cit.
4. Cabanis, op. cit., p. 180.
5. See Appendix 4.
6. Chateaubriand, *Essais historiques sur les révolutions anciennes et modernes*, Paris, 1859, II, pp. 94–5.
7. Gastellier, op. cit., pp. 94–5.
8. The instantaneousness of the instant is paradoxical: the instant, though indivisible, irreducible and the phenomenal manifestation of the present, also consists of a separation, an infinitesimal and dynamic rupture between past and present. Each instant is a *syncope* out of which the linear continuity of time is constructed. Cf. Aristotle, *Physica*, IV, 13–14: 'The instant is in one way a potential dividing of time; in another it limits and unites both parts (past/future) ... for where the 'instant' is, there also is the distance from the instant.'
9. *Opinion du Chirurgien Sue, Professeur de Médicine et de Botanique, sur le Supplice de la Guillotine*, Paris, *Brumaire* Year IV, p. 1.
10. *Encyclopédie*, article on 'Death', Livourne edition, 1770, X, p. 662: 'One should be ... very circumspect about pronouncing that absolute death has ensued, for a little more confidence might overcome the obstacles. Absolute death may be deemed certain when putrefaction begins to set in ... There is a first stage of death during which res-

urrections are clearly possible, as is shown by a very simple argument and by well-established observations ... Moreover the strange revolution, the prodigious changes that the machine then undergoes, can be advantageous to some chronically ill persons ... This axiom is widely agreed.'

11. Auberive, *Anecdotes sur les décapités*, Paris, Year V, pp. 7–8. 'It is easier to cut a rope neatly than to replace a head. The latter experiment has nevertheless been attempted ... to find out if it was possible to detain the departing soul and prolong life for a few moments after the fatal blow. The subject of the experiment was a young man, sentenced to be decapitated for a crime. No sooner had he been executed, than surgeons stopped the flow of blood from the trunk with styptics, while others who had held up the head placed it back on the neck with all possible precision and dexterity, vertebra on vertebra, muscle on muscle, artery on artery. The incision was wrapped around with compresses, which were mechanically held in place. Finally strong spirits were placed beneath his nose. The head then seemed to come back to life. A perceptible movement of the face muscles occurred, and the eyelids twitched. A cry of surprise and wonder was heard. The young man was gently lifted up and taken to a nearby house where, after having given some very slight signs of life, he expired. This much seems to me to be established. But it appears that the experiment was ill-conducted and the arrangements most unsatisfactory.'

12. Villiers de L'Isle-Adam, *Le Secret de l'échafaud*, in *Akëdysséril et autres contes*, Plan-de-le-Tour (Editions d'Aujourd'hui),1978, p. 43: 'If, *at that moment*, whatever other facial twitches there may be, you can, by this triple wink, communicate to me that you have heard and understood me, and prove it by thus altering, with an act of surviving will and memory, your palpebral muscle, your zygomatic nerve and your conjunctiva – mastering the horror, the great swell of other impressions that your existence will be undergoing – this deed will be enough to illuminate science and revolutionize our beliefs. And you may rest assured that I shall make the facts known in such a way that, in the future, you shall be remembered rather as a hero than a criminal.'

13. The debate was opened by Soemmering in Year III. His essay *Sur le Supplice de la Guillotine* was presented by Oelsner to the readers of the *Magazine encyclopédique*. It favoured the likelihood of survival, and was supported in Year IV by a surgeon, Sue (op. cit.). From Year IV onwards refutations came thick and fast. In addition to the two monographs previously mentioned, by Cabanis and Gastellier respectively, there appeared the *Dissertation physiologique* by Léveillé, surgeon of the Hôtel-Dieu in Paris, and the *Réflexions historiques et phy-*

siologiques sur le Supplice de la Guillotine by Sédillot the Younger, a doctor of medicine.

14. Oelsner, op. cit., p. 2: 'Our minds measure time according to the number and kind of sensations that we experience.'

15. Soemmering, op. cit., p. 7.

16. Sue, op. cit., p. 7. La Pommerais might well have been a little chary of proving any such thing, and it is less than surprising if he called upon the 'discretion' of Dr Velpeau, so that 'his head might be left peacefully to bleed out the last of its life into the tin bucket provided to this end'.

17. Soemmering, op. cit., p. 9.

18. Camille Desmoulins, *Oeuvres complètes*, Paris, 1906, II, p. 382.

19. Soemmering, op. cit., p. 10.

20. ibid., p. 11.

21. The works of Cabanis, Gastellier, Léveillé, and Sédillot use similar arguments and I will cite medical detail here only in so far as it helps to elucidate the role of the imagination in this debate.

22. Sédillot, op. cit., p. 4

23. Gastellier considers the case closed and he concludes with an argument using the term 'mask', the implications of which we shall discover later: 'These heads preserve the mask they had at the instant of death and   the muscles of the face remain as they were. The wretch condemned to death, prone on the fatal board, waiting for the cruel instrument which is to cut off his days, may gnash his teeth or have other such convulsions, which continue after the head has been separated from the body.' (Op. cit. p. 15.)

24. ibid.

25. Sue, op. cit., p. 14: 'Intellectual life in the head, with the eye consequently as its seat; moral life in the breast, and the heart is then its centre; animal life, which is a form of vegetation, extends as far as the organs of reproduction, which must therefore be considered as the seat or centre of such life.'

26. Cabanis, op. cit., pp. 173–4: 'Microscopy has discovered that life is everywhere; that, in consequence, pleasure and pain are everywhere, and, in the very organization of our fibres, there can exist innumerable causes of individual lives whose correspondence and harmony with the entire system, via the nerves, constitute the self. From this there follows nothing of what citizen Sue claims; for the self exists only in the general life.'

27. As the 'meeting point of most of the intense sensations' (Cabanis, op. cit., p. 178) it is an 'organ essential to life' (Gastellier, op. cit., p. 18), which 'ensures the unity of the system of nerves', which are in

their turn the 'only organs of feeling' (Léveillé, op. cit., p. 463).

28. Léveillé, op. cit., p. 462.

29. Sédillot, op. cit., p. 22.

30. Auberive, op. cit., p. 18.

31. Auberive censures the 'modern philosophy', which 'with the excuse of freeing us from the yoke of superstition . . . never even reaches the intellectual plane. It cannot perceive the chain that unites all beings, still less be cognizant of that soul which imparts motion to matter, which regulates the course of the celestial spheres, and maintains order, beauty and harmony in all the parts of this vast universe. Questions about the human soul, however simple, can be answered only by reference to the principles of the true philosophy.' (Ibid., p. 29.)

32. Villiers de L'Isle-Adam, op. cit., p. 40.

33. Cabanis, op. cit., pp. 179–80.

34. A 'sense' that Rousseau's *Rêveries du promeneur solitaire* had done much to diffuse; cf. in particular the famous outburst in the *Cinquième Promenade*: 'What is it that one so enjoys in this situation? It is nothing external to one; it is nothing but oneself. While the mood lasts, one is entirely self-sufficient, like God.' (Cf. *Oeuvres complètes*, Paris, 1959, I, p. 1047.)

35. Auberive, op. cit., p. 17.

36. Robespierre, *Oeuvres complètes*, X, p. 354.

37. Cabanis, *Oeuvres complètes*, III, p. 188: 'It is not yet known what constitutes the unity of the brain, spinal cord, and the nervous system in general. What is certain is that it is possible to cut off considerable portions of the system without damaging the sensory efficiency of the intact portions, and to do so without causing any apparent disorder in the operation of the intellect.'

38. Cabanis, *Lettre sur les causes premières* in *Oeuvres complètes*, V, pp. 64–5.

39. Sue, op. cit., p. 14: 'The face may be regarded as the synopsis of the three sensations: the forehead down to the eyebrows is the mirror of the intelligence; the nose and cheeks are the mirror of the moral life and the sensibility; the mouth and chin, the mirror of the animal life. We can thus summarize by saying that intellectual life is the sanctuary of the soul, because from it flash out the lightnings of thought.'

40. cf. R. Démoris, 'Le Corps royal et l'imaginaire au XVII° siècle: Le portrait du Roi par Félibien' in *Revue des sciences humaines de l'université de Lille III*, 1978, 4, p. 23: 'If the king is the State, and the State a body, it follows that the king is the place where the State thinks itself, and has the privilege of grasping the sense of what occurs there, a sense which it produces itself. This suggests an image of the king as

the soul of the Body-State; or, if we are to remain in the realms of what can be illustrated, as the head ... of this body.'

41. He was a friend of Pinel, who was also present at the Bicêtre tests of the guillotine and who 'freed' the madwomen of the Salpêtrière in an act of 'democratic indignation'; cf. G. Didi-Huberman, *Invention de l'hystérie*, Paris, 1982, p. 10.

42. From this point of view, *Quelques considérations sur l'organisation sociale en général* and the better-known *Mémoires sur les rapports du physique et du moral de l'homme* should be read together. Just as the reaction against the Terror and its 'batches' restored respect for a localized and unitary self which the medical science of the guillotine had, as it were, broken up, so political thought returned to the idea of a united and strong executive.

43. Cabanis, *Quelques considérations* ..., in *Oeuvres philosophiques*, Paris, 1956, II, p. 475: 'Everything is done for the people and in its name; nothing is done by the people or at its intemperate demand. And while its colossal force animates all parts of public organization ..., it lives calmly under the protection of the law ... In short, it enjoys the two fruits of real liberty, a liberty guaranteed by a government, and a government always strong enough to protect it.'

44. ibid., p. 471.

45. ibid., pp. 466–7. Cabanis is here very close to the thought of Robespierre and Saint-Just and to their hostility to all forms of direct democracy. Saint-Just was of the opinion that 'the fundamental principle of the Republic [was] that the national representatives should be elected by the people as a body' (*Discours sur la Constitution à donner à la France*, 24 April 1793, in *Oeuvres complètes*, Paris, 1908, I, p. 431). In his *Rapport sur les principes de Morale politique qui doivent guider la Convention* (5 February 1794, in *Oeuvres complètes*, X, pp. 352–3), Robespierre clearly sets out his opposition to direct democracy: 'Democracy is not a state in which the people, continually assembled, itself deals with all public affairs, still less one in which a hundred thousand fractions of the people, by isolated, precipate and contradictory measures, decide the fate of society as a whole. No such government has ever existed, and its existence could serve only to drive the people back to despotism ... Democracy is that state in which the people is sovereign, and, guided by laws that are its own handiwork, does of itself all that it can do well, and through its delegates all that it cannot do for itself.' For Cabanis the Terror was a 'commotion' undergone by the body of society. But the remedy was not to reduce the power of the executive; on the contrary, in terms again reminiscent of Robespierre, Cabanis proposes that a strong, that is 'united', execu-

tive be reconstituted, one capable of governing without falling under the sway of particular factions.

46. Cabanis, op. cit., pp. 477–8: '. . . one person must have in his hands the power to put an end to debate, to bring everyone round to the same opinion, to determine by his casting vote the uncertainties which numerical equality on both sides of a question might give rise to . . . Unity of thought and action must always regulate the central power whence all actions radiate.' This point suffices, moreover, to show how strongly the influence of Montesquieu is still felt. 'The executive power must be in the hands of a monarch, because this part of government, which almost always needs instantaneous action, is better administered by one than several.' (*Esprit de lois* in *Oeuvres complètes*, Paris, 1951, II, XI, 6, pp. 401–2.

47. Quoted in Mathiez, *La Révolution française*, Paris, 1927, III, p. 4.

48. Cabanis, *Mémoire* . . ., op. cit., IV, p. 279: 'All the parts of this system communicate amongst themselves via the spinal cord and the brain . . . The common centre, the partial centres and the extremities are linked by constant and mutual relations . . . [To the] common centre come, from all parts of the body, the innumerable sensations from which judgements derive . . . [From the] common centre, to the organs which are the object of the volition, go the motor reactions which these same judgements decree.'

49. Démoris, op. cit.

50. Cabanis, op. cit., IV, p. 408.

51. Cabanis, *Adresse au peuple français* in *Oeuvres philosophiques*, op. cit., p. 458.

52. Chateaubriand: *Essais historiques*, p. 323. This 'orgy of darkness' anticipates *René*: 'How often [this vague longing for something] has forced me to leave the spectacle of our cities, and go and watch the sun set far off in some wild place! How many times have I, escaping from the society of men, stood motionless upon some lonely strand, contemplating with that selfsame disquiet, the philosophical prospect of the sea! It has made me follow, in the surrounds of their palaces and in their stately hunting parties, those kings who left behind them an enduring renown. And, with this same longing, I have loved to sit in silence at the door of the hospitable cabin, close to the savage who passes unknown through this life as the nameless rivers pass through the wilderness he inhabits.'

PART II, CHAPTER 2

1. Lamartine's description is problematic because it bears little or no relation to the way in which the guillotine really worked. Not only were there never any 'weights attached ... under the scaffold', but the notion of 'movement part horizontal, part vertical' is less than clear. Had Lamartine never seen a guillotine? Or is his description based on a foreign engraving, of the kind that were very soon circulating, which illustrates a mechanism such as has perhaps never been seen? This may explain the otherwise inexplicable fantasy of a blade cutting the neck of the victim horizontally. Cf. D. Arasse and V. Rousseau-Lagarde, op. cit., and see illustration.

2. Lamartine, *Histoire des Girondins*, Paris, 1884, II, pp. 548–9.

3. Albert Sorel, *L'Europe et la Révolution française*, Paris, 1908, III, p. 267.

4. Robespierre, *Opinion sur le jugement de Louis*, 3 December 1792, in *Oeuvres complètes*, IX, p. 128.

5. On the politico-theological tradition of the body royal, cf. E. H. Kantorowicz, *The King's Two Bodies, A Study in Medieval Political Theology*, Princeton, 1957. This concept seems to have lost much of its strength by the eighteenth century but, as we shall see, was ready in case of need.

6. De Sèze, *Défense de Louis*, ed. A. Sevin, Paris, 1936, p. 10

7. Grégoire, in Lamartine, *Histoire des Girondins*, op. cit., p. 297.

8. M.-E. Blanchard, *Saint-Just & Co. La Révolution et les mots*, Paris, 1980, p. 37.

9. Saint-Just, *Discours sur le jugement de Louis XVI*, 13 November 1792, in *Oeuvres complètes*, VII, p. 367.

10. Robespierre, *Discours sur l'inviolabilité royale*, 14 July 1791, in *Oeuvres complètes*, VII, p. 555.

11. Saint-Just, op. cit., pp. 87–8.

12. Robespierre, *Discours sur le jugement de Louis XVI*, 3 December 1792, in *Oeuvres complètes*, IX, p. 121.

13. ibid.

14. ibid., p. 123: 'When a nation has been forced to resort to the right of rebellion, it returns to the state of nature as regards the tyrant. How can the tyrant invoke the social contract? He himself has destroyed it ... What laws replace [the Constitution]? Those of nature, that law which is the very foundation of society: the safety of the people. The right to punish the tyrant, the right to overthrow him, these are one and the same ... The trial of the tyrant is the insurrection. His judgement is his fall from power; his punishment, whatever the freedom of the people necessitates.'

15. ibid., pp. 122 and 129–30. Robespierre had argued for the abolition of the death penalty. Taking as his premiss that the Assembly had maintained it, he refused to countenance an exception in favour of the 'one person who might legitimate it'.

16. ibid., p. 129: 'You have proclaimed a Republic, but have you delivered it? ... A Republic! And Louis still lives! And still you put the person of the king between us and liberty!'

17. ibid., pp. 122 and 186.

18. ibid., p. 123: 'Peoples do not judge as tribunals judge: they give no verdict, but hurl their thunderbolts; they do not sentence kings, but return them to the abyss whence they came; and this is a justice which outweighs that of the courts.'

19. Robespierre, 5ᵉ lettre à ses Commettants, in Oeuvres complètes, V, p. 60.

20. Robespierre, Oeuvres complètes, IX, p. 184.

21. Saint-Just, Discours sur la Constitution à donner à la France, 24 April 1793, in Oeuvres complètes, I, pp. 423–4: 'Our corruption under the monarchy was in the heart of all its kings; corruption is not natural in the people ... Tyranny depraves mankind ... The weakness of the people is in the interests of monarchy ... Monarchy it is that corrupts the human heart and depraves those under its yoke. It acts upon the soul like a sleeping potion ... The ancient Franks, the ancient Germans had almost no magistrates: the people was prince and sovereign. But when the people lost the taste for assemblies that might negotiate and conquer, the prince split off from the sovereign and, by usurpation, became sovereign himself.'

22. Saint-Just, Discours sur le jugement de Louis XVI, op. cit., p. 370: 'I cannot imagine a greater neglect of social principles and institutions than that a court should decide between a king and the sovereign ... How can the general will be summoned before a tribunal!'

23. cf. R. Démoris, op. cit., p. 17.

24. ibid.

25. Robespierre, Oeuvres complètes, IX, p. 256.

26. ibid., p. 130 (3 December 1792). Legendre stated a similar idea at the Jacobin club on 13 January 1793, but his metaphor, as befitted the premisses, was a more brutal one: 'We want the head of the tyrant ... The tree of liberty will be planted in vain in the eighty-four départements; it will never bear fruit, if the tyrant's body does not manure its roots.' Revolutionary rhetoric was again taking over the monarchic theme pro patria mori, inverting it for its own purposes. Cf. E. H. Kantorowicz, op. cit., pp. 239ff, and Mourir pour la patrie, Paris, 1984, pp. 105ff.

27. Robespierre, *Oeuvres complètes*, IX, p. 256.

28. 'He mounted the scaffold with the majestic, religious air of a venerable priest who goes up to the altar to celebrate Mass. These are the very words of an eyewitness who was standing close to the scaffold.' (*Annales de la République française*, 23 January 1793, quoted in Beaucourt, *Captivité et derniers moments de Louis XVI*, Paris, 1892, I, p. 335.) Ballanche presents a more exalted picture: 'It was the father of the country who came, in religious resignation, to leave upon the scaffold the last vestiges of his sad crown; who came, at his last hour, to implore the sovereign Master of peoples and kings alike to accept the sacrifice of his life in expiation of the parricide . . . It was royalty in person, which, pure and without stain, gloried in its inevitable resurrection.' (*L'Homme sans nom* in *Oeuvres*, Paris, 1883, III, p. 224; cf. also p. 264: 'The king has redeemed France as Jesus Christ redeemed the human race.'

29. *Acta Quibus ecclesiae catholicae calamitatibus in Gallia consultum est*, Rome, 1871, II, p. 34: '*O dies Ludovico triumphalis! cui Deus dedit et in persecutione tolerantiam, et in passione victoriam. Caducam coronam regiam, ac brevi evanescentia lilia, cum perenni alia corona ex immortalibus angelorum liliis contexte feliciter illum commutasse confidimus.*' We note here a specifically Roman and pontifical articulation of the theme of 'two crowns' which had long been a feature of the theory of the divine right of kings, cf. Kantorowicz, op. cit., pp. 336ff.

30. Madame de Staël, *Considérations sur les principaux événements de la Révolution française*, Paris, 1818, II, pp. 52–3.

31. See below for the meaning of each of these movements.

32. Joseph de Maistre, *Les Soirées de Saint-Pétersbourg*, Paris, I, p. 32.

33. Goncourt, *Histoire de la société française . . .*, op. cit., p. 439.

34. Proof of this is not lacking. I have chosen to quote four particularly revealing examples: 'I have silenced in myself the groan of nature. I lend ear to the voice of justice and the voices of the victims sacrificed to the fury of the tyrant. Since the law must be equal for all, since it is necessary to give an unforgettable example . . . I vote for the death penalty' (Pierre Lombard-Lachaux, Protestant pastor). 'What punishment must he suffer? The same as his accomplices who have fallen beneath the axe of national justice . . . Free men acknowledge nothing but principles' (Louis Louchet, professeur). 'I open the book of nature, the most certain guide, and I see that the law must be equal for all; I open the penal code and I see the punishment prescribed for conspirators. I hear the voice of liberty, the voice of the victims of the tyrant, whose blood has drenched the pláins of our border *départements*.

They demand justice of me, justice is what I owe their memory: I vote for death' (Jean-François-Marie Goupilleau, notary). 'The law must be equal for all, I vote for death' (Claude Siblot). (Quoted in *Dictionnaire historique et biographique de la Révolution et de l'Empire, 1789–1815*, Paris.)

35. cf. Beaucourt, op. cit., I, pp. 357–8.

36. Mercier, quoted in G. Maugras, *Journal d'un étudiant pendant la Révolution*, Paris, 1910, p. 315; Ballanche, op. cit., pp. 226–7.

37. The 'objectivity' of the account is suspect, given the events with which it embroiders the 'last instant' of Louis XVI; see below and Beaucourt, op. cit., I, pp. 355–6. But objectivity is here a question of the tone or mode of the narrative.

38. Beaucourt, op. cit., II, p. 308.

39. ibid., I, p. 390.

40. Quoted in Chateaubriand, *Essais historiques . . .*, op. cit., p. 95.

41. This rumour was used by Balzac in his *Episode sous la Terreur*.

42. Quoted in Chateaubriand. *Essais historiques . . .*, p. 97.

43. *Annales de la République française*, 22 January: 'Paris is plunged into dismay and stupefaction. Pain wanders the street speechless, and terror, which constrains the expression of all feelings, can be read engraved upon the foreheads of the citizens.' (Beaucourt, op. cit., I, p. 353.)

44. *Détails authentiques sur les derniers moments de Louis XVI*, quoted in Beaucourt, I, p. 393.

45. 'I saw the people processing arm in arm, laughing and chattering, as though returning from a festivity. Their faces were unchanged. The day of the execution made no impression. The theatres opened their doors as usual; the bars which gave onto the blood-stained square emptied their jugs as usual; cakes and pastries were hawked around the decapitated body.' (Mercier, in Maugras, op. cit., p. 316.) 'The death of the king in Paris was like the banishment of the Tarquins from Rome. The people exhibited a calm and a majesty that would have graced the great days of the Roman Republic.' (*Journal d'une bourgeoise*, quoted in Maugras, op. cit., p. 315.)

46. cf. Beaucourt, op. cit., I, pp. 367–8.

47. Robespierre had foreseen this when he rejected the appeal to the people that had been proposed for the judgement of Louis. The working people would not have participated in the assemblies called to hear this appeal, and their absence would have allowed 'the schemers of the Republic' to get round that 'majority of the nation that they ignobly call the people . . . and to term the true friends of liberty "cannibals".' (29 December 1792, in *Oeuvres complètes*, IX, p. 189.)

48. C. Desmoulins, *Histoire secrète de la Révolution*, in *Oeuvres*, I, p. 347.

49. *Le Véridique ou l'antidote des journaux*, February 1793, in Beaucourt, I, p. 373.

50. Beaucourt, I, p. 399: 'After a damnable Norman-style trial which lasted four months and which set the ministers of the Convention at one another's throats, justice has at last been done ... the Pope is going to make him a saint; priests are already buying his old clothes and making relics of them; old women are telling stories about the miracles of this new saint.'

51. *Annales de la République française*, 26 January (Beaucourt, I, p. 353): 'A great many people hastened to obtain locks from his head; others soaked paper or even their handkerchiefs in his blood. For whatever purpose, several certainly bought locks, and were seen holding out their hands, shouting: "Five pounds for one! Here, ten pounds!"' *Journal de Perlet*, 22 January (Beaucourt, I, p. 342): 'Many people seemed anxious to have bits of his clothing. Blood that had flowed onto the square was collected with paper or with white handkerchiefs by people who gave no sign of being actuated by political superstition.'

52. *La Révolution de 92*, 22 January (Beaucourt, I, p. 351): 'Volunteers immediately dipped their pikes, others their handkerchiefs and even their hands, in the blood of Louis XVI.' *Annales de la République française*, 28 January (Beaucourt, I, p. 357): 'The executioner, astounded by the enthusiasm shown by several people for soaking their sabres or swords in the blood of Louis, cried out, "Wait a moment, I'll get you a bucket in which you can dip things more easily!"'

53. *Lettre historique sur la mort sublime de Louis XVI*, (Beaucourt, I, p. 396): 'Pieces of paper soaked in blood served as playthings for the fanatics, while the virtuous obtained locks of hair as if these were the precious relics of a martyr.'

54. *Les Souvenirs de l'histoire ou le Diurnal de la Révolution de France pour l'an de grâce 1797*, quoted in Beaucourt, I, p. 398.

55. *Journal de Perlet*, 22 January (Beaucourt, I, p. 343; cf. *Annales de la République française*, 25 January (Beaucourt, I, p. 356): 'A well-dressed young foreigner was to be seen. There were also two other well-dressed young people: one of them, who seemed to be foreign, gave fourteen *livres* to have his handkerchief soaked in the traces of blood; the other seemed to be very anxious to get hold of some locks, for which he paid one *louis*.'

56. The attempt to explain this enthusiasm as merely the well-known popular preference for the concrete was quickly abandoned: 'His blood

flowed. The competition was on, one soaking in it the tip of his finger, another a quill, another a piece of paper. Someone tasted it and announced: "It ain't half salty."' (Mercier, quoted in Maugras, op. cit., p. 316.)

57. Beaucourt, I, pp. 366–7.

58. 'Poetry needs something outrageous, barbarous, savage. It is at times when the madness of civil war or fanaticism sets daggers in men's hands and blood flows in streams upon the earth that Apollo's laurel rustles and grows green. It needs to be watered with blood.' (Diderot, *De la poésie dramatique* in *Oeuvres complètes*, Paris, 1875, VII, pp. 371–2.)

59. Beaucourt, I, pp. 365–6.

60. He preferred hanging to the guillotine because 'no blood is shed. Frequent sight of blood hardens the heart and brutalizes the eye.' (Quoted in Goncourt, *Histoire de la société française . . .*, op. cit., p. 436.)

61. An account that its author, the gentle Abbé Morrellet, a former member of the Académie française, did not publish, shows to what lengths of cruel irony one could be driven by the repulsive spectacle of the audience of an execution. The account is entitled *Nouveau moyen de subsistance pour la nation, proposé au comité de salut public en Messidor d l'an II*: 'I propose to those patriots who butcher their fellow men that they should eat the flesh of their victims, and, given the state of famine to which they have reduced the nation, should feed those that they allow to live on the flesh of those that they kill. I would even propose that a *national butchery* be established in accordance with the designs of the great artist and patriot David, and that a law be passed to oblige all citizens to buy supplies there at least once a week, under pain of being imprisoned, deported or having their throats cut as suspects, and [I] demand that at every patriotic festival there should be a course of this kind, which would be the true communion of patriots, the Eucharist of the Jacobins.' (Quoted in Goncourt, op. cit., pp. 447–8.)

62. *Le Républicain, journal des hommes libres de tous les pays*, 22 January: 'He proffered these words only: "I pardon my enemies"' (Beaucourt, I, p. 340. *Le Moniteur universel*, 23 January (Beaucourt, I, pp. 345–6): 'He said, in quite a firm voice: "Frenchmen, I die innocent. I pardon all my enemies, and I desire that my death serve the people." He seemed to wish to say more.'

63. Mercier, *Mémoires inédits*, quoted in Beaucourt, I, pp. 355–6.

64. cf. Beaucourt, I, p. 355: 'We have said that he was unwilling to have his hands tied behind his back. The truth is that his hands were bound before he mounted the scaffold. And whilst they were being

bound, he shuddered. He shuddered also when the executioner cut his hair. But suddenly regaining his stoical courage, he mounted the scaffold with the majestic, religious air of a venerable priest who goes up to the altar to celebrate Mass ... When he was strapped to the fatal board, he momentarily lifted his eyes to the sky and then bowed beneath the axe.'

65. 'Mémoire écrit par Marie-Thérèse Charlotte de France', in *Journal de ce qui s'est passé á la Tour du Temple, par Cléry*, Paris, 1968, p. 145. The expression clearly shows that the politico-theological conception of the body royal (cf. Kantorowicz, op. cit., pp. 314ff) was still current, at least in the mind of the royal family. It also found expression among supporters of the monarchy in the concept of dynastic continuity, which was reaffirmed immediately following the king's death. As early as February 1793 *Le Véridique* ... was remarkably sanguine: 'The death of Louis XVI has created one more saint and a new king. We will deal with the saint at some time to come, for the urgent question now is that of a king. By our estimate this king is the son of Louis XVI. The only difficulty is that of finding a regency for him.' (Beaucourt, I, p. 374.)

66. *La Révolution de 92*, 22 January (Beaucourt, I, pp. 350–51): 'He arrived at ten minutes past ten in the place de la Révolution. He disrobed and mounted the scaffold with great steadfastness. He wished to harangue the people; but the public executioner, following the orders of General Santerre, obliged him to submit to his judgement. Louis's head fell. It was shown to the people.'

67. '[He] got calmly out of the carriage, took off his frock coat, opened his shirt in order to expose his neck and shoulders, and knelt down to receive the last blessing from his confessor. He stood up again immediately and mounted the scaffold alone. At this horrible moment, his confessor, as though inspired by the sublime courage and heroic virtue of the king, threw himself down on his knees and, raising his eyes towards him, in a voice inspired by heaven said: "Now, son of Saint Louis, you go to heaven." The king asked to speak to the people. The three ruffians who were in charge of the execution replied that first of all they had to bind his hands and cut his hair. "Bind my hands!" the king replied rather curtly. Then, immediately recovering his composure, he told them, "Do whatever you wish, this is the last sacrifice." When his hands were bound and his hair cut, the king said: "I hope I may now be permitted to speak," and immediately he walked along the left-hand side of the scaffold. He made a sign for the drums to cease, and said in a loud, steady voice: "I die entirely innocent of the crimes of which I am accused. I pardon those who are the cause of

my misfortunes. I go so far as to hope that the shedding of my blood will contribute to the happiness of France and you unhappy people..." Here that ferocious brewer, whose exploits have made him general of the Paris Guards, interrupted him and said: "You were brought here not to make speeches, but to die." At once the drums drowned all voices and the three wretches seized upon their victim, strapping him to the fatal instrument, and the head of the monarch fell.' (Beaucourt, I, pp. 371–2.)

68. Beaucourt, I, p. 374. This detail of the narrative confirms that the author of *Le Véridique* was not present at the scene. To describe the mechanism of the guillotine, which has become an 'axe' in his metaphor, he probably made use of an engraving, in all likelihood the one published at the time of Guillotin's proposal.

69. This detail of the staging was invented by Louis Claude Bigot de Sainte-Croix, the king's Minister for Foreign Affairs, who resigned after the *journée* of the tenth of August and wisely and promptly departed for England. It was published, predated 21 January, as an appendix to his *Histoire de la conspiration du 10 août*, which appeared in London in 1793 (cf. Beaucourt, I, pp. 392–3).

70. 'The steps to the scaffold were extremely steep. The king was forced to support himself on my arm; with the difficulty he seemed to have mounting the steps, I was momentarily afraid his courage might have begun to wane. What then was my astonishment when on reaching the last step, I saw him, as it were, slip out of my hands.' (Beaucourt, I, p. 335.) The uncertainty as to the position of the confessor at the moment of execution is exploited in a version that elaborates the role of Edgeworth on the scaffold: 'Abbé Edgeworth, who had been kneeling on the scaffold throughout the execution, and who had remained in this position, would have been covered in blood, if an involuntary movement, which he subsequently regretted, had not made him fall over as the monster [the young 'cannibal' who showed the head to the people] came towards him.' (Beaucourt, I, p. 337.)

71. Beaucourt, I, p. 381. See Appendix 5.

72. cf. Jean Adhémar, 'L'Exécution de Louis XVI? Un dessin davidien' in *Gazette des Beaux-Arts*, May–June 1983, pp. 203ff.

PART II, CHAPTER 3

1. Alexis de Tocqueville, *L'Ancien Régime et la Révolution française*, Paris, p. 16.

2. C. Desmoulins, *Le Vieux Cordelier*, no. 6, in *Oeuvres complètes*, II, p. 240.

3. Thus, after the assassination of Lepelletier de Saint-Fargeau, Robespierre declared to the Assembly on 23 January 1793: 'Citizens, Friends of Liberty and Equality, it is for us to honour the memory of the martyrs of this truly divine religion of which we are the missionaries.' (*Oeuvres complètes*, IX, p. 257.)

4. Quoted in Lamartine, *Histoire des Girondins*, (XLV, 29), Paris, 1884, III, p. 382.

5. Quoted in Walter, *Actes*..., op. cit., p. 392.

6. Quoted in H. Fleischmann, op. cit., p. 255.

7. ibid., p. 223.

8. cf. Delarue, op. cit., pp. 160 and 258.

9. In Walter, op. cit., p. xiv.

10. This is no doubt the most interesting of the connotations of the song 'Les Forges républicaines': 'Mines give us fire,/Blacksmiths have work,/Let us make hell-fire everywhere./Frenchman, let us be ever more courageous.../One by one, let a republican courage,/Fill our hearts,/Under the orders of Vulcan./Work, work, jolly blacksmiths,/ Through your courage we shall triumph. [refrain] Despite the traitors within,/And foreign tyranny,/We wish to defeat the tyrants,/Or we shall wage war for ever./The guillotine is working apace,/Forge the iron, melt the bronze/Work, . . .'

11. Desmoulins, *Histoire secrète de la Révolution*, op. cit., p. 225.

12. Desmoulins, *Le Vieux Cordelier*, op. cit., p. 225

13. Madame de Staël, op. cit., II, pp. 139–40.

14. B. Constant, *Des effets de la Terreur*, Paris, Year V (a refutation of the ideas propounded in a pamphlet entitled *Des causes de la Révolution et de ses résultats*): 'Government had to become savage if the State was not to collapse. It was the Terror that consolidated the Republic. It re-established obedience within and discipline without ... The successes that occurred only after the Terror were nevertheless the effects of the impression it had made.' (p. 9.)

15. Saint-Just, *Oeuvres*, op. cit., II, p. 379 (15 April 1794).

16. Goncourt, op. cit., p. 434.

17. Saint-Just, op. cit., pp. 83–4. Lord Stanhope emphasized the fear that this arrangement caused ministers: 'In France ministers speak, write and act in the shadow of the guillotine.' (quoted by Desmoulins in *Le Vieux Cordelier*, no. 7, op. cit., p. 257.)

18. Quoted in Delarue, op. cit., p. 165.

19. Quoted in Guy Thuillier, *Témoins de l'administration*, Paris, 1967, p. 41. And Camille Desmoulins, before his notion of 'A Committee of Clemency' (which was to prove fatal for him), opposed clemency because 'so great an impetus, imparted to the machine of government

in a direction contrary to its first momentum, might break the springs of its action.' (*Le Vieux Cordelier*, no. 4, op. cit., p. 189.)

20. cf. in particular 'La Machine dans l'imaginaire, 1650–1800', *Revue des sciences humaines de l'université de Lille III*, 1982–3.

21. In Desmoulins's words, see note 19.

22. 'They reached the foot of the grim scaffold ... The orator knelt down, rose to his feet and then, turning towards us, thanked and *eulogized* the guillotine in the name of liberty, selecting phrases so gracefully fearsome, with an adulatory manner so terrifying, that I felt cold sweat flow off my forehead and over my eyelids. I should like to forget everything grim about my memories; but I am writing my *memoirs* and I still cannot forget that fanatical procession of the Propaganda which had the executioner for pontiff and the guillotine for altar!' (Nodier, *Souvenirs et portraits de la Révolution*, Paris, 1841, pp. 23–4.)

23. Saint-Just, *Oeuvres complètes*, II, p. 76. And, on 26 February 1794, he makes the image more precise: 'Our goal is to create an order of things such that everything inclines towards the good, such that the factions find themselves suddenly projected off this slope onto the scaffold.' (*Oeuvres*, II, p. 235.)

24. Desmoulins, *Histoire secrète* ..., op. cit., pp. 347–9.

25. Quoted in Walter, op. cit., p. 395.

26. He condemns those who slander and blaspheme the people 'incessantly representing them as ... wicked, barbarous, and corrupt': 'The attempt is made to divide the nation into two classes, the one armed, apparently, to keep the other in check ... and the first is supposed to contain all the tyrants, all the oppressors, all the leeches upon the body politic; the second the people!' (*Oeuvres*, op. cit., VI, p. 265.)

27. cf. Delarue, op. cit., pp. 156–7.

28. op. cit., p. 29.

29. Saint-Just, 15 April 1794, *Oeuvres complètes*, II, p. 377.

30. 16 February: 'On the subject of the guillotine, the people say that it's good, but that things are not going fast enough. It is astonishing, they say, that the numbers do not frighten the others.' 26 February: 'A citizen in one group was saying that he would like to see fifty people a day guillotined until there were no more conspirators ... In a revolutionary government, he said, you have to act revolutionary.' (In Caron, op. cit., III, pp. 158 and 357.)

31. cf. Delarue, op. cit., p. 168. After *Thermidor* the anti-Robespierre propaganda obviously made use of these facts: 'The blade of the guillotine was not working fast enough for his taste. They talked to him about a guillotine that would strike off nine heads at once. He

liked the idea.' (In Galart de Monjoie, *Histoire de la conspiration de Robespierre*, quoted in Fleischmann, op. cit., p. 257.

32. cf. Delarue, op. cit., p. 168.

33. Robespierre, *Oeuvres complètes*, X, p. 353 (5 February 1794). The national representative body, the Convention, was 'the sanctuary of truth', to the extent that 'no individual interest could usurp the supremacy of the general will of the Assembly and the indestructible power of reason' (ibid., p. 345).

34. Robespierre, 1 December 1790, in *Oeuvres*, VI, p. 619.

35. Robespierre, *Oeuvres complètes*, X, p. 356 (5 February 1794).

36. De Tocqueville describes the social structure of the *ancien régime* in terms which are remarkably consistent with Robespierre's thought. Whereas 'men had grown very similar to one another', 'within this vast uniformity there grew up a prodigious number of little barriers that divided it into a great many parts, and within each of these enclosures there appeared, as it were, an individual society that considered only its own interests, and took no part in the life of the society as a whole'. Try as royal legislation might to become general and uniform – 'everywhere the same, the same for everyone' – the fact remained that 'the barrier that separated the nobility of France from the other classes, though it remained easy to cross, was still fixed and visible, and those it excluded could not help but recognize the blatant and odious signs which marked it'. (*L'Ancien Régime et la Révolution*, op. cit., pp. 115 and 133.) In 1818 Madame de Staël had made the same diagnosis: 'Pride knew no limits but placed barriers everywhere. In no other country have the nobles been so alien to the rest of the nation.' (*Considérations . . .*, II, p. 116.)

37. Saint-Just, *Discours pour la défense de Robespierre*, in *Oeuvres complètes*, II, pp. 483–4: 'Pride fathers factions . . . Factions are the most fearful poison for the social order . . . By dividing the people factions replace liberty with partisan fervour . . . If it is your desire that factions be snuffed out, and that no one attempt to raise themselves upon the ruins of civil liberty through the axioms of Machiavelli, then rid politics of its menace by reducing everything to the impassive rule of justice.'

38. Robespierre, *Oeuvres complètes*, X, p. 354 (5 February 1794).

39. Quoted in Walter: *Actes . . .*, op. cit., p. 23. Her *Adresse aux Français*, written the day after her arrival in Paris, begins significantly: 'Oh unhappy Frenchmen, will your delight in schisms and uncertainty never end? For far too long factious and villainous men have placed their own interests and ambitions above the interests of the nation.' (Cf. Walter, ibid., p. 28.)

40. Desmoulins, *Oeuvres . . .*, II, p. 262.

41. ibid., II, p. 251: 'As soon as ... France has become a republic, we must expect parties, or rather coteries and intrigues, to be springing up endlessly. Liberty seems inseparable from this succession of cliques – and especially so in this country of ours, where the spirit of the nation and the native character have from the earliest times been factious and turbulent.'

42. ibid., II, p. 252.

43. Robespierre, *Oeuvres complètes*, X, p. 227 (25 December 1793).

44. 'Our forefathers did not have this word "individualism", which we created for our own use. For, in their time, there was indeed no individual who did not belong to a group and who could consider himself absolutely alone; but each of the thousand and one little groups of which French society was made thought only of itself. It was, if I may so put it, a sort of collective individualism, which prepared people's minds for the true individualism of today' (de Tocqueville, *l'Ancien Régime...*, op. cit., p. 143).

45. Saint-Just, *Oeuvres...*, op. cit., II, p. 508.

46. ibid., II, p. 76 (10 October 1793).

47. The attention focused upon the individuality of each case within the series is a feature of the specialized press that reported on the executions. The most famous journal was Tisset's. Its title is an example, as clear as it is longwinded, of this wish to emphasize the individuality of those who had placed themselves outside the body politic: *An account rendered to the* sans-culottes *of the French Republic by the most potent and expeditious Dame Guillotine, lady of the Carrousel, of the places de la Révolution and de la Grève and other sites, containing the names, Christian names, and details of those men and women to whom she has delivered passports to the next world; the place of their birth, their age, their day of judgement, since its foundation in the month of July* [sic] *1792 to this day.* (Cf. Delarue, op. cit., p. 161.) Shorter, but just as revealing, is the title of a competing pamphlet: it advertises a 'revolutionary gallery', and suggests a gallery of portraits in which the parasites on the body of the people would each be shown in effigy: *The Sword of Vengeance of the French Republic, or the Revolutionary Gallery, by a friend of the Revolution, or morals and of Justice.* Concerning the portrait of the decapitated, see Conclusion. Lastly, in 1796 Prudhomme drew up a list of those who had died under the guillotine. It is again revealing that he should have chosen to do so in the form of a 'dictionary of persons': *Dictionary of persons sent to their deaths during the Revolution and under the reign of the National Convention.*

48. Saint-Just, *Oeuvres...*, op. cit., II, p. 428.

49. The more illustrious victims were sometimes executed in solitary

splendour, like Marie-Antoinette. Her execution was, moreover, the object of precautions similar to those taken for the death of the king. Even so, the production-line aspect of executions subsequent to 21 January 1793 left their trace on hers. Whereas the king had gone to the scaffold in a closed carriage, his hands free and his hair intact, the queen received the standard treatment: her hands were tied behind her back; her hair was cut; and, above all, she was transported in the common tumbril.

50. Walter, op. cit., p. 225. Cf. Delarue, op. cit., p. 177: 'In Paris the art of guillotining has attained the utmost perfection. Sanson and his pupils guillotine with such rapidity that you would think they had taken lessons from Comus in the art of making men disappear. They disposed of twelve in thirteen minutes.' (Comus was the stage-name of a magician then at the height of his fame.)

51. cf. Walter, op. cit., p. 396.

52. This indifference to the reasons for any particular sentence reached its culmination in the case of Hébert. Whereas Desmoulins, who was guillotined for 'leniency', had portrayed Hébert as a wretch who 'needs to reach a state of intoxication stronger than wine can supply and to lick up the blood at the foot of the guillotine' (*Le Vieux Cordelier*, no. 5, op. cit., II, p. 225), just three weeks after his execution and scarcely ten days after Desmoulins had been guillotined, Saint-Just presented Hébert as the 'head of the faction favouring leniency under violent auspices' (15 April). This was not an oversight: Saint-Just was confirming the levelling effect of the guillotine by confusing *a posteriori* and *ultra* and *citra* factions, the memory of whose violent dispute was still vivid.

53. cf. Walter, op. cit., pp. 396–7.

54. Quoted in Lenotre, *Le Tribunal révolutionnaire*, Paris, 1908, p. 197.

55. ibid., p. 206.

56. Chateaubriand, *Essais historiques*..., op. cit., p. 59.

57. cf. F. Furet, *Penser la Révolution française*, Paris, 1978, p. 230.

58. Madame de Staël, *Considérations*..., op. cit., II, p. 142.

59. Robespierre, *Oeuvres complètes*, X, p. 554. His last speech aspired only to refute the 'odious slander' alleging that he wanted to seize power and become a tyrant. He could leave behind him only 'the terrible truth ... and death': 'What am I? A slave of the homeland, a living martyr to the Republic' (ibid., p. 555).

INTRODUCTION TO PART III

1. Goncourt, *Histoire de la société française . . .*, op. cit., p. 442.
2. Quoted in Walter, op. cit., p. 445.
3. Desmoulins, *Oeuvres*, op. cit., p. 185.
4. ibid.
5. ibid.: 'Crowned heads fell beneath the guillotine's blade, but Punchinello, who was also being guillotined on the same square, shared the attention.'
6. *Journal des spectacles*, 16 July 1793: 'Two new pantomimes are in rehearsal at the Théâtre du Lycée. The titles are *Adèle de Sacy* and *La Guillotine d'amour*. We know nothing of the stories of either, but the horrible and strange title of the second may well tickle the curiosity of the public.'
7. Lenotre, *La Guillotine . . .*, op. cit., pp. 310–11.
8. cf. Foucault, op. cit., pp. 37–8.
9. ibid., p. 39.
10. Getting down from the carriage; disrobing; haircut; farewell to the confessor; ascending the scaffold; strapping to the board; decapitation: for Louis XVI these seven events took two minutes and this was a most royal indulgence in time. At all events, the elimination of the interval between getting down from the tumbril and mounting the scaffold – the victims were already 'prepared' on arrival – allowed a satisfying increase in productivity.
11. Lenotre, op. cit., p. 309.
12. Desmoulins, *Histoire secrète . . .*, op. cit., p. 349.
13. Robespierre, *Discours et rapports . . .*, op. cit., pp. 327ff. The 'very sublimity' of the object of the Revolution was both its strength and its weakness. The Revolution was 'a sublime drama' which required a 'sense of the sublime' in its actors, so that they might prefer 'the public interest to all private interests'. Precisely for that reason the Festival of the Supreme Being constituted the 'sublime gathering of the first people in the world'.
14. E. Burke, *A Philosophical Enquiry into the Origin of our Ideas of the Sublime and the Beautiful*, London, Scolar Press, 1970, pp. 58 and 95–6.
15. Such, at least, was the opinion expressed on 22 January 1794 by Bourbon, deputy for the Oise. The day before, the members of the Assembly, accompanied by the Jacobins, had gone to the place de la Révolution to celebrate the anniversary of the death of the king by symbolically burning effigies of the monarch. But the members of the Convention found themselves simultaneously attending the four

executions. And they were not happy about this. They reacted with indignation: 'Why then were four wretches brought there at the same time to pollute us with their blood? This is a plot woven by mischief-makers who want it to be said that the representatives of the nation are cannibals . . . We went to celebrate the death of a king, the punishment of a true devourer of men, but we had no desire to have our eyes soiled by this disgusting and hideous spectacle.' (Delarue, op. cit., p. 166.) The sensitivity of the members of the Convention is all the more striking when we note that it is contrasted with the barbarity of a man-eating king . . . But the king was a man-eater in image rather than in reality. On the scaffold the guillotine sacrificed men in very deed, and if the theatre of the guillotine was not always able to remain within the confines of the sublime, this was due to the difficulty of making image and reality coincide.

16. Verninac de Saint-Maur, op. cit. (Goncourt, op. cit., p. 436).

PART III, CHAPTER I

1. A woman had fainted as the tumbrils passed.
2. Quoted in Fleischmann, op. cit., p. 279.
3. cf. Delarue, op. cit., pp. 267–8.
4. Baron de Frémilly, *Souvenirs*, published by A. Chuquet, Paris, 1908, p. 182. We will return to this 'reading of expressions' – it was one of the essential theatrical functions of the procession. Each witness gave his own interpretation: thus, Hérault seemed to Des Essarts to be 'holding his head high without the least affectation', and 'there was not a trace of agitation in his bearing' (ibid.).
5. cf. Walter, op. cit., p. 382.
6. ibid.
7. ibid., pp. 383–4.
8. cf. Delarue, op. cit., pp. 109–11. The letter written by the artist and deputy, Sergent, to the Extraordinary Criminal Tribunal about the Corday affair articulates very clearly the philosophical image which was supposed to inspire public behaviour: 'Philosophy and humanity . . . both tell us that he who, by the loss of his life, is to offer society a stirring example of the respect due to the law, becomes thereby an unfortunate and sacred being. The people of Paris, so often slandered, . . . possesses this character, and if some sentiment should draw it to the courts, to the passage of the criminals or to the foot of the scaffold, a majestic silence, broken only by the cry "*Vive la République!*" at the moment when the conspirator's head falls, shows that it knows well enough how to respect a being that the law is about to strike down.

Let us maintain this sensibility which does it great honour; for, in order to preserve this sensibility the legislators abolished torture and the appalling deaths of the Wheel and the Stake.' (Quoted in Cabanès, *Le Cabinet secret de l'histoire entr'ouvert par un médecin*, Paris, 1875, II, pp. 408–9.)

9. Beaucourt, op. cit., I, p. 379. The royalist version of this sublimity is given, for example, in an English account which was written as the caption for three versions of a print representing *The Massacre of the French King*: 'The stamping and whinnying of the horses, the shrilling sound of the trumpets and the uninterrupted drum-roll pierced the ears of every spectator and increased the terror of the awful scene.'

10. cf. E. and J. de Goncourt, *Histoire de Marie-Antoinette*, Paris, 1925, p. 399; Lenotre, *La Guillotine . . .*, op. cit., p. 266.

11. cf. Delarue, op. cit., p. 170.

12. cf. Walter, op. cit., p. 297.

13. 'There is a general outcry against those who daily insult not only the condemned as they are brought to their deaths, but also those who are only accused of conspiracy. The practice is an attempt to lower the French nation in the esteem of other nations. To bring this abominable scandal to an end, nothing less will suffice than a decree which severely punishes these individuals who seem to think of nothing but blood and carnage.' (24 January 1794, quoted by Caron, op. cit., III, p. 128.)

14. *La Chronique de Paris* received an edifying letter: 'Persons being interrogated are no longer placed on the stool of repentance. We should also dispense with the tumbril that brings the condemned to their deaths. Under the unfortunate necessity of bringing them beneath the sword of the law, we should at least eliminate anything that may add to the horror of their situation. Would it not be more humane to bring them to the scaffold in an open carriage, accompanied only by the minister of the religion they request, and even by a friend, if one could be found loyal and courageous enough to give this last and painful mark of their attachment? The condemned should not have their hands tied behind their backs until the moment of execution. The guards by whom they are surrounded are sufficient to ensure that they do not escape, and the executioner placed in the hindmost carriage should not appear before them till called upon to perform his cruel task. This endeavour of humanity would give a more august character to the death penalty, and the people would see that the death of a condemned man must be very necessary to the homeland if it allows a man it treats with such care to die upon the scaffold.' (In Lenotre, *La Guillotine . . .*, op. cit., pp. 251–2.)

15. A. Ubersfeld, *Lire le théâtre*, Paris, 1978, p. 157.

16. cf. *Le Père Duchesne*, no. 199: 'Well, buggeration, I should like to tell you how happy the *sans-culottes* were when the archtigress crossed Paris in the coach with thirty-six doors. It was not her handsome white horses, so beautifully harnessed, so splendidly plumed, that drew her; it was two old nags that were harnessed up with Master Sanson sitting behind them.' (Quoted in Walter, op. cit., p. 138.) Hébert was himself to meet with this public joy as he went to the scaffold: 'I have never seen anyone guillotined, but I will happily go and see them, especially Hébert and Chaumette.' (Walter, op. cit., p. 378.)

17. Walter, op. cit., pp. 382–3.

18. Police report of 5 February 1794: 'One of the five criminals shouted as he went to his death: "I am innocent! We die innocent!" The other three [*sic*] kept a serene countenance and seemed as calm as if they had been sitting at their own firesides. The spectators were astonished and said that the more steadfast the condemned the more moving they found it.' (Caron, op. cit., IV, p. 106.)

19. 'What a brilliant triumph for us./Martyrs of holy liberty,/ Immortality awaits us,/Worthy of such a destiny,/To the scaffold we go without fear,/Immortality awaits us./To die for our country (*bis*) Is the finest, the most enviable fate.' (cf. Lenotre, *La Guillotine...*, op. cit., p. 269.)

20. Letter to Barbaroux, quoted in Walter, op. cit., p 25. The same Roman tones feature in her letter to her father, which was clearly inspired by Corneille: 'Forgive me, dear papa, for having determined my fate without your permission. I have avenged many an innocent victim ... Adieu, my dear papa. I beg that you will forgive me or rather rejoice at my fate, for my cause was a great one ... Do not forget this line of Corneille: "The crime and not the scaffold is the source of shame." I am to be judged tomorrow at eight o'clock. On the 16th of July.' (Ibid., pp. 25–6.)

21. 'This imperturbable calm and complete self-denial which show her to be entirely without remorse, when she is, as it were, in the presence of death, this calm and this self-discipline, sublime though they are in one regard, are unnatural; they are explicable only by the raptures of political fanaticism that armed her hand.' (Quoted in Walter, op. cit., p. 27.)

22. 'The people had seen this woman pass, had brought her to the scaffold, without insult for her last moments... The more righteous and fierce their indignation with the unfortunate creature, the more proud and generous her attitude and calm countenance made them.' (Sergent, quoted by Cabanès, op. cit., loc. cit. Other accounts, however,

contrast the dignity of Charlotte Corday with the 'barbarous' cries of the crowd.)

23. cf. Walter, op. cit., p. 279.

24. ibid., p. 280.

25. Des Essarts, quoted in Walter, p. 279.

26. Marat, *L'Ami du peuple*, 7 July 1792, quoted in Walter, op. cit., p. 8.

27. Bailly may be taken as an example. The former Mayor of Paris, held responsible for the massacre of the Champ-de-Mars (17 July 1791), showed a truly Roman fortitude. He had to suffer a procession which the actions of the public (insults, stone-throwing, pushing) made doubly humiliating. Bailly twice gave utterance to his stoic courage. On the first occasion he explained to the comte de Beugnot, who had come to take a last farewell, why he had put some diluted coffee on his chocolate: 'As I have a rather difficult journey to make, and do not altogether trust my temperament, I have put a little coffee on top ... With this repast, I hope I shall make it to the end.' (Walter, op. cit., p. 296.) Further, when Sanson protested at the crowd's throwing stones, the former Mayor of Paris is honoured with the following comment: 'It would be a sad thing to have learnt to live honourably for fifty-seven years, and then find myself unable to bear courageously the fifteen minutes before my death.' (Walter, op. cit., p. 298.)

28. '... the spectacle of a queen brought to her death amid the silent satisfaction of a great people! And it would have been enjoyed, had it not been for the ridiculous order, given by I know not which despot, to prevent men from being at their windows with their wives and children. This long rigmarole spoiled everything. The majesty of the people was eclipsed by this stupid insolent sound: "Head down! Head down!" There were even some sticklers for orders forcing citizens to remove their hats.' (Walter, op. cit., p. 139.)

29. Quoted in Fleischmann, op. cit., p. 216.

30. Walter, op. cit., p. 138.

31. This ambition would also explain the fact, recorded in several accounts, that there were persons 'employed' by the government to encourage the people to express its revolutionary anger. The State's ideology, with its preferred model, the sublime, was quite at odds with its practice of inciting to revolutionary anger.

32. Quoted by Fleischmann, op. cit., p. 281.

33. Caron, op. cit., II, pp. 142–3. Cf. ibid., p. 323: 'The Mayor of Montpellier was in the tumbril, about to suffer on the place de la Révolution the penalty for his misdeeds, when he began laughing

and said: "Adieu, my brothers!" The spectators replied: "To the guillotine!" He went on laughing.'

34. cf. Delarue, op. cit., p. 252, and Lenotre, *La Guillotine* ..., p. 303.

35. Delarue, op. cit., pp. 267–8.

PART III, CHAPTER 2

1. cf. the report, an official report it should be said, of 26 August 1792: 'Everything went off in the most orderly fashion and the people applauded enthusiastically, making way for the gendarmerie.' (Quoted in Delarue, op. cit., p. 157.)

2. Delarue, op. cit., p. 156.

3. ibid.

4. cf. Walter, op. cit., p. 294.

5. cf. Introduction to Part III, note 15.

6. The significance of placing the guillotine where the Bastille had stood, on place Saint-Antoine, is clear, and the name given by the Revolution to the former Barrière du Trône Renversé sufficiently explains the meaning of the guillotine's transfer to that site.

7. Robespierre, *Oeuvres complètes*, X, p. 561; 'O forever happy day, when the people of France as one man rose to render to the author of Nature the only homage worthy of him! What a moving forgathering of all those objects that might enchant a man's heart or eyes! Old age, how you are honoured! O generous ardour of the children of the homeland! O naive and pure joy of the young citizens! O sweet tears of mothers whose hearts are melting! O celestial charm of innocence and beauty! O majesty of a great people rejoicing solely in the sense of its strength, its glory and its virtue! Being of beings! The day in which the universe arose from the hands of the omnipotent, did it shine with as pleasant a light in your eyes as on this day in which, throwing off the yoke of crime and error, it appeared before you, worthy of your attention and of its destiny?'

8. ibid: 'But when the people, in whose presence all private vices disappear, return to their homes, the schemers reappear and the role of the charlatans recommences.'

9. cf. Walter, op. cit., pp. xxviii–xxxi.

10. Marat, *L'Ami du peuple*, 18 December 1790, quoted in Walter, op. cit., p. 6.

11. Desmoulins, *Oeuvres*, op. cit., p. 139.

12. Saint-Just, *Oeuvres complètes*, op. cit., II, p. 508.

13. The risk that a surfeit of executions would cause indifference had been noted by Collot on 7 November 1793 in a report on the situation

in Lyons, where, to respect the Convention's decree that 'Lyons no longer exist', firing-squads and guillotine had been working overtime. Collot in person stated: 'Even executions do not have quite the effect expected ... Yesterday a spectator returning from an execution remarked: "Well, that wasn't so very tough. What exactly would I have to do to be guillotined? Insult a representative?"' (Quoted in Mathiez, op. cit., p. 445.)

14. Delarue, op. cit., p. 325. The term 'play-acting' confirms that the guillotine can always be perceived as theatrical in nature. The desire that it be hidden was reinforced by the disrespectful joke practised by one Peugnez, who, coming out of prison on 1 February 1899, had shouted: 'Present arms!' and the soldiers in the protective cordon had mechanically complied. Peugnez died in state.

15. Foucault, op. cit., p. 20.

16. F. Furet, op. cit., p. 231.

17. This fear was vindicated by the arrangements made at the scaffold of the Barrière du Trône Renversé: 'A hole has been dug for the blood of the dead. When the execution is over, the hole is simply covered with some planks, and this is not sufficient to seal in the smell of the rotting blood, of which there is no small quantity ... To avoid noxious emanations during this season of the year, it would be as well to place, on a little wheelbarrow with two wheels, a lead-lined case in which the blood of the dead might collect. This could afterwards be emptied into the Picpus sewer. The Department of Public Works will, I trust, hasten to adopt this measure, and I do the more exhort it to do so, since the place of execution and the sewer are not far apart, and the effluvia might attract one another and give rise to a concentration of noxious substances which would be all the more dangerous, in that, if this occurred, it could not fail to pollute the atmosphere considerably.' (Quoted in Lenotre, *La Guillotine* . . ., op. cit., p. 287.

18. cf. Dauban, *La Démagogie en 1793*, Paris, 1870.

19. cf. Lenotre, *La Guillotine* . . ., pp. 284–5.

20. Verninac de Saint-Maur, op. cit.; see Part I, Chapter 3, note 6.

21. 'This method of execution is open to criticism under another head, which is that, though it reduces the pain of the condemned man, it does not sufficiently protect the spectator from the sight of blood: he sees blood on the blade of the guillotine and it flows copiously on the *pavé* under the scaffold. This repugnant spectacle should not be set before the eyes of the public, and it would be very easy to remedy the drawback, which is greater than generally considered since it familiarizes people with the idea of murder – murder, it is true, committed in the name of the law, but with a cold-bloodedness that incites pre-

meditated savagery. Have we not already heard the crowd say that this kind of death is much too soft for the villains who have so far been executed, several of whom have indeed seemed to scoff at death. The people disgrace themselves by seeming to desire vengeance, instead of confining themselves to seeing justice done.' (*Révolutions de Paris*, 27 April 1793, quoted in Lenotre, *La Guillotine . . .*, p. 259.)

22. cf. Lenotre, *Le Tribunal révolutionnaire*, Paris, 1947, pp. 250–51.

23. Fleischmann, op. cit., p. 185.

24. ibid., p. 292. Report of 25 March 1794.

25. This is described in Lamartine's *Mémoires*, and is confirmed by the moving account given by an abbé who came to give absolution as close as possible to the last instant: 'My earliest memories take me back to when my father was in prison and my mother a captive . . ., to the strains of the 'Marseillaise' and 'Ça ira' in the streets . . ., the dull thud of the instrument of death in our town squares.' (*Mémoires inédits*, Paris, 1870, p. 5.) 'The sacrifice is about to begin. The raucous joy, the vile taunts of·the spectators grow louder, adding to the anguish of a death that is not in itself cruel, but which is rendered terrible by the sound of the three successive strokes and the sight of so much blood.' Quoted in Lenotre, *La Guillotine . . .*, op. cit., p. 174.

26. 'I did not see the condemned mount the scaffold. I watched as they appeared upon the fatal stage, immediately to disappear with the movement of the plank or bed on which eternal rest began for them. The remainder of the operation was hidden from me by those who directed it. Only the sudden fall of the blade told me when the moment came, or rather, had come.' (Arnault, *Souvenirs d'un sexagénaire*, in Walter, op. cit., pp. 444–5.)

27. cf. Walter, op. cit., p. 384.

28. ibid., p. 262.

29. According to A. Robert, in the *Dictionnaire historique et biographique de la Révolution et de l'Empire, 1789–1815*, Paris, II, pp. 78–9.

30. Walter, op. cit.

31. Saint-Just: *Oeuvres complètes*, op. cit., II, p. 87. All the witnesses were struck by the fact that, in response to the guillotine's extreme 'laconicism', the sublime role that Saint-Just offered the victim was limited, at its culminating point, to complete and apparently impassive silence.

32. See p. 68.

33. Madelin, *Les Hommes de la Révolution*, Paris, 1929, p. 225.

34. This final *coup de théâtre* unveils the true face of the traitor, in his death mask.

35. Letter quoted in Cabanès, op. cit., p. 408.

36. Lafont d'Aussone, *Mémoires secrets et universels des malheurs et de la mort de la Reine de France*, Paris, 1836, quoted in Fleischmann, op. cit., p. 218.

37. In Walter, op. cit., p. 136. The *Mémoires de Sanson* offers a touching variation of this detail: 'On arriving at the place de la Révolution, the tumbril stopped just opposite the *grande allée* of the Tuileries. For a few moments the queen was overwhelmed with painful thoughts. Her face grew suddenly paler, her eyes moistened, and she was heard to murmur in a stifled voice: "My daughter! My children!"'

38. 'The tumbril drew up before the scaffold, and, though her hands were still bound, she got down quickly and nimbly without any assistance.' (*Le Magicien républicain*, quoted in Walter, pp. 135–6.)

39. Quoted in Dauban, *Madame Roland et son temps*, Paris, 1864, CCXLIII.

40. Quoted in Walter, op. cit., pp. 386–7.

41. ibid., p. 383.

PART III, CHAPTER 3

1. Quoted in Lenotre, *La Guillotine . . .*, op. cit., p. 174.

2. Joseph de Maistre, *Les Soirées de Saint-Pétersbourg*, op. cit., I, pp. 30–31.

3. 'The exclusion of public executioners is not founded on a mere prejudice. It is in the heart of all good men to shudder at the sight of one who assassinates his fellow man in cold blood. The law requires this deed, it is said, but does the law command anyone to become a hangman?' Quoted in Delarue, op. cit., p. 50.

4. 'A few old men of the town of Rennes still fondly remember the virtues of Jacques Ganier, who died some thirty years ago, having been for many a year the city executioner. This gentle man never put a criminal to death without first going to communion to expiate, as it were, the action he was about to commit. The magistrates of the *parlement* used to come and play *boules* outside his house . . . and, though he was not of their company, they nevertheless showed the greatest respect for him and used him as an umpire in all the disputes arising in their game. He gave to the poor all that he received above the strict minimum he needed to live on. For them his death was a calamity. They wept bitterly and ran through the streets, proclaiming in tones of pitiful distress: "We have lost a father!" For many years the people visited his tomb like that of a saint.' (Quoted in Lenotre, *La Guillotine . . .*, op. cit., p. 333.)

5. cf. Delarue, op. cit., p. 49.

6. Lenotre, op. cit., p. 174.

7. Delarue, op. cit., pp. 188–9.

8. Desmoulins, *Révolutions de France et de Brabant*, in Lenotre, *La Guillotine*..., op. cit., p. 132: 'We are assured that this journal is an anthology of the witticisms and drinking songs of the aristocratic dinner-parties held at the house of the Paris executioner. Whether out of spite towards the gibbet and Monsieur Guillotin, or because the visit of so many distinguished people went to his head, Monsieur Sanson feasted his guests as best he could.'

9. cf. J. de Maistre, op. cit, loc. cit.

10. cf. Delarue, op. cit., p. 307.

11. Sanson's assistant in Paris, Desmorets, was sent to Grenoble. He wrote in 1803 as follows: 'Citizen minister; my sufferings are unspeakable, I should need a quill dipped in blood to express them. Allow me, dear citizen, to set out in brief the succession of misfortunes that have afflicted me over the last six and more years ... On my arrival in Grenoble I was placed in an isolated house a league distant from the town, and as the executioners for this part of the world were, till my appointment, common criminals taken by the judges directly from their cells to perform these functions, I am considered a poor sort of fellow. What makes this prejudice even more damaging in my own case, is that when I arrived at Grenoble with my commission, the public prosecutor had just appointed two villains, the one sentenced to irons, the other to deportation, and these men were in the house where I live. I am thus set at one with the basest of men, and from that time forth insulted, despised and continually threatened. I live in fear of my days, and my tears fall daily upon my meagre repast.' (Quoted in Delarue, pp. 198–9.) When Sanson was consulted on this subject in 1798, he replied that it would be wise to respect the traditional connection of executioner and 'his' population: 'The only places where it may be possible to resist are in the neighbourhood of Paris within, say, sixty leagues. And then only if the appointees are honest men. For the lack of prejudice in these places is due to the old executioners having stayed there. It only needs one dishonest individual for the prejudice to start up again, and make honest people leave the profession.' (Quoted in Delarue, p. 200.)

12. cf. the letter of the Minister of Justice Duport-Dutertre to the Assembly, dated 3 March 1792: 'There are few important towns in which there is not still some individual bound to this grim activity, and isolated from the other citizens by the invincible horror that nature inspires in them for the man who, albeit in the name of justice and

society, makes of himself an instrument of death ... I am nevertheless confident that the Assembly will consider that it cannot in justice refuse to provide for the subsistence of these unfortunate individuals, to whom the Constitution has already granted citizenship, but who, having already, as it were, renounced their humanity to take up their profession, will, for many years to come, in a prejudice that it is difficult to overcome, because it is rooted in the heart, encounter a repugnance for their own persons, which will prohibit their obtaining the least resource for keeping themselves in body and soul.' (Quoted in Lenotre, op. cit., pp. 26–7.)

13. Letter to the Convention from the executioner Bourcier; cf. Lenotre, op. cit., p. 341.

14. These criticisms were answered by Schmidt, who pointed out that the executioner and not the machine was at fault, the executioner having 'failed to attend to the need to attach the two ends of the cord which holds up the drop-hammer, and to hold them in such a way that they could not impede its movement'. (Cf. Delarue, op. cit., p. 369.)

15. *Lettre écrite le 27 mai 1806 par le Procureur général de Sa Majesté l'Empereur à Son Excellence le Grand Juge Ministre de la Justice*, Archives nationales, BB³212.

16. cf. Foucault, op. cit., pp. 63ff.

17. cf. Delarue, op. cit., pp. 173–4.

18. Decree of Cales, representative of the *départment* of the Côte-d'Or: 'Being only now informed that the instrument of death, which must be exposed to public view only when the execution of the law so requires, and which in all other circumstances cannot help but revolt those of sensitive disposition and erode the sentiments of humanity which should be the mark of a free people, is permanently established upon one of the squares of Dijon: it is decreed that, upon receipt of this letter, said instrument shall be removed by the prompt action of the national agent of the municipality ... It shall be [exposed] for one hour only before an execution and will be immediately and without delay removed after the execution.' (Quoted in Delarue, op. cit., pp. 170–1.) Letter from the Prefect of les Landes to the Minister of Justice: 'Monseigneur, in the past it was felt necessary to distinguish in society those men who had taken up the profession of executioners of criminal sentences ... In some provinces, it had been found that the best method of providing for this was a distinctive uniform which did not permit of error and which reassured honest folk. It is more than ever advisable to revive these ancient customs.' (21 March 1806 quoted in Delarue, op. cit., p. 43.)

19. The slap given to Charlotte Corday's head by one of the execu-

tioner's assistants, the carpenter François Legros, is the most notorious of these excesses, and was immediately condemned. But see note 22 below for the executioner whose enthusiasm caused him, while showing a head to the public, to fall from the scaffold, head in hand, to his death.

20. Quoted in Lenotre, op. cit., p. 172.

21. Marquise de la Tour du Pin, *Journal d'une femme de cinquante ans (1778–1815)*, Paris, 1913, pp. 312–3. This event was probably the inspiration for Galart de Montjoie's inventive account, whose sole purpose is to show that the cruelty and barbarity of the event were not to be ascribed to the executioner but to the official who gave the order. The latter is, of course, 'a henchman of Robespierre's': 'a third [henchman] ordered that the children be tied one to each corner of the guillotine. The eldest of the children was sixteen. While they were so attached, the blood of their father and mother flowed out onto the scaffold and dripped down on their heads.'

22. 'One of the sons of the executioner, who was showing the head to the people without looking where he put his feet, fell off the scaffold and cracked his head open on the ground. His father was convulsed with grief.' (*Chronique de Paris* quoted in Lenotre, op. cit., p. 250).

23. 'This abominable sight made such a strong impression on Sanson that he fell ill, and he never again practised his cruel craft. He died some six months later.' (Cf. Lenotre, op. cit., p. 147.)

24. ibid., p. 348.

25. Joubert, *Carnets*, Paris, 1938, p. 460. My thanks to Professor A. Pizzorusso who drew my attention to this most eloquent passage.

26. Quoted in Lenotre, op. cit., pp. 1–3.

27. F. Furet, op. cit., p. 224.

28. cf. Lenotre, *Le Tribunal révolutionnaire*, op. cit., p. 348.

29. cf. Lenotre, *La Guillotine . . .*, op. cit., p. 206.

30. ibid., p. 208.

31. *Journal officiel de la Commune*, quoted in Delarue, op. cit., p. 295.

32. Quoted in Delarue, op. cit., p. 378.

33. ibid.

34. ibid., p. 283.

CONCLUSION

1. I use the terms 'motif' and 'theme' in their art-historical sense, cf. E. Panofsky, *Studies in Iconography*, Oxford University Press, 1939, pp. 17ff.

2. cf. de Manet, op. cit., pp. 359–61.

3. This well-known term is given in one of the fundamental treatises of the theory of 'humanist' painting, the *De Pictura* of Leon Battista Alberti, 1435 (ed. C. Grayson, Bari, 1975, pp. 44ff.).

4. Fénelon, *De l'éducation des filles*, quoted in R. Démoris: 'Original absent et création de valeur: Du Bos et quelques autres' in *Revue des sciences humaines de l'université de Lille III*, 1975, 1, p. 67.

5. cf. especially the *Lettres philosophiques sur les physionomies* by Abbé J. Pernetti (The Hague, 1768), one of the most important texts for an understanding of the significance of this theme in the eighteenth century.

6. cf. J. Adhémar, 'Les Musées de cire en France, Curtius, le "banquet royal", les têtes coupées' in *Gazette des Beaux-Arts*, December 1978, pp. 203–14.

7. R. de La Sizeranne, *Les Masques et les visages à Florence et au musée du Louvre*, Paris, p. ii.

8. Italo Calvino, quoted in R. Barthes, *La Chambre claire*, Paris, 1980, p. 61.

9. R. Barthes, ibid.

10. Robespierre, 5 February 1794: 'Though not all have had a change of heart, how many faces are masked! How many traitors interfere in our affairs only in order to bring them to confusion!' (*Oeuvres complètes*, X, p. 361.)

11. cf. Delarue, op. cit., p. 321.

12. R. Barthes, op. cit., pp. 122–3.

13. ibid., p. 120.

14. G. Didi-Huberman, *Invention de l'hystérie*, Paris, 1982, p. 51.

15. R. Barthes, op. cit., p. 27.

16. 'Since I have yet some instants to live, might I hope, citizens, that you will allow me to have myself painted? I should like to leave my friends this sign of my remembrance. Besides, just as the image of a good citizen is cherished, so curiosity sometimes makes people seek out the image of a great criminal, and thus the horror that his crimes inspire is perpetuated', in Walter, op. cit., p. 30.

17. R. Barthes, op. cit., p. 153.

APPENDICES

Appendix 1

Charles Henri Sanson's report to the Minister of Justice on the mode of decapitation (quoted by Jules Taschereau in Revue rétrospective, *Paris, 1835)*

For the execution to arrive at the result prescribed by the law, the executioner must, with no impediment on the part of the condemned man, be very skilful, and the condemned man very steadfast; otherwise it will be impossible to carry out an execution by sword without dangerous scenes resulting.

The sword is not fit to perform a second execution after the first. The blade is liable to chip, and must absolutely be reground and sharpened again. Were there several executions to perform at one time, it would be necessary to have a sufficient number of swords, all of them ready prepared. It should also be noted that swords have often been broken during executions of this kind. The Paris executioner has only two, which were given to him by the former Parlement de Paris. They cost six *livres* each.

A further consideration is that, when there are several condemned men to execute at once, the terror of the execution, caused by the vast quantities of blood, will bring terror and faintness to the hearts of even the most intrepid of those to be executed. This faintness will prove an invincible obstacle in the way of execution, as the persons will be unable to hold themselves still. If the attempt is made to proceed despite this, the execution will become a struggle or a massacre. Yet it seems that the National Assembly only decided on this method of execution in order to avoid the long-drawn-out methods previously in use.

To judge by executions of another kind – which do not require anything like the same degree of precision – the condemned have been known to be taken ill at the sight of their executed accomplices, and, at least, to feel unsteady or fearful: all this is an argument against an execution in which the head is decapitated by sword. How indeed should a person tolerate the sight of the bloodiest form of execution without feeling faint? With the other forms of execution, it was easy to hide this faintness from the public, because they could be carried out without the condemned man having to remain steadfast and fearless; but, with this form, if the condemned man flinches, the execution will fail. How can one deal with a man who cannot or will not hold himself up?

With regard to these humane considerations, I am bound to issue a warning as to the accidents that will occur if this execution is to be performed with the sword. It would, I think, be too late to remedy these accidents if they were known only from bitter experience. It is therefore indispensable, if the humane views of the National Assembly are to be fulfilled, to find some means by which the condemned man can be secured so that the issue of the execution cannot be in doubt, and in this way to avoid delay and uncertainty.

This would fulfil the intentions of the legislators and ensure that no breach of public order occurred.

Appendix 2

*Doctor Louis's proposal concerning methods of decapitation (*Avis motivé sur le mode de décollation, *quoted by Ludovic Pichon,* Code de la guillotine, *Paris, 1910)*

The Legislative Committee has been kind enough to consult me about two letters written to the National Assembly concerning article 3 of the first title of the Penal Code, which stipulates that all those condemned to death shall have their heads cut off. On the basis of these letters, the Minister of Justice and the director of the *département* of Paris, subsequent to the representations that have been made to them, are of the view that it is necessary to determine immediately and precisely how to proceed with the application of the law. They fear that if, by a defect in the means employed, or through inexperience, or through clumsiness, the execution became horrible for the condemned man and for the spectators, the people might have occasion to be unjust and cruel towards the executioner, a thing it is important to prevent.

In my opinion, these representations are correct and their fears justified. Experience and reason both show that the method previously used to cut off the head of a criminal expose him to a death much worse than the simple privation of life which is the formal requirement of the law, and which, in order to be achieved, requires that the execution be the instantaneous effect of a single blow. Examples show how difficult it is to attain this.

It should be remembered at this stage what occurred during the execution of Lally. He was kneeling and blindfolded. The executioner struck him on the back of the neck. The blow did not separate the head from the body, nor could it have done. Nothing now prevented the body from falling. It toppled forward, and the head was finally separated from the body by four or five sabre blows. This hacking, if we may use the term, was witnessed with horror.

In Germany, the executioners are more experienced owing to the frequency with which this form of dispatch is used; it is the only form of execution for persons of the female sex, whatever their status. Yet a perfect execution is rare, despite the precaution, taken in certain places, of fastening the seated victim to an armchair.

In Denmark, there are two positions and two instruments used for decapitation. What one might call the honorific execution is performed with the sabre. The criminal is blindfolded and kneeling; his hands are free. If the execution is to be ignominious, the patient's hands are tied and he lies prone beneath the axe.

It is well known that cutting instruments have little or no effect if the stroke is perpendicular. When examined under the microscope, they are seen to be saw-blades of greater or lesser thickness, which can operate only by sliding across the body they are intended to cut. It would be impossible to decapitate with a single blow from an axe or cutter whose blade was straight; but with a convex blade, as on the old-style battleaxe, the blow is perpendicular in effect only at the centre section of the circle; but the instrument, as it penetrates further into the parts it divides, acts obliquely on each side and attains the goal with certainty.

If we consider the structure of the neck, the centre of which is the spinal column, we note that it is composed of several bones which overlap at their junctures, so that there is no joint to be found. It is not therefore possible to guarantee immediate and complete separation, if this task is to be confided to an agent whose dexterity may be affected by moral and physical causes. If the procedure is to be infallible, it must needs be carried out by invariable mechanical means, whose force and effects we can also establish. This is the course adopted in England. The criminal's body is laid prone between two uprights surmounted by a cross-piece from which the convex axe is made to fall onto the neck by means of a trigger. The back of the device must be sufficiently strong and heavy to act efficiently in the manner of a drop-hammer driving piles. It is well known that the force increases with the height from which it falls.

A machine of this kind is easy to construct and is infallibly effective; decapitation would instantly ensue, in keeping with the spirit and demands of the new law. It would be easy to test it on corpses, and even on a live sheep. We will see whether it is necessary to fix the patient's head by a crescent which would grip the neck at the base of the skull. The horns or extensions of the crescent could be fixed by cotters under the scaffold. This piece of apparatus, if it proved necessary, would not cause the least sensation and would scarcely be noticeable.

Consulted at Paris, the 7th of March 1792

Appendix 3

Complaints of the Public Executioner against those who have exercised his profession without having served out their apprenticeship

Saviours of the homeland, hereafter do not make such a hasty end of criminals who fall into your clutches. Put it to those extreme patriots of excess that it is no service to their fellow citizens to eradicate, by their slapdash zeal, the only way to come at the root of the catastrophes that were then being prepared. Put it to them that they owe me compensation for the executions of which they have deprived me. Each of the heads of the four scoundrels, if my sword had put them off their shoulders, would have been worth twenty *écus* to me. Put it to them that the work would have been much more neatly done and that a great many spectators would have enjoyed the spectacle of the sacrifice of these vile victims, if the tragedy had been played at my theatre.

The lovers of gory scenes who would have liked the death of the criminals to be prolonged for the amusement of their ferocious tastes had only to inform me of their preferences, and if our ordinary and extraordinary tortures seemed means inadequate to overcoming the discretion of the guilty parties, and to extract from them useful denunciations and confessions, I would have written to the Reverend Fathers of the Holy Office, those of Madrid *and* those of Lisbon, to ask them to lend me some of those ingenious gewgaws that their holy atrocities have invented to force the innocent to declare themselve guilty of crimes that they did not commit.

If the torture of the rope, or that of the wheel, or beheading seem to them too insipid to inspire horror at the thought of crime, I shall write, at their petition, to my colleague in London. I shall beg him to cross the sea, and to come and show me how to disembowel a man in the best traditions, to tear out his heart and entrails and beat the cheeks of the corpse therewith. For thus it is that they treat crimes of treachery on the banks of the Thames. If this torture seems to them too gentle, too insignificant, I will call upon my colleague of Avignon, and learn from him how to knock my man out with an iron bludgeon, open his stomach, tear out his entrails, cut him into four quarters, and array them at the four corners of my theatre, as a butcher does with a bullock, a *charcutier* with a pig, a roast-meat merchant with a lamb – and all this to teach a good lesson to anyone who felt some inclination to imitate the four villains whom the usurpers of my functions so incompetently dispatched. And let these usurpers consider that they, much more than I, deserve that ignominy with which I am myself visited. For it is not I who kill the criminals who die beneath my blows; it is Justice that sacrifices them, it is Justice that makes me the avenger of society. Should not this appellation rather honour than abase me? Can it then be true that in Africa there was more good sense than in Europe, and will philosophy not succeed in making my profession a glorious one?'

Paris, 1789

Appendix 4

*Dr Sédillot's account of the 'unprecedented crimes' committed during the Terror (*Réflexions historiques et physiologiques sur le supplice de la guillotine, *Paris, Year IV of the French Republic, pp. 24–5.)*

May it be forgiven, if we here offer a harrowing outline of the unprecedented crimes that have, in our time, been committed upon so many wretched people by that machine. Such calamities deserve the tribute of some expiatory tears.

The guillotine was no sooner discovered than its formidable appearance carried terror from town to town, from village to village; France bristled with scaffolds. Then, dragged and piled aboard innumerable carts, side by side with their executioners, their heads bare, their hair hacked off, their hands tied behind their backs, men, women, children, and old people were everywhere to be seen, at all hours of the day, passing slowly through the ranks of the cannibal devotees of the tyrants, who, by threats, curses and savage cries, insulted humanity, honour, virtue, misery, and old age. When the victims arrived at the square, the public square that every day ran with blood, they were presented with the sight of the scaffold still reeking with the carnage of the victims who had preceded them. There, often, by a refinement of cruelty that has no parallel in the annals of the most corrupt peoples known to history, wretched parents suffered a thousand deaths before they came to execution, as, amid the raucous joy of a horde of cowardly and barbarous brigands, they saw the murderous blade of the guillotine fall upon those to whom they were bound by their very hearts and bodies. After this horrible tragedy, the mutilated bodies were tossed pell-mell into tumbrils, like so many animals; whence they were taken to their mass grave and there, without funerary pomp, a little earth scarcely covered them, allowing infection to spread far abroad . . .

Appendix 5

Authenticity of Rouy l'Aîné's description of the people dancing at the foot of the scaffold after the execution of Louis XVI

In his book, *La Démagogie en 1793* (Paris 1870), Dauban quotes Rouy's account and, in an attempt to refute the doubts that arise from its exceptional narrative, cites a drawing by Peyron, a follower of David, which does indeed show the scene of dancing round the scaffold. He takes the similarity of text and drawing to confirm the reality of the event he described. It is however possible to regard the drawing as having been inspired by the narrative, and to suppose that in the narrative the image found what the classical theory of painting calls its *programme*, its *invention*. But it is also possible that the opposite happened, and that Rouy used the episode depicted in the drawing to enrich his own description. For, upon reflection, it is clear that in a graphic representation, dance is the simplest and most effective gesture by which to show the joy that a written description can simply explain. It is, in any case, of interest to read Dauban's own words: he accepts the image at face value, and his description of the drawing, which in itself constitutes an excellent *ekphrasis*, produces a last narrative variant on the theme. His tone is thus inevitably republican, and yet the author can hardly be suspected of sympathy for the events of 1793:

> This scene brings together all the comments made about the death of the king by Montagnards and extremists ... This was the day on which slaves attained the dignity of free men. On the barrel of the cannon they swear to defend their liberty against the foreign hordes. Citizen and soldier, embracing one another, repeat this same promise. To the right, two terrified youths throw themselves into the arms of an old man of severe and grim countenance who declares that the nation's cruel act is necessary for the safety of the homeland. To the left a Montagnard wearing the red bonnet points out the instrument of death to some women citizens. So die all tyrants! These groups, with their expressive attitudes from which we divine

their opinions, form a sort of apology for the picture, the moral that the painter draws from the event. On one side history proceeds, the deed itself is seen: the guillotine, the executioner holding up the severed head; men, panting with blood-lust, bodies raised on tiptoe, calf muscles straining, strive to reach up to Sanson's blood-stained hands; half mad with joy, they dance beneath the figure of the executioner ... This is the story, this is history, as the historian Rouy l'Aîne saw and recorded it that day.

We seek in vain to know which of the two was the origin of the other. Though the historical narrative normally models the image, the relation can perfectly well be inverted and the narrative become a form of *ekphrasis*: the spectacle he pretends to have witnessed is described by the 'historian', who plies his rhetoric to convince the reader of the morality of the event.